I0645495

OLIVIA, AMONG OTHERS

A NOVEL

Olivia, Among Others

A Novel

Charlie Torino

CORREDORA
INDEPENDENT PUBLISHING

Copyright © 2021 Corredora Independent Publishing
All rights reserved.
Printed in the United States of America.
First Edition, October 2021

All of the characters and events portrayed in this novel are fictitious. Any similiarity to real persons, living or dead, is coincidental and not intended by the author.

The Library of Congress Cataloging-in-Publication Data
Names: Torino, Charlie, author.
Title: Olivia, Among Others
Description: First edition.
Identifiers: ISBN: 978-0-9995768-4-7 (paperback)

Cover Design: Ashley Santoro

Chapter One

Most so-called epiphanies are overrated and overstated. They're nothing more than the stammering recitation of some banal nugget of pseudo-wisdom, which everyone other than the self-indulgent idiot having the supposed revelation understands intuitively and accepts as common sense. But it occurred to me while I was sitting in English class during my sophomore year of high school—rocking back and forth in a wobbly chair with the desk welded attached, and using a mechanical pencil to color in the knifed-in initials of some kid who probably was slumped over in the same rusted-out seat listening to the same old-bag teacher twenty years prior—that I could never allow myself to become dependent on the fickle good graces of a man for my survival. Every choice I've made since then has been shaped by that realization.

You'll want to paint me as some kind of villain, but I never took from anyone who didn't have it coming. Each one of my "victims" deserved it and could afford it, which is precisely why I've been able to get away with all this for as long as I have (if you can fairly consider me to have gotten away with anything at all). Nothing I've done in the past was reported to the police, or if it ever was, the cops couldn't be bothered to intervene. This is an opportunity for an epiphany of your own: doesn't their ubiquitous indifference say it all?

Chapter Two

I was born Olivia Ann Marie Fletcher. Fletcher is my biological father's last name, but I haven't seen or heard from him since I was four. My mother, Lillian, claims that she hasn't spoken to him since then either, and if his parents know anything about his whereabouts, they aren't disclosing it in the Christmas card they send us each December—always a cartoon of a happy family of gingerbread men or polar bears in striped hats, never their own miserable faces—which is the only time they bother contacting us at all.

My mother kept their house in Snellville, Georgia. With the help of her own mom, Rosaline, who drove up from Valdosta after Bio Dad bailed, Lillian promptly sold off or trashed every item of his that he had left behind. Looking back on it, Rosaline probably transferred all of Bio Dad's money out of the joint bank accounts he'd held with Lillian before Lillian filed for divorce too. Lillian wouldn't have had the foresight to do it herself, and I don't think that her salary as an executive assistant in the Department of Administration of the Snellville city government would have been enough to cover our mortgage payments and expenses otherwise. But Meemaw Rosaline was smart like that.

Rosaline took care of me and my little brother Milo all the time during that first year after Bio Dad took off. Milo was a baby, only a couple months old, and having Meemaw watch over us saved Lillian the expense of daycare. But after a year or so, my grandmother went back to Valdosta. Most nights, while Lillian went out on dates or hit up the bars in Snellville or Lawrenceville with her other single-mom friends, our babysitter Moira, a high school junior who lived five houses down the street from us, was the presiding semi-adult authority. Moira was a plump, pale white girl with long jet black hair and honey brown roots. She dressed goth, which I imagine initially made Lillian nervous—although on second thought, Lillian probably was too drunk and desperate back then to care—but Moira was the sweetest person I had ever met. She never complained when my mother returned home three hours later than promised, plastered, if Lillian slipped her an extra fifteen bucks for the trouble.

When Moira came over, she did her homework and let me watch cartoons and grown-up shows for as late as I wanted as long as I got into my pajamas and brushed my teeth first, and then darted off to my room and pretended to be asleep whenever Lillian got back. She taught me a litany of cusswords that made me the star of my kindergarten class. When I caught her smoking in the backyard one time, she let me have a puff of one of her Carolina Skinnies on the assumption that I'd find it so disgusting that I'd never want to smoke again. She was right, and a decade later, when I was working retail, I only feigned a pack-a-day habit so that I wouldn't lose out on cigarette breaks. I promised Moira that I wouldn't snitch on any of the reckless shit she did or let us do while she was taking care of us, and I've kept that promise up until this very moment.

Back then, Milo liked Moira better than he liked our mother. He fussed whenever Lillian held him, but he calmed down as soon as she handed him off to Moira. Moira's dad was gone too, but she didn't have any siblings and her mother was a lot older and never left the house. I think Mrs. Moira's-Mom might have had cancer, but I don't really remember for sure. I was only in kindergarten, after all. Besides, Moira didn't like to talk about it. She needed the money and she probably liked the excuse to get out of her crappy, rundown house with the overgrown lawn and fallen trees that no one ever got around to removing. But even if her life sucked, she never took it out on me or Milo, which automatically makes her a better person than ninety-nine percent of the population. I don't remember her last name, but sometimes

I wonder if she still dresses goth and if she ended up having any kids of her own. She would be a good mom, or at least the version of her that I remember from back then would be.

Then, my mom met Raymond Ray. I was six. With a name like "Raymond Ray," it's understandable if you assume that he'd be a total douchebag, but he turned out to be not that bad of a guy. He was employed by the City of Snellville too, as a public works manager, but they met (unsurprisingly) at some random shithole bar in Lawrenceville. Once she and Raymond started getting serious, Lillian toned down her bullshit. This was true in general, but especially true whenever he was around. It was like she was trying to show him what a good housewife she'd be to him. Our bathrooms got cleaner, our dinners got less revolting, and Moira started coming over only once or twice a week, rather than every night.

I missed having Moira around, but on balance Raymond was a positive presence in our household. Meemaw Rosaline was initially skeptical, mostly because Raymond is a Black guy, and Meemaw told us that she was raised to believe that people shouldn't date outside their own race. But even she came around quickly enough. How could she not? Raymond was handy and repaired all the fixtures and appliances in our house that had been broken since before Bio Dad left; he read books to me and Milo and he was there with open arms and a steadying hand while my little brother figured out how to pedal his tricycle without toppling off of it; he gave me a rag doll that his own mother had sewn and sent from West Tennessee just for me, which I've been told I carried around with me literally everywhere for ten weeks straight; he made my mother's face light up in a way that none of us had ever seen, whether by stealthily grabbing her hand as they sat at the dinner table or by gently touching the small of her back when he squeezed past her in our crowded kitchen; and he comported himself with the impeccable manners of a southern gentleman and spoke to Meemaw with unwavering respect, even when she was being icy and standoffish, until finally, on their fourth or fifth in-person encounter (between each of which, she was bombarded with near-daily updates on what a good and decent man he was), she warmed enough to tell him that he was welcome to call her "Rosaline" or "Mama Rose," rather than "Mrs. Ellsworth" or "ma'am."

Raymond occasionally tried to pull some disciplinary father-figure bullshit with me when I was a teenager—grounding me when I broke curfew, scolding me for failing tests, sending me to my room for backtalk—but he never smacked us around, so even though I still think he was overstepping, I've mostly forgiven him. He seems to love my mother, and he's been the only dad that Milo has ever known. Raymond and Lillian had two new kids together, Finn and Matilda, whom they obviously love the most. Especially Matilda. She's the youngest, a freshman in high school now, and she has no idea how easy she has it.

Anyway, my mother and Raymond married when I was nine, and Raymond adopted me and Milo six months later. They legally added "Ray" to my last name at the same time that Lillian changed her surname entirely. When I was fifteen, it occurred to me that she probably needed to get my bio dad's permission to do that, so I asked her bluntly: Had she found him? Did Grandma and Grandpa Fletcher find him on her behalf? Or did she forge his signature, knowing that if he gave any sort of shit about me and Milo being stripped of his last name, it would only be because he would want to extort her for a few hundred dollars to get his written consent first?

The question struck a nerve, although for once, I really wasn't trying to piss her off. She took her sandal off her right foot and hurled it at my head. It was a move she had stolen from her own mother and which she pulled out for those special occasions in which she deemed my or Milo's offense to be especially egregious.

"The audacity of this one," Raymond muttered, shaking his head but remaining seated at the kitchen table.

Lillian hurled her left sandal at me, but she missed by a long shot. It knocked over a half-empty plastic cup of juice that was on the kitchen counter, which fell to the floor with a crash. Matilda went ballistic. I knew better than to laugh.

"Now look at what you've made me do," Lillian shrieked.

"I know she doesn't have this kind of a sass mouth at her job," Raymond stated to no one in particular as he pushed back his chair and scooped up Matilda.

"Clean up that juice and go to your room," my mother hissed at me as she stroked Matilda's arm.

"What happened?" Finn poked his head around the corner and asked gleefully. "Did Olivia misbehave again? Is she going to be punished?"

"Finn Aurelius Ray." Raymond's voice was stern, but there was no chance that the little brat was going to have a shoe whipped at *his* head. "What do we say about minding our own business?"

"Umm... that we should do it, sir?" Finn pouted.

"Good boy. Go back to the TV room with your brother."

I rolled my eyes and patted the juice with a wad of paper towels, which I crammed into the trash quickly, before Lillian could reprimand me for being wasteful. Then I darted to my room. Being sent there was far from a punishment, at least while Matilda was still downstairs. It was borderline criminal that I was forced to share a bedroom with a three-year-old, but it was better than rooming with Milo, who was thirteen and probably learning to jack off around this time, or God forbid, that six-year-old tattletale little shit, Finn. Some of my friends from school had their own bedrooms, but I needed to enjoy my moments of solitude whenever I could find them.

Although I'm exceptionally well-read and you won't find a prep school brat who speaks with more eloquence and insight than I, my formal education was nothing special. I went to South Gwinnett, which is one of the public high schools in Snellville. Good ol' Snellville: "Where Everybody's Proud to be Somebody." My mother regularly attended town hall meetings (as a requirement of her job, not out of some latent sense of civic duty), and when I was thirteen or so, I proposed that she enter a motion for adopting an alternate motto: "Where Everybody's Proud to Say They're From Atlanta, Even Though They Actually Live a Solid Forty-Five Minutes East of Downtown." She wasn't amused.

All things considered, though, Snellville wasn't the worst place to grow up. I didn't love South Gwinnett High, but I didn't hate it either. Raymond and Lillian were far from rich but, to their credit, they at least had decent, stable employment with the city. I got my first part-time job halfway through my sophomore year, and by shoplifting clothes, accessories, and makeup (mostly to compensate for how my bitchy managers shorted me on my paychecks) and supplementing my income through various quasi-legal schemes, I was able to maintain my status as one of the best-dressed and most attractive girls in my grade. I'm not being conceited. I've had these perfect C-cup breasts and this toned hourglass physique since eighth grade; my hair is so long and thick that people always assume I've gotten extensions; my lips are naturally this full, without injections or implants; my skin is flawless; my teeth are almost totally straight despite the fact that Lillian and Raymond couldn't afford to get any of us braces... need I go on? I could pretend to be modest or insecure, but I'm trying to be completely honest with you from the start. The one thing Bio Dad gave me that he can't take away is good genes.

My friend group in high school defied all the standard classifications. We weren't the dorks or jocks or metalheads or preps or dealers. We weren't the Black kids or the white kids or the Latino kids. Or, at least, we weren't any of those things exclusively. This was unusual at my school, where people tended to group together based on their racial identity or the sport they played or some other notable trait or interest. But I didn't see why I should have to define myself based on a single characteristic, and I guess the rest of my friends felt the same way. If any commonality bonded the six or eight of us in my core circle, it was that we all knew how to assimilate into, or ingratiate ourselves with, or get what we needed from, any of the other cliques, without drawing undue scrutiny as to our motives. Incidentally, although I've lost touch with basically everyone from my class, all signs on social media indicate that the same six or eight of us are the only ones who have managed to escape our hometown and do anything remotely interesting with our lives.

I didn't learn shit from my classes. What South Gwinnett offered me, if anything, was the chance to learn through experience how to read and manipulate people who would otherwise have power over me. The school administration, for example, got off on requiring us to provide parental notes for every idiotic circumstance you can imagine. Knowing this, the first time I forged a note, I intentionally left off my student ID number. Then, when I went into the office and presented it to Ms. Potter, a hook-nosed bitch whose tits sagged down to her bellybutton, and she pointed out the omission, I wrote in my ID number at the bottom in a different color pen and using different handwriting so she could see how my penmanship was distinct from "my mom's." I told Ms. Potter that I'd remind my mother about including my ID number in the future. As anticipated, Lillian never bothered to return Ms. Potter's phone call verifying the validity of the note, so the school used it as the basis for comparison going forward; and since "Lillian's" handwriting was, of course, my own, I never once had any of my written excuses second-guessed.

The other thing I figured out was the importance of keeping the notes simple. Some of my friends insisted on writing two paragraphs of an elaborate excuse, and they got caught every time. Their spelling and grammar sucked, so the extra sentences merely provided more opportunities for them to make the kinds of stupid mistakes that would tip off the administration that a dumbass functionally illiterate kid was the note's true author. More importantly, most parents don't have time to spend twenty minutes writing out all that shit, and every other adult knows it. A sentence is all that is required, because that's all an actual parent would do.

This was doubly true for doctor's notes. What medical professional is going to write two hundred words of flowery prose about some dipshit teenager's diarrhea? I forged as Lillian about eighty percent of the time, and as Raymond or the doctor's office the other twenty percent, and whenever I chose to do a doctor's note, I wrote it as the office receptionist or a nurse, never as the doctor herself. There are templates for this online. All you need to do is find the right kind of paper in the school supplies section at CVS and type in some random doctor's letterhead in black and white. I tried to explain this to my friends, but they always thought they knew better. Fools. I was the only one who never got caught. Thankfully I've always had the good sense to trust my own superior instincts rather than abide the "wisdom" of the crowds.

Chapter Three

I had one boyfriend in high school. Or, rather, one boyfriend that I actually cared about. His name was Manny Rodriguez. He lived in a well-maintained ranch-style home with his happily married mom and dad, his two younger sisters, and his eighty-five-year-old great-grandmother. The Rodriguezes even had a black Labrador puppy. Whenever I went to his house, there was always someone—usually his great-grandmother or one of his aunts visiting for the afternoon—cooking fresh food, calling me "flaquita," and trying to entice me and Manny to hang out in the kitchen and eat and talk about our day. They were a nauseatingly wholesome family.

Manny was six foot four, and although he could dunk and he bench-pressed more than most of the guys on the football team, he was satisfied with being a mediocre varsity baseball player. At heart, he preferred to spend his time learning hair metal cover songs on his guitar and writing fan fic for some random late-'90s TV show called *Buffy the Vampire Slayer*. I think the only reason he got so jacked or bothered with sports at all was because he needed the "jock" rep to cover for the fact that he was secretly a huge geek, and because he wanted to look out for his sisters and scare off any boys who tried to date them. He put stickers and pins of the Puerto Rican flag on all his stuff (his textbooks, backpack, jackets, bicycle, it was endless) and on any other available surface, including and especially school property. It was technically petty vandalism and it was the closest he ever came to engaging in any type of juvenile delinquency, although he'd front like he was some kind of badass when he was around his older cousins.

I heard that Manny joined the Army a few months after we graduated, but I haven't tried to find him on Insta or Snap to verify. When a relationship is over—whether it's a boyfriend, a female friend, a hookup, or a family member—it's better to leave that person behind entirely. I don't have an active social media presence under my real name anymore anyway, but when I did, I would always unfollow and block my exes immediately. I guess I can admit I'm a little curious about how Manny's doing: what his new girlfriend looks like, or whether he got married or has a kid by now, whether he moved back to Snellville, stuff like that. Not curious enough to degrade myself by adding him under a dummy account, though. Besides, he probably got tricked into knocking up some gross tag chaser who doesn't deserve him, and I don't need that visual tarnishing my memories.

Anyway, Manny and I started going out during sophomore year when we both got busted for dress code violations on the same day: I was wearing a spaghetti strap tank top and my red bra straps were visible, and he had on a red Nike sweatband, which the administration had randomly, and quite incorrectly in Manny's case, decided was a symbol of gang affiliation. We were seated next to each other in an open classroom along with twenty other students who had been rounded up for various asinine reasons on that morning's dress-code sweep. Although everyone was supposed to be completely silent until it was their turn to be written up, Manny and I whispered to each other our speculations about which arbitrary rule each of our fellow hoodlums had violated.

Manny was hot and funny, and we started texting each other every day after that. Technically we were together until the beginning of our senior year. I never cheated on him unless it was for business purposes. I was always emotionally faithful to him, and anyone who said otherwise is a damned liar. I didn't tell him about the other guys because they didn't count and I knew it would needlessly upset him.

I met all of those random douchebags through my various retail jobs, and for Manny's sake, I was meticulous about making sure none of them had any connection to South Gwinnett High. That got a lot easier once I figured out that my best options were guys out of high school, in their early twenties, with middling jobs and adequate income but no illusions of power or status.

It wasn't complicated. Other women *make* their relationships with men complicated, and unnecessarily so. Intentionally or not, they do it to themselves. I'll leave it to you to create your own psychological theories as to why this is true; my point is simply that they do, and I don't, and I'm better off for it. Most men think of women as one of three things: one, a hole to fuck and discard at their leisure; two, a functionally insentient accessory to make them look cool in front of their friends; or three, a housekeeper/ mommy to mend and rehabilitate their garbage existence, while simultaneously ensuring that they don't feel pathetic for needing the help. Most women don't realize this until they're old as fuck—like, in their late thirties, when it's too late for them anyway. They'd be lucky to get a broke sixty-year-old's attention at that point.

But I've always been wise beyond my years—and don't try to say that Lillian's bullshit made me mature faster, because she doesn't get credit for anything that I've achieved—and I realized these truths by the time I had turned fifteen. Moreover, since the guys I was dealing with back then were teenagers and slightly older losers, I knew that most of them probably had their "mommy" needs covered by the real thing, and were therefore looking for one of the other two alternatives.

I became substantially more sophisticated with my approach to men in the intervening years, but initially my technique barely varied from one guy to the next. Scoping out the right target was easy, especially when I was working at the mall and had an endless stream of guys from which to choose. The ones I pursued always displayed some ostentatious sign of parental wealth and disposable income (or for the older ones, at least a general lack of concern for their credit score). They always had trouble concealing their attraction to me. They were never so ugly that it would arouse suspicion about why I was with them—although it's not like these clowns had the self-awareness to realize that a woman like me was out of their league anyway—but they exhibited enough dorky, awkward traits that I could be assured the upper hand from the start. I made them visibly nervous. They alluded to possessing the attributes of a good boyfriend during our first interactions, and they were a little too excited when they discovered a mutual interest or other trite commonality with me. Above all, there was something intangible, some pheromone of desperation that they were secreting, or some unconscious movement or posture that whispered "I'm an easy target" to those who know how to look for it, that they all shared and that I had a knack for spotting.

So I'd see him, this insignificant loitering townie or generic Mr. Mall Rat McFuckface, and... oh, I'm almost embarrassed to explain this part of my story out loud. Candidly, even allowing for the fact that I was still in high school, it all seems so callow compared to how my methodology has evolved, to say nothing of how drastically the caliber of man to whom I'll give so much as a second glance has improved. You want to call the guys that came later my "marks"? Fine. That makes this germinal set of losers my Skid Marks. But you're the one who wants to know the whole story. You're the one who asked me to start from the very beginning, and I have nothing to hide.

Anyway, I'd see a potential Skid Mark, and I'd give him that look that says, "Come talk to me, if you have the balls." I rarely made the first approach, for the same reason that I never offered up my number without being asked and I always waited for the guy to invite me to hang out. I could be flirtatious, but Skid Mark needed to believe that he initiated the whole affair and was in total control.

I would make the guy take me out at least four or five times before I fucked him so that he wouldn't think I was just another ho. Being "girlfriend material" makes you inherently more trustworthy, and these were formal dates. I guess that doesn't sound like a big deal to older people, since that's how things were always done in the 1950s or whatever, but for people my age, one-on-one dating was typically limited to exceptional girls whose boyfriends knew that they had to work continuously to keep her affection. Mostly, everyone just hung out in groups or hooked up at parties. Even with Manny, other than some school-sponsored dances and similarly lame shit, we didn't go on many official dates. That was different, though. Manny knew that I was exceptional, but he didn't have the extra cash to spend on nice restaurants, and I was kind enough not to hassle him about it.

Anyway, on the third or fourth date while running this scheme, I would treat Skid Mark to dinner at a place like Five Guys or Chick-fil-A, which seemed halfway decent to my underdeveloped palette at the time. It wasn't a huge expense, and I'd expect him to pay for mini-golf or bowling or whatever other cheesy, low-class activity he had planned for that night after we ate, but it illustrated that I wasn't like other girls and proved I wasn't after his money.

When I eventually got around to banging Mr. Skid Mark, I'd ask if he had a condom only if I was pretty sure he didn't. This was tricky and I never quite got this part down to a science. Ideally, the scenario would go like this: I'd ask, he'd say he didn't but beg to go on anyway, I'd pretend to waver but eventually give in "only if he promised to pull out." This way, I had a basis to get mad at him later. You know, "I told you that we needed to use a condom, and you bullied me into having sex with you without one anyway."

Of course, if I told him to wrap it and he obliged, that meant I'd be stuck having sex with him for no reason. Once I got super lucky and the condom broke, but mostly it meant that I'd have to keep having sex with him until he slipped up, or I'd have to dump him if he turned out to be one of those guys who insist on protection every time.

I'd drag things out with the dumbass for another few weeks until it would make sense for me to say I took a pregnancy test and, big surprise, it is positive and I don't know what I'm going to do (cue the waterworks), there's a Planned Parenthood in East Atlanta that performs abortions and I can get my cousin to drive me there, but where am I going to come up with eight hundred bucks? Even though a baby will cost us (and it was definitely "us") so much more than that in the long run, how can I possibly afford an abortion when I'm barely making minimum wage? Sobs, lamentations, you get the picture.

I ran the scam on two high school guys. One of them was a dude from Buckhead named Noah. He wasn't going to pay up until I told him that I had found his mother's Facebook account and was going to confess everything to her if he hadn't helped me by the end of the week. I guess knocking up "white trash" from South Gwinnett would have gotten him disinherited, because suddenly Noah was absolutely giddy to pay out a full seven hundred dollars in cash that he borrowed from his older brother. Idiot.

The other high school guy was a sophomore from a private school in Decatur. Jake or Blake or Drake, something like that. Oh, how that one cried when I told him that I would not be keeping the (totally fictitious) baby. He told me that abortion was a sin, that we'd both be going to hell, that he'd marry me, that he'd raise the child on his own without me if he had to. I started worrying that this blubbering, apparently super-Christian (although not Christian enough to refrain from unprotected premarital sex with a girl he'd known for less than a month) dipshit was going to track down my own parents or show up at my school and the whole story would get back to Manny. I was doing this *for* Manny, so he wouldn't have to take a second job to pay for all my shit or force me to break up with him so I could get a richer boyfriend. Ultimately, I accepted the $118 (paid in three twenties, and the rest in singles and fives) that the stupid kid scraped together, blocked his number, and nearly gave up the scam completely.

Fortunately, I had the sense to try one more time with a twenty-three-year-old electrician who had recently started his own contracting business. Jackpot. He paid me $850 in cash to cover the full cost of the "abortion," plus fare for an Uber or a cab, with any left over as an implicit bonus for me to go away. Indeed, half of these older guys offered to pay for the full cost of the ol' fetus deletus immediately, no questions asked. Those who wavered, or who only wanted to contribute a portion of the cost, had an abrupt change of heart when I told them that, surprise, I'm still in high school (had I forgotten to mention that?). The optics of spermatizing some girl a decade their junior typically was enough for them to shut up and pay.

I cycled through this process about ten times over the course of two and a half years, averaging a little over six hundred dollars per dude. Nowadays that's basically spare change for me, particularly given the amount of time and effort involved in the process, but back then it was huge, especially in comparison to the lousy wages I made at my crappy retail jobs.

Manny never found out about any of this, but he broke up with me three weeks after the homecoming dance our senior year anyway. Can you believe that? After everything I did for him all those years, after I bought him $250 Jordans for his birthday, after I turned down multiple guys from our school who were just as hot as he was, he had the nerve to dump me. He couldn't even give me a good reason for it. It was a bunch of convoluted bullshit about how he felt like I never had time for him and he thought I was hiding things from him and it was weird that I never wanted to bring him around my family or be affectionate with him in public. Like, I would hug him in the cafeteria and we made out at house parties all the time. If we had fooled around in the hallways, we would have gotten after-school detention for PDA, and then he would've missed baseball practice and I would've been late to my job.

I was so furious when he ended it that I nearly ran the abortion-money scam on him! I deserved to do something to make us even, but I'm too soft-hearted of a person. All I did was chuck a brick through the passenger-side window of his precious Dodge Neon, which was the perfect crime. The next day at school, I overheard him in the cafeteria bitching about the crackheads who had passed through his neighborhood searching for spare change or shit they could pawn, and how his car was totally empty, while his neighbor three doors down left a shotgun and a .45 in the trunk of his Cavalier all the time, but his was the only vehicle on the street that suffered any visible damage. It cost him almost three hundred dollars to fix the window. He had no idea it was me. After that, I considered his debt to me discharged and forgave him.

I didn't have another boyfriend until after I had graduated high school. It wasn't because I was sad about Manny. We said hello to each other in the hallways and we could sit at the same table during lunch without any drama (as long as he didn't flirt with anyone else in front of me, obviously). He went to senior prom with some inexplicably popular sophomore girl with dyed-pink hair and a humungous ass, and I went with the dude who had let me copy his math homework before class every day for the past two semesters.

At the time, I told myself that it was probably for the best. When Lillian shared the photos with Meemaw Rosaline, Meemaw probably would be relieved to see her granddaughter's arm around a white guy. I don't think that Meemaw would have disinherited me if I had gone with Manny or with one of my Black or Latino guy friends, but I remember thinking that she must have been in her seventies or eighties by then, and that perhaps being complicit with her latent racist bullshit one last time would induce her to bump me up in her will.

Meemaw is still chugging along in Valdosta, as spry and sassy as she was ten years ago. And with Lillian or her washed-up sister as the eventual executor of Meemaw's modest estate, I doubt I'll ever see a dime.

Chapter Four

I graduated high school on time, which was less of an accomplishment and more of an expectation in the Fletcher-Ray household. I don't know what provoked it, but during the summer before my senior year Lillian started partying again, the way she used to before Raymond came into our lives. Her proclivity this time around was for pills rather than booze, but the same cast of trashy friends from a decade prior spontaneously reemerged, sprouting up on the TV room couch on a random Tuesday before school or hogging the shower when I needed to get to my job on a Sunday mid-morning. The parade of drug-addled deadbeats persisted for months, until Raymond finally took charge: he banished all the unwanted guests from our property, purged the house of all alcohol and drugs, dragged Lillian back to AA and NA meetings every single day for two weeks straight, and otherwise worked his magic in ways I don't fully understand. On the one hand, I'd never let anyone control me the way he controls her. On the other hand, I can admit that something needed to be done, and he was the one who stepped up and did it. Like I said before, all things considered, Raymond's always been a pretty decent guy.

Even through all those months of bullshit, Raymond made it crystal clear that I was expected to keep up with my homework assignments and tests, and that neither my retail gigs nor any melodrama caused by Lillian and her idiot friends would constitute a valid excuse for falling behind in my classes. If anything, he got stricter with us during that time—even with Finn and Matilda, who were both too young to cause any real trouble, but his tolerance for their sass mouths dropped to zero. I wasn't, like, inspired by him to do better or any lame shit like that, but I maintained my C+ average and walked with the rest of my classmates who managed to graduate on time too. For twenty minutes or so that day, Lillian took a modest break from making everything about her. The six of us went to Chili's to celebrate after we left the graduation ceremony at the Infinite Energy Center arena and they let me choose the appetizer.

For the record, I chose the Bloomin' Onion. Mostly because Milo and I love them, and a little bit because, to this day, Finn hates anything with onion or garlic in it.

I bombed the SAT, but it wasn't my fault because I didn't want to take the damn thing in the first place, and I didn't really try, and I didn't get to attend one of those fancy prep courses like all the rich kids at Brookwood High School do. The only reason I agreed to sit for the stupid test at all was because Raymond wouldn't stop pestering me about registering. He even paid the fee for me. I don't know why he was so insistent on it. My grades in school were pretty crappy, but I guess he understood that it was because the teachers were all terrible and annoying, and I had figured out how to do the minimum amount of work necessary to pass (and not an iota more). And actually, I'm so good at math that I managed to consistently make Bs, even though I never studied and I always cheated on the homework. Plus, I spent my free time back then the same way that I do now, reading as much as possible: fiction and non-fiction, books, articles, blogs, whatever. I should have been a star in English and history, but my teachers were imbeciles and I could have exposed them, so they needed to discredit me. The easiest way to do that was by giving me bad grades. Luckily, I don't need academic awards to know that I'm well-read and smart as fuck. My intelligence is how I've survived.

But I loathe standardized tests, and Raymond knew that. I guess he had some twisted idea that since I like to read and since I'm much more intelligent than my GPA suggested, I'd be able to get a perfect score simply by showing up. He should have known better and saved his money. Or he should've given the registration fee to me in cash.

Anyway, between my mediocre grades, my abysmal SAT scores, and my total lack of high school extracurricular activities (other than working thirty or more hours a week since I was a sophomore, but college admissions officers don't give a shit about actual life skills), I knew I wasn't cut out for university. When I was nineteen, I did try a semester at Georgia Gwinnett College. I thought I might be a business major, even though the idea of sitting in a cubicle every day, surrounded by brainless douchebags who'd think they're better than me because they went to some fancy college in New England, made me want to slit my wrists. A business major or a nursing student; I despise old people and children and blood and vomit and weird smells, but I thought that I might be able to suppress my revulsion if it meant the chance to cozy up to rich doctors on a daily basis. Ultimately, though, four years of that crap seemed like way too much work and way too much money per semester, despite the decent financial aid for which I was eligible. I cut my losses and, within two months, I dropped out.

Instead, I ended up getting my associate degree in hospitality management from Albany Technical College. My credit rating sucked, but I had paid off my car note and had only a couple hundred dollars of debt since I'd never stopped working full-time. I was barely twenty-two, and back then this felt like a real accomplishment, because back then I didn't yet know any better.

I have always been wise beyond my years; it just happens to be in ways that the educational system doesn't value or under-stand. So, upon coming to my aforementioned epiphany—that I would need to rely on myself, and not a boyfriend or a husband or a father, to make it in this world—I took action. I got my first job a few months after my fifteenth birthday, and working retail gigs remained my most consistent, if not most lucrative, source of income until I was almost twenty-three. It was through these jobs at various clothing stores, a jewelry store, two shoe stores, and a high-end accessories boutique that I learned that almost all people are shitheads, and the wealthier and more powerful they are, the shittier their shitheadedness is likely to be.

Every store was the same. Spoiled teenagers from Atlanta's ritziest private schools swiped hairclips and nail polish from the checkout counter for giggles while, courtesy of daddy's credit card, they paid four hundred dollars for a neon green romper that would be out of season and out of style within six weeks. Of course, the cost of the missing merchandise was deducted from my or my coworkers' paychecks. Urban-hippie MILF-wannabes allowed their screaming brats to run amok, getting greasy orange-tinted fingerprints all over the clothes and displays, crashing into random customers, and shoving their siblings into mannequins, while the braless bitches offered breathy praise for the "infinite wealth" of their "little moon's creative self-expression" or obliviously prattled on about how motherhood is the hardest job of all. The rich old white ladies, with their frozen foreheads, pinched nostrils, and dead eyes, sighed in exasperation whenever I approached: they always either "had just walked in and just want to browse, I'll come find you when I'm ready if you're so worried about your commission," or "had been waiting for over half an hour for anyone in this store to so much as make eye contact, don't you know how much money I spend here?" And then I'd be forced to skip my break to clean up the disaster left behind when Madame Botox-face decided that, notwithstanding multiple allusions to her husband's wealth and importance, if we couldn't give her an extra twenty-five percent discount, then she'd have to wait until the midseason sale to make her purchase, or maybe (horror of horrors) she would never return at all.

My managers were worse than the customers. Three months into my job at the luxury clothing franchise Gracieux, I got cussed out by the then-manager, Ellen, for letting my cousin use my employee discount to buy a prom dress. That hypocrite regularly walked out of the store at the end of the day with new $450 heels on her feet. Didn't those morons at corporate ever notice the odd coincidence that all the "missing" or "damaged" inventory happened to be in women's shoe size 7.5 and dress size 4, which in turn happened to be Ellen's sizes?

We called her "Hell-en," thinking we were clever. It didn't dawn on me until a year after I had left that "Helen" is a relatively common female name, and since Ellen fancied herself more on the level of the store's upper-class customers than its low-wage employees, she probably attributed the recurring error to the poor pronunciation and deficient short-term memory that she smugly associated with our lesser socioeconomic status.

Ellen fired me two months after the prom dress incident. Manny had visited me in the store a few times that particular week, and since Ellen was undoubtedly a lady incel, she resented us. We tried to pretend like he was looking for a gift for his mother or sister, but since I was actually smiling and laughing for a change, she saw through the ruse. After she canned me, I immediately sent an anonymous letter from a burner email account to Gracieux's corporate HR suggesting that they look into the misreported inventory. I hope those stolen Ferragamo pumps were comfortable during your eight-hour shifts scooping fries at Mickey D's, bitch.

Ellen wasn't an aberration, though. Other managers clocked me out early, or refused to pay me overtime, or would deduct the most unfair charges from my paycheck to cover mistakes that weren't my fault. At The Willow Wisp—another waking nightmare of an upmarket boutique, this one featuring "bohemian chic" clothes (such as the heinous crochet shawl that cost more than my last three electric bills combined) and home décor (a $249 Native American dream catcher with the "Made in Taiwan" engraving on the back half-disguised by a barcode sticker, or for the more frugal, seventeen delightfully tacky strands of beaded curtains for $99.95)—the assistant manager, Bethany, was a deranged racist, although she'd fervently deny it and claim that *she* was the one being victimized if confronted. Bethany's hobbies included following three steps behind each and every Black person who entered the store for the duration of their visit or, almost as often, demanding, under threat of written reprimand for insubordination, that I or one of my coworkers "be vigilant" in her stead.

Bethany eventually fired me, as all the others before and after her did during that tortuous eight-year period of retail perdition, most of them purporting to do so "for cause" while waving around a mound of documentation that supposedly showed a consistent pattern of tardiness, or no call/no shows, or my cash register coming up short with undue frequency, or endless other bullshit allegations of disobedience and misconduct. In reality, the only "cause" of my termination was that they were afraid that I would expose their gross incompetence, or that I'd supplant them as manager, if they didn't fire me on a pretense first.

So yes, I learned early on that in the real world, everyone is an asshole. Everyone steals. Everyone looks out for their own interests, if not exclusively, then at least as their first and foremost priority. What I've done isn't any worse. In fact, it's morally superior. I have never *stolen* an identity; I've merely borrowed it. I never robbed anyone at gunpoint; in fact, most of the gifts and cash I've received over the years were given to me freely. Sometimes I wonder if the system is targeting me simply because they can tell how powerful I would become if they didn't intervene.

Chapter Five

A few weeks before my twenty-third birthday, I was hired as part of the reception and front office staff at The Roosevelt, a high-rise apartment complex located in a posh section of Atlanta's Buckhead neighborhood. In addition to being my first opportunity to make some semblance of use out of my hospitality management degree, it was also my first job outside of the retail sector. Notwithstanding Raymond's praise about this "huge step" in my career, however, I wasn't feeling particularly proud or excited. I did get a burst of joy, I suppose, when I saw how jealous Lillian was when Raymond surprised me with a $250 gift card to Banana Republic for new work clothes. And, having just quit a job at a boutique shoe store in Midtown where they had banned flats or any other frumpy footwear despite the requirement that we schlep up and down a steep staircase to the basement stockroom in order to fetch merchandise fifty times a day, the prospect of getting paid four dollars an hour more to keep my ass in a chair had a certain appeal. All things considered, I figured the residents of an upscale place like The Roosevelt would be insufferable, but ultimately no more or less obnoxious than the patrons of any of my former retail employers. It's not like I had been discovered by a talent scout who was going to whisk me off to Hollywood. It was a little bit more cash and a little bit less manual labor, but hardly the life-changing opportunity I had been waiting for.

The Roosevelt's reception and front office staff comprised four employees, one of whom was me, plus the property manager, Bradford Carmichael III. The third. The douchebag actually introduced himself to me that way during my first interview for the position, and he looked exactly as smug as you'd expect when he got to "the third" part, thereby leading me to assume that his grandpa was a rich prick, who spawned his rich prick father, resulting in this twat of a son.

Bradford promptly confirmed my intuition, boasting that his dad owned several other major apartment buildings, among other real estate and investment holdings, in Buckhead and Midtown Atlanta, as well as in Savannah, Augusta, and St. Simons Island. Alas, due to some unspecified misdeed by one of his siblings, all the Carmichael children were being forced to suffer the indignity of working "full-time"—that is, a maximum of six hours per day, three or occasionally four times per week—at six-figure salaries, in order to continue to receive their additional monthly trust fund distributions (which indubitably quintupled their income) and retain access to the family's private jet.

Bradford was approaching two full years of post-collegiate experience when he hired me. He was a legacy at Princeton, by the way, in case you didn't know, which he made sure to mention twice within the first ten minutes of our initial meeting, and at least once a week every week thereafter. Bradford prided himself on holding his employees to the highest standards—or, at least he did whenever he bothered to show up to the building and tear himself away from his cell phone long enough to observe what we were doing—and by the time I arrived to The Roosevelt for my first day of work, two of the three clerks who were employed when I was interviewed had been replaced. David, a twenty-eight-year-old whose pale skin, white-blond hair, and feeble appearance reminded me of the ghost of a Victorian peasant boy, had been working there since two months into Bradford's tenure.

"There's a lot of turnover," David said, his voice barely above a whisper, five minutes after I had sat down at one of the desks and Bradford had excused himself to watch Netflix in his office. "Mostly with the desk clerks and assistants, but among the maintenance staff too." Like a good little servant-boy poltergeist, David offered me no further explanation and busied himself with a stack of manila folders on top of the filing cabinet.

"I started four days ago," a forty-something woman named Margaret told me later that afternoon. "Maybe you met that guy Liam when you interviewed?"

I nodded.

"Yeah, so he's gone too. He resigned two days ago. But before he left, he told me that about eighty percent of the staff gets fired within two or three months. The other twenty percent last about the same amount of time before they quit. I worked at Canvas Lofts for six years before this. You know, that fancy gated complex over by Emory? There's no way that the tenants here will be worse than the spoiled shits over there. Not only did we have to deal with them, we constantly had to deal with their asshole parents. So far Bradford doesn't seem like as much of a tool as Liam said. David's a little odd, but he's nice enough and I can tell that he's a hard worker. I think I'll be able to stick it out until I find something that pays the same but is closer to home. I'm driving from Austell, so the commute here is a little bit better than it was for my last job, at least. I'd love to find a position like this somewhere in Cobb County though."

Margaret finally stopped talking and smiled encouragingly at me, as if waiting for me to respond. I paused. Whatever marginal benefit I might glean from the inisghts of four extra days of experience was drastically outweighed by the mindless chatter I'd have to endure for the indefinite future if I humored her right then. I didn't want to befriend any of these people. I wanted to spend as much time as possible sitting by myself at the receptionist stand in the lobby, rather than at one of the three tiny desks in the front office, and regardless of where I was located on any given day, my goal was to pass my time reading books or screwing around online, not listening to my coworkers whine about their trivial problems.

"Well, even if Bradford isn't as intense as all of his ex-employees say, I don't want to risk ticking him off on my first day," I mumbled after several seconds of silence. Incurring the reputation of being an obedient, unobtrusive ass-kisser would accrue to my advantage, regardless of what policies I might want to bend or rules I might want to break in the future. "I'm going to set up my work station at the receptionist desk out front. I'm pretty sure that's what Bradford wanted me to do, but his door is shut and I don't think we should knock on it to double-check."

With that, I escaped to the lobby and evaded any more painful small talk for the rest of the day.

I guess Bradford's obligation to continually interview potential replacement employees was cutting into his yachting and international luxury travel schedule, so for several months he forsook the joy of shit-canning members of his staff on a whim. During that time, Margaret, David, and I, plus Antonia, the fourth employee who primarily took the weekend and late shifts and whose hours barely overlapped with mine, worked together relatively harmoniously. We were all polite to each other and occasionally got a good group laugh at a resident's expense, but mostly we minded our own business. The work itself ranged from tedious to soul-destroying, but unlike most of my former retail jobs, no one at The Roosevelt (other than Bradford) felt the need to exacerbate an already-rotten situation by instigating petty interpersonal drama.

I lasted for seven excruciating months and sixteen excruciating days before Bradford got another hard-on for spontaneous layoffs and fired me and Antonia back-to-back on a Friday afternoon. My only regret is that it didn't occur to me until the very end of my miserable tenure there to start collecting the residents' personal information. It had been readily accessible to me since my first day, had I been prescient enough to start gathering it from the beginning. But I accumulated enough for my modest purposes at that time, and in a sense, that experience is what set me on the path that led to this conversation today.

The overwhelming majority of the people living in that building were assholes who flaunted their wealth and privilege in my face, but I only targeted the worst of the worst. This included, above all, one Ms. Marissa Annabelle Clinton, then age thirty-four, born October 24 (a Scorpio, of course), social security ending in -6402, originally from Houston, Texas (with her prior two home addresses on file), and a resident of The Roosevelt for the preceding eighteen months when I first made her acquaintance.

Marissa came into the front office on an almost-daily basis to pick up her packages: shit from Amazon, shit from multiple meal preparation services and vitamin supplement companies, shit from Rent the Runway, shit from Lululemon, shit from Nike, shit from Skinceuticals, just a ceaseless parade of shit. Marissa lived in a two-bedroom penthouse by herself. She was a management consultant, a job that apparently paid her a small fortune, but which, as I heard her whine to Bradford, required so much travel that it was impossible for her to find time to date or to take care of a pet. Poor little princess.

She and Bradford were both acquainted with some rich fucker who lived in Tuxedo Park and who was currently being investigated by the SEC for securities fraud. Around the time that whispers about the governmental inquiry began to circulate through their social circle, it was revealed that, for the past eight months, this same sleazebag had been cheating on his second wife with a man fifteen years his junior. A man with whom, coincidentally, Bradford had gone on several lackluster dates two years prior.

The revelation that Bradford was gay was the first time that their daily inane conversations captured my interest rather than provoked my scorn. Up until then, I had assumed that Bradford was straight and that the reason he tolerated Marissa's intrusions on his Netflix time, appeasing her insatiable need to gossip about their mutual acquaintances, was because he wanted to bang her. After all, that was the only reason the building's custodians and handymen put up with her clumsy attempts to converse with them in Spanish, spoken with her godawful gringa accent. Her butter-blond hair extensions, bleached-white teeth, and stapled-on tits turned men stupid.

Marissa had the option to come into the front office, fetch her packages, blab about the latest revelation in the Ponzi-scheme/secret-gay-lover scandal to Bradford, and sod off directly to her apartment. But instead, she made it a point to linger, to greet me, David, and anyone else who was working or busy handling other business in the office at the time, and to undertake cursory attempts at exchanging pleasantries with us as well. Did she think that she was doing us a favor? Was this her way of convincing herself that she was down-to-earth, someone who could connect with the plebes who work for an hourly wage, so that she could justify the rest of her existence as a spoiled, stuck-up bitch? Her smile was as phony as everything else about her, but I was the only one smart enough to see through it. Even meek, frail David offered to help her carry her packages up to her penthouse—an offer that she always declined, making some repulsive joke about how she wanted to put her personal training sessions to good use. With my head down and fist clenched, somehow I always managed to repress the urge to scream, "We get it, you insufferable bitch. We all understand that you're filthy fucking rich and you can afford to waste more money in a week on bullshit than everyone else in the front office makes in a month combined. Congratu-fucking-lations. Now go away."

At the Roosevelt, we were instructed not to give away any information about our residents over the phone, regardless of who was calling. Bradford said that this was a security measure, imperative to protect our "celebrity" clientele—a term dubiously defined to include a gorgeous but short male Instagram model with a butt-ugly girlfriend who never left his side; an overhyped style influencer who received a dozen unsolicited packages each week for her sponsored posts, whose meticulously filtered and edited photos couldn't fix her sagging jowls and visible stomach fat in real life; a hetero couple who were more famous around the building for their vanity and overblown egos than for the fact that they both had achieved a modicum of success in the IFBB physique competition circuit; a C-list rapper who made an appearance at The Roosevelt once every six or eight weeks with an entourage of twenty people that took over the rooftop pool, but who was unwaveringly polite and almost as soft-spoken as David the handful of times that he came into the front office alone; and some old guy who allegedly won several Academy Awards for animation, although from the looks of him, it probably happened in the 1940s. As an afterthought, we also were supposed to make sure that we didn't expose any of the non-celebrities to threatening exes or stalkers or process servers. The rule was, no matter who the person on the other end of the line claimed to be or what organization they claimed to represent, we had to demand a court order before we could so much as confirm whether the individual in question lived in the building.

I had moved out of Raymond and Lillian's house when I was nineteen. I had spent most of the time since then living in what was essentially a converted traphouse, in a neighborhood where gentrification had tried but failed to take root, with my cousin Jana, her gross then-boyfriend Derek, and some random girl they found on Craigslist. Jana broke up with Derek and bailed on the house around the same time I finished up my associate degree. I moved out too, and thereafter proceeded to circle the perimeter, living with random whiny bitches in Douglasville, Norcross, and Forest Park for about six months each. I even managed to sneak into the graduate student housing at Georgia Tech for two glorious months, living in the "spare" bedroom of a timid foreign guy who was pursuing his doctorate in robotics, until the dork's real roommate—some chick who was getting her PhD in civil engineering—returned several weeks early from the clean water program she was running in rural Guatemala and immediately realized that a stranger had been sleeping in her bed and living in her space. But a few months after I got the job at The Roosevelt, I found a single-bedroom apartment in East Point for a little over seven hundred dollars per month, and once I started living alone, I vowed never to have a roommate again.

I doubted that the management team at my place in East Point would be as sensitive to residents' privacy as The Roosevelt required us to be. But I also knew from trying to get my broken kitchen sink faucet fixed that they were unlikely to answer the phone at all, and even if they did, those idiots were far too lazy to look up my information for a nosy caller who wasn't searching for a rental and who therefore couldn't earn them a commission. Besides, my tenancy in East Point was going to be temporary, and by the time anyone caught on to what I was doing, I'd be long gone.

So I treated myself. I opened accounts, using Marissa's name and social security number but with a service location at my new East Point address, for a premium cable TV package and high-speed internet. The utilities companies required far too much proof of identity to make transferring those bills to Marissa's name worth my while, but I had no trouble opening two credit cards, each with a six-thousand-dollar credit limit, using her information. With one, I spent the day at Lenox Mall, splurging on a new wardrobe befitting my rising social status and on two years' worth of makeup and haircare products from NARS, Urban Decay, and Olaplex at Sephora. I stopped at Publix on the way back to East Point to stock up on nonperishable groceries and household essentials, just in case the cards were cancelled sooner than anticipated. For the same reason, after spending about twenty-five hundred dollars on a new laptop, luxury bed linens, a Dyson supersonic hairdryer, and a safe and a door jammer for my apartment, I used the other credit card to purchase a little over thirty-five hundred dollars in untraceable gift cards to cover me in the event of any future cash-flow shortages. I meticulously tracked my expenses and maxed out both credit cards (with a buffer of forty-eight cents on one, twenty-two cents on the other) within a day of receipt.

I paid the monthly minimum on both credit cards via money order a couple of times, until a snail-mail letter from my TV and internet provider informed me (or rather, informed Marissa A. Clinton) that they were sending the thousand dollars' worth of unpaid charges I had accrued to collections. By then, Bradford had fired me from The Roosevelt for unrelated reasons, and it was only a matter of time before Marissa realized that her credit score had tanked and uncovered all the other accounts I had opened with her information. I was unconcerned. After a few weeks of unemployment, I recently had accepted a new job in Dunwoody, and the commute was killing me. It was time to move on, from both the East Point apartment and from the Marissa scam.

Chapter Six

I don't talk much about my romantic history, and not because it consists almost exclusively of a series of fictions created for profit. Unlike most people my age, I understand the concept of discretion. I don't need to blast my business all over the internet in some pathetic attempt to impress my former high school classmates. There's no competition to be had when I've already won.

With that said, I know you're wondering, as others before you have wondered, whether I have ever been in love, whether I have tried to make a so-called "normal" or "real" relationship work, presumably with some mediocre dipshit with a mediocre job from my mediocre hometown. And when I'm unable to disguise my contempt at this line of questioning, you want to know, what's wrong with me? Have I given it an honest try? What happened in my past that made me hate men or become so embittered and cynical? On and on with a progressively more absurd and abhorrent line of questioning, stemming from the psychology degree you think you've earned from absorbing ten thousand hours of clichéd plotlines from the sixty-minute criminal profiler dramas that you watch on network television every night in order to distract yourself from the hollow echoes of your empty mind.

So let me disabuse you of your hackneyed diagnoses, Professor McMoron. I have no childhood trauma. Yes, my piece-of-shit bio dad left my mother when I was a toddler, as thousands of other crappy fathers do to their crappy families every day. That was Lillian's doing and Lillian's problem, not mine. I sure as hell am not his victim. If anything, I was the one who held the household together until Raymond came along.

And as for Raymond, don't you dare so much as insinuate any improprieties on his part. Raymond can be a pain in my ass, and he takes it way too easy on Finn and Matilda, especially compared to how strict he was with me and Milo. But he always was kind to me. He stuck around through all of Lillian's bullshit, helping her to pull her life back together time and time again, and he never took it out on us. He treats me and my brother almost the same as he treats his own kids. He doesn't have much in the sense of money and power and resources, and we both know that I'm destined for much bigger things, but to this day, if I were to ask for his help, he'd give me whatever he could. How many people can say that about their step-dads? If anything, Raymond is the one decent man I know.

So, no, I'm not working out "daddy issues." I'm not targeting men who are doppelgangers of a childhood sexual abuser to regain a sense of domination or control. These fools aren't surrogates for me to act out some revenge fantasy on a boyfriend who slapped me around or a male teacher who made me feel like I was inferior. But please, keep trying to profile me, please toss your other idiotic pop-psychology theories my way. I'm happy to dismantle them one by one.

The unpleasant truth that no one wants to hear or admit is that men are utterly useless, and yet they've managed to obfuscate this fact with their oversized egos and unjustifiable sense of entitlement to... well, to everything, including to me and my body and my attention and my love, without any obligation to give me anything in return. And women haven't just accepted this fabrication, they've embraced it! They've embraced it so wholeheartedly, in fact, that it makes my job easier. It is so incomprehensible to these worthless, dickless men that I might have seen through their system of lies and adapted so that I can get my due, that I am able to operate above suspicion.

I'm getting ahead of myself. You want to know, if my behavior isn't dictated by your easy narrative of childhood abuse and neglect, then surely some guy must have irreparably broken my heart? Have I tried at all to let down my guard and permit myself to feel and receive genuine love?

It's comical.

I've already told you about Manny, but that was childish puppy love and it was bound to fail eventually. Let me tell you about one of my futile endeavors into "honest" dating as an adult. I need only tell you one, because the men are interchangeable and fundamentally the tales all start and end the same way. For that reason, I suppose I can choose a story where the details are marginally more interesting, or at least it seemed that way to me at the time. In retrospect, the whole affair was as stupid as any of the others that I had experienced in the past or that I would find myself embroiled in over the years to come.

A little over three years ago, right around the same time I started ripping off residents' personal information from The Roosevelt's records and accounts, my cousin Jana and I went to see the band Six Times Country play at the Tabernacle in downtown Atlanta. Are you into that kind of music? Six Times Country has been nominated for a Grammy and a couple of CMT awards since then, but three or four years ago they were just starting to blow up and were still playing in mid-sized venues rather than stadiums. Milo drove us to the concert, but five minutes after we arrived at the Tabernacle he realized that he had gone to high school with one of the hot bartenders, so he ended up spending the whole night hovering around her workstation, ignoring us and the music.

Anyway, Six Times Country was touring to promote their third album, *Background Check*, which I suppose isn't bad as far as country records go. Jana was and still is obsessed with them. I had a good enough time at the show. Jana isn't as naturally pretty as me, and she's two years older, but she's blond and a makeup artist, plus she bought herself a pair of fake tits for her twenty-second birthday that she loves to show off. Suffice to say, we were able to wiggle our way toward the front of the stage without much hassle, situating ourselves in the second row and slightly off-center in between the lead guitar player and the singer. No doubt half the guys in the venue were looking at us rather than the band.

The audience was stuffed with desperate groupies who were going nuts throughout the band's entire performance. Their shrieks were obnoxious, but overall I didn't mind being surrounded by a bunch of washed-up fatasses because I knew it made me and Jana look that much hotter in comparison. This one cow took it upon herself to flash her ugly tits at the stage, and I could tell by the way the guys in the band were exchanging glances with each other and suppressing smiles that they all had noticed. Part of me was tempted to flash them too. Hell, letting them see my perfect breasts would have been a public service after they'd been traumatized and half-blinded by that dumb bitch's ugly rack.

But I kept my cool. I had been wordlessly flirting with the hot lead guitar player throughout the whole show, and I knew I stood out. Every single girl at the venue, including Jana, was dressed in denim and plaid or gingham, or in a flowery sundress, and brown leather cowboy boots and fringe-covered bags were ubiquitous. I, on the other hand, looked like a sexy rocker chick. And although I was enjoying the concert, I wasn't losing my mind fawning all over them. I nodded my head to the beat of the music, but unlike one of the hideous beasts to my left, I didn't look like a heaving hippo wheezing through a misguided attempt to twerk to a country tune. In other words, I was the only person in the audience with badass style and timeless grace. Of course the guitar player would take notice.

The show ended and, as the crowd applauded and cheered for a second encore, guitar-boy tossed his pick in my direction. I could tell he intended it for me, even though hippo-girl practically barreled me over to snag it for herself. The venue started to clear, which was how Jana and I finally managed to find Milo, who had been ignoring his phone for the past two hours, still chatting with that cute bartender from his high school history and math classes.

In an effort to justify hovering around the bar, Milo had polished off at least eight beers. He was holding himself together surprisingly well, all things considered, but he was in no position to drive. Jana snagged his keys and he finally introduced us to his friend, Kara, who promptly tossed down the rag she had been using to wipe up the bar top and greeted us with a smile. I think

Kara must have been harboring a crush on Milo since they were teenagers, because she immediately began to suck up to me and Jana, offering us both a drink on the house and inviting us to hang with her after she got off her shift.

"I've been working here since we graduated high school, so I have seniority among the girls and a little bit more say than most of the rest of the staff as far as which nights I work," Kara started. "I lived here, downtown, for a while, in those lofts off Pryor Street over by the courthouse. Obviously the building was a fucking free-for-all—I lost track of how many times we had some coked-out Airbnb guest banging on our door at 5:00 a.m. because they forgot what unit they were staying in, and the cops had to come to break up parties and fights every other night—but I was picking up shifts at the Glenwood in East Atlanta whenever I wasn't working here and I rarely got home before 4:00 a.m., so I didn't really give a shit."

Kara paused to hand me and Jana each a bottle of Sweetwater 420.

"Anyway, rent was dirt cheap since I was living with three other girls, but long story short, one of them turned out to be an absolute psycho and a thief, so I've been back in Snellville living with my mom in my childhood bedroom for the past two months or so. It was fucking humiliating to have to ask to move back in, but she let me do it and she's not charging me anything, so I guess I can't complain. It's still worth it to drive here for work a few nights a week, but the Glenwood shifts were too erratic so I had to drop that gig and start working at the Mellow Mushroom in Snellville instead."

Jana and I exchanged glances. Like, was there a reason she was telling us her entire life story, and were we supposed to pretend like we cared just because she gave us a free beer? But Milo was looking at her with hearts and rainbows and butterflies practically shooting out of his eyeballs, so I smiled patiently and Jana murmured some encouraging bullshit about how yeah, roommates are the worst and Atlanta's housing market sucks a dick, especially if you want anything ITP. Kara, who hadn't stopped cleaning while she was carrying on about all her personal drama, flung a container of garnishes into the trash and paused to look up at us before continuing.

"Oh yeah! So I was telling Milo earlier that normally I would have invited y'all to crash at my place and we could get as fucked up as we wanted. Obviously that's not an option anymore since I had to move, but if you want to stick around, we could go to Sidebar after I finish up here. I had to open today and I met the guys in the band while they were doing soundcheck. They were all really cool, and the drummer invited me to hang out after the show until their bus call." Kara glanced at Milo, who didn't seem to register that she was referring to his competition. "He told me to 'bring friends,' so I think some of the other guys in the band are single too."

Kara suddenly became a lot more interesting.

"To be honest, a lot of the band dudes that pass through here are fucking losers and creeps. Like, they think they're so much cooler than they actually are, and I almost never accept their propositions. This is the first time in months that I actually think it could be fun to hang with them. They seemed like normal, good-looking dudes that happen to play music for a living. But no pressure." She glanced at Milo again. This was hilarious; whether it was because he was hammered or naturally oblivious or both, Milo still didn't seem to understand that Kara was insinuating how easily she could ditch him for a rockstar tonight, and somehow his lack of jealousy or concern was turning her on. "Milo, I'm down for whatever you want to do. I just think it'd be fun for the two of us to catch up when I'm not distracted by a hundred different people in my face demanding drinks."

"Yes, let's do Sidebar! Please!" Jana exclaimed. I swear, sometimes she has absolutely no chill. "I promise I won't fan-girl too much and embarrass you, but I love Six Times Country so, so much."

"I'm down for Sidebar too," I said, much more subdued. "We don't have any other solid plans for tonight, but I'm not ready to go home. If Sidebar sucks, we can walk somewhere else. And Jana and I barely drank the entire show, so unless things get crazy, either one of us should be fine to drive Milo's car back when we're done."

All three of us turned to Milo, who shrugged. "Yeah, whatever. Sidebar is fine. Kara, I'm buying you a tequila shot when we get there. You need to catch up."

Kara blushed. The two of them were nauseating. But it was settled. By the time Jana and I had finished our beer, Kara had cleaned up the rest of her section and cashed out. She took the three of us out one of the back exits, into the parking lot where Six Times Country's tour bus was parked. As we approached, the drummer, the band's tour manager, and the merch guy were finishing loading up the last few boxes of t-shirts and gear. The bass player was pacing at the edge of the lot as he FaceTimed his girlfriend, who was ripping him a new ass about God knows what. And the singer and guitar player were leaning against the bus, talking to three fat groupies, one of whom was that stupid bitch with the heinous titties and an even uglier face who had flashed them during the show. I immediately caught the guitar player's eye again, stifled a laugh, and gave him a look that dared him to approach me.

"Yo, Kara!" the drummer called out. His timing couldn't have been more perfect. Kara grabbed my hand and walked me and Jana over to him, with Milo trailing behind.

"Hey again, Chris! These are my friends, Jana and Olivia." She turned her body and pulled Milo next to her in a way that made it clear that she had decided which of them she wanted. Credit where credit is due, Kara had some finesse. "And this is Milo. Guys, this is Chris, and this is the band's manager, Mark, right? And I'm sorry, I didn't catch your name earlier today."

"I'm Josh, what's up," the merch guy said indifferently. "Okay, that's the last of this shit. I need food and a beer. Mark, when's bus call tonight?"

"Our driver has the full night off. He's asleep at the motel. We leave here for Greenville, South Carolina, at 6:30 a.m. sharp." Mark looked up from his phone. "I don't give a shit if you stay out all night, but no noise or guests on the bus after 3:00. We have back-to-back interviews with local media starting at 11:00 on the dot tomorrow morning, so let the other guys know that they better plan on being showered and having their shit together by then."

"Yeah, yeah," Josh said. "I'm not sure why *we* don't get to have a hotel room tonight too, if it's a fucking 6:30 bus call, but what the fuck do I know after ten years of doing this shit, right?"

"Hey, where the fuck is Carlos?" Chris asked. Having processed the hint that Kara was otherwise spoken for this evening, he was gradually inching his way over to me and Jana. "He's the only one you need to worry about."

"He's already gone," a voice behind us said. "He's with that chick he met here during our last tour."

"The one who was DMing him upskirts of her dirty thong?" Chris asked.

"The very same." I turned to my left. The guitar player had abandoned the groupie whales and had positioned himself so close to me that I could practically feel the heat radiating off his upper body. He was scruffy and sexy, and he smelled freshly showered, like Old Spice and virility, exactly the way a man should. "Didn't you see her hanging around backstage all night?"

"She filters the fuck out of all her photos. Except for those unholy close-ups of her snatch," Josh said. "You wouldn't have recognized her in real life unless Carlos told you it was the same chick."

"I've been texting that little shit for the past hour," Mark fumed. "That's why he bailed on load-out? So help me God, I will leave his ass in Atlanta. I can tune a guitar myself. The tour will go on just fine without him."

"Carlos is my guitar tech, and the tour will not go on without him," Mr. Scruffy whispered to me. "He'll be here before dawn, Mark," Scruffy said more loudly. "I vouched for him, you can count on it." He turned back to me. "I'm Alex, by the way. Alex Montalvo-Moore. I saw you standing toward the front of the pit, right? I was hoping I might get a chance to talk to you."

"I'm Olivia Ray," I said. I held out my hand and gave him a wary look, as if I wasn't ready to fuck his brains out right there. "I had a nice time tonight. That's my cousin, Jana. She's the real fan. But I'm glad I joined her."

Jana looked giddy as she shook Alex's hand, but she quickly turned her attention back to Chris, who had already shamelessly put his arm around her waist.

"I'm glad you did too," Alex smiled. "Hey, Kara! Good to see you again."

"You too," she replied sweetly, but without letting go of Milo's hand. "We were thinking we'd all go to Sidebar to hang."

"I don't give a shit what the rest of you do, but all I've eaten today is those gas station taquitos because the fucking openers once again demolished our catering before I had the chance to get anything." Josh scowled. "I'm going to Sidebar now. Come find me if you decide to join." Josh stormed off into the night.

"Does he know where he's going?" Alex asked.

"Well, he's heading in the general direction of the bar, and there are a few other good places close by, so he'll probably be okay," Kara laughed.

"Are we following him or what?" Chris asked. "It's not even 1:00 yet."

"I don't give two shits what the rest of you do either, but I'm serious: no outsiders and no noise on the bus after 3:00 tonight. If any of you wake me up, there will be hell to pay." With that, Mark turned his back on us and walked away.

"He's not normally such a prick," Alex said to me, apologetically. "We've been sleeping in the bus and showering at the venues for the past three stops, and Carlos is driving him insane. We'll get hotel rooms in South Carolina tomorrow, and I'll make Carlos apologize for slacking on his responsibilities today. Mark will calm the fuck down."

"I'm not mad," I shrugged. "If I were in my fifties and had to wrangle up a bunch of dudes in their twenties every night, I'd have a stick up my ass too."

At this, Chris and Alex began howling with laughter.

"I'm pretty sure he's, like, thirty-eight," Chris sputtered. "Holy hell, that's a lesson for all of us. That's what too many years of too much cocaine and too many filthy women will do to you."

"Yeah, plus he's vain as fuck," Alex added. "He's convinced that he can almost pass for our age. He'd lose his mind if you said that to him. I wish you *would* say that to him."

"My bad," I shrugged again.

"Hey, so this girl that Milo and I know from high school is having a house party in Decatur," Kara said, holding up her phone as if to evidence the text conversation she'd been having. "I think we're going to go there instead. If you don't mind sitting on each other's laps, my car can fit all of you."

"I'm not going anywhere too far from here," Chris said. "Jana, if you want to hang on the bus with me, you're welcome to."

"Didn't that guy just say no outsiders though?" Jana blushed. She always has been the kind of girl to seek permission for the smallest things.

"That rule isn't in effect until 3:00, and he won't say shit about it later either, as long as you're with me."

"Okay, then, wow! Awesome! I've never been on a tour bus before." Jana is also the kind of girl who doesn't know when to play it cool.

"We can smoke some weed and I'll give you the grand tour," Chris replied. Alex must have seen me roll my eyes, because he stifled a laugh.

"Is that okay?" Jana asked me. She turned back to Chris. "I mean, can Olivia come too?"

I gave Jana my most contemptuous glare. As if I needed her to run interference for me. And for what, the dubious privilege of giving one of these guys a blowjob in his bunk? Please.

"I spend enough time on that bus as it is and wouldn't mind seeing downtown Atlanta at night," Alex jumped in before I could respond. I could tell by his tone that I already had him hooked. "We have a couple bottles of Bud Light and I think some vodka and rum and a few mixers in there, but I wouldn't mind sitting down for a real drink either. If you wanted to join me?"

"Yeah, that works," I replied. I paused, then added with a smirk, "We can smoke some weed and I'll give you the grand tour. Of downtown Atlanta, that is."

Although my snide remark went completely over Chris's head (as he was undoubtedly distracted by thoughts of the dozen different ways he was planning to bang my cousin within the hour), Alex snickered and looked delighted.

And so, we parted ways: Milo and his high school crush to some shady party in Decatur, Jana to play the part of band-slut with the drummer of her dreams, and Alex and I a few blocks down Luckie Street to Sidebar.

"Josh must've gotten lost or sidetracked," Alex said when we entered the bar. The conversation had flowed easily between us on the walk over, and I was happy that Josh wasn't around to interrupt the dynamic. "Unless he's hiding at a table in the back, I don't see him anywhere."

"I bet the kitchen is closed," I said. "He probably bailed to find a place that's still serving food at this hour. I'm sure there's a Waffle House or something somewhere nearby if you're starving. Text him if you want."

"No, I'm fine," Alex said. "He wasn't kidding about the opening band eating all our food at the venue, though. The Tabernacle provided us with a nice spread, but Josh was busy setting up the merch booth when they put it out and he didn't get any of it. I don't blame him for being pissed. But we don't need to babysit him."

"So, let's hang at the bar, then?"

"Wherever you want to go."

Alex and I sat there for about an hour until closing. Alex had a few locally brewed beers and I had a gin and tonic, which he paid for. I talked a little bit about getting my "business degree" (I didn't mention that it was a two-year program in hospitality management) and how I was currently the assistant building manager at a high-end apartment complex in Buckhead (technically I was still a desk clerk with no formal title, but given how useless everyone else in the front office was, I was effectively Bradford's second-in-command). Even with embellishments, my job seemed humiliating compared to the life of a rockstar, so I made up some stuff about being an aspiring entrepreneur too. I acted like that was my true passion and told him that the management job was a way to maintain a certain quality of life for myself until my side businesses generated enough income for me to quit The Roosevelt and focus on operating my own enterprises full-time.

Alex lit up at that remark and started reminiscing about how, when Six Times Country was just getting started, his bedroom consisted of an air mattress in a walk-in closet in a rundown house that he rented in Knoxville, Tennessee, with seven other guys, all musicians or roadies. He had paid $140 each month for his six-by-ten-foot windowless "room," which included his share of utilities. This arrangement meant that he could cover his living expenses by giving a couple of private guitar lessons whenever he was in town, thereby allowing him to dedicate the rest of his energy to pursuing opportunities for the band and working on his craft. By temporarily sacrificing space, privacy, and comfort while chasing his musical dreams, he never needed to take up some shitty, exhausting, time-consuming job doing landscaping or working as a busboy or dealing weed, which was how the majority of his peers made ends meet.

Most of his bandmates and the crew were from Knoxville too, Alex explained, although their tour manager, Mark, had recently moved from Los Angeles to some random town outside Baltimore, Maryland, where his parents owned a pharmacy, and their bass player, Ezra—the one who had been bickering with his girlfriend over FaceTime, which happened almost every night they were on tour, and who had joined Six Times Country about two years prior after the last guy quit for "a more stable lifestyle"— lived in a suburb of Raleigh, North Carolina.

Alex, for his part, had since substantially upgraded his own living situation from the walk-in closet of the band's early days (thank God), having saved up enough money to buy himself a converted loft between Downtown Knoxville and Old City. He swelled with pride as he raved about its high ceilings and exposed architecture.

"I think I have a knack for real estate investing," he boasted. "I'd seen how the neighborhood was ripe for revitalization and I got in just in time. I don't normally talk numbers, but you're a businesswoman so you'll know I'm not just bragging. I bought this place for a little over two hundred thousand almost three years ago, and it's already worth almost three hundred fifty K today. I've put some work into it, but that's still an insane return on my investment. So now I'm looking at similar properties that I can buy now, rent out for passive income while I'm on the road, and sell in however-many years when the market is right. Six Times Country is my priority, but the music industry is fickle and I'm looking to build lasting wealth."

I'll admit that, overall, I was impressed. The part about being poor and living in a closet had been a huge turnoff, but I told myself to have some compassion for that period of his life; after all, I've been in situations that were beneath me too. The important thing was, those struggles were in his past, and I was making a connection with him just as his career prospects were burgeoning on two fronts. Hell, if his ambition was to be a rockstar real estate magnate, maybe my expertise in hospitality and property management was an asset after all. I wanted him to have the revelation on his own about how our skills and interests could align, but before I could say anything to nudge him in that direction, he paused and smiled at me.

"Do you know how refreshing it is to talk about this stuff with a chick?" he said. I raised an eyebrow. "Not a chick. A smart, savvy woman. You know what I mean. Most of the females I meet only care about the band. Half of them just want me to introduce them to Sean. You know Sean, our lead singer? The other half want to be able to tell their friends that they fucked one of the guys in Six Times Country, and they don't care which one. They ask the same damn questions about 'where did your band name come from?' and 'do you guys get along?' that we constantly get from hack interviewers at dying media outlets, and beyond that, all they want to do is take selfies with me for their Instagram."

"Yeah, I don't really do social media," I shrugged. "I'm happy Jana dragged me along tonight, though." I silently congratulated myself on having had the good sense not to scream along the lyrics to the two songs they played to close out the show, even though they were my favorites. If Alex was attracted to my casual indifference about his music, it would be easy enough for me to continue the act.

As if on cue, a chubby girl in a loose-fitting floral blouse and too-tight jeans approached us. We already had been interrupted several times by dudes slapping Alex on the back and offering him shots of tequila, accompanied by their trashy girlfriends who glared at me as they stuffed their pathetic cleavage into Alex's face and got their cakey drugstore-brand foundation all over his clothes when they nuzzled into his chest to beg for a picture. This time, however, I was happy for the interruption. The dumb cow was only underscoring how different I was from all of Alex's fawning groupies.

"You are my absolute favorite guitar player," she cooed. "Is Sean here too?"

I choked down a spiteful laugh.

"Just me, I'm afraid," Alex said patiently.

"You're my absolute favorite," she said again. "Can I please take a picture with you?"

"Of course," Alex said. How he managed to show unwavering kindness to these imbeciles defies my comprehension.

She held her phone at arm's length to take a selfie and proceeded to make a dozen different adjustments to the angle and her pose, trying to find the right shot. Like, bitch, iPhone is going to capture all three of your chins no matter how your head is tilted. Finally, she looked up at me with desperation.

"Can you take the photo from a few steps back so it shows our whole bodies?" she asked.

I rolled my eyes, took her phone without comment, snapped three shots, and handed it back to her for review and approval.

"The first one is great," Alex said. Clearly he wanted her to get lost too.

"I'll post that one!" she said excitedly. "I'm @ShamuThe DumbBitchWhoWillNotGoAway on Snap and Insta. I'll tag you!"

"That'd be great," Alex said. "Thank you so much for supporting us. We really appreciate you. We'll be back in Atlanta for Shaky Knees in May. I hope you come see us."

She squealed, gave Alex another hug, and finally, blessedly, scampered away.

"I was going to say that you made her night, but I think you made her whole year."

"Imagine if Sean had been here, though," he snorted.

"She'd be telling that story to her grandkids."

We shared a laugh, but there was a total absence of cruelty in his. So I continued, "I think it's really sweet though. Loyal fans like that must be a blessing, ultimately. You can count on her to buy your t-shirts and memorabilia and download your albums and talk up how great your band is to everyone she knows for the rest of your career."

"You know what, Olivia? You are absolutely right."

The bartender announced last call. The whole point of me telling you this story is so that you'll stop speculating about some deep-seeded psychological trauma that impels me to do what I do, and you'll stop acting like I've never tried to make a so-called "real relationship" work (or at least, not after Manny). So I'll be vulnerable for a second here. In that moment, when I heard "last call" that night, I was genuinely disappointed. Nervous, even. I liked Alex a lot more than I had expected to when I saw him onstage or when he introduced himself in front of his tour bus, and I didn't want my time with him to end. Normally I know instinctively how I need to act to get what I want from a guy, but my emotions were screwing with my judgment. I didn't want to part ways yet, but I didn't want to look clingy. I wanted to sleep with him immediately, but not if that meant it would be a one-off thing. I wanted him to want to spend more time with me, but it was unclear whether the best way to achieve that was to make my exit right then and leave him wanting more, or to get him hooked on me by creating an even more memorable night together over however many hours we had left before his tour bus took off for the next city. Part of me was so furious with myself for caring at all that I had to force myself not to do something outrageous, like slap him across the face or ask him to hook me up with Sean, in order to bring the whole situation to an immediate and irrevocable end on my own terms.

"So, what do you think, Miss Olivia Ray?" he asked as he threw down a twenty and a ten to cover our tab. "Are you hungry? Josh texted me while we were talking, but I ignored it. He's back on the bus. I guess he found some burger joint, but he said that he left a half hour ago and they were already starting to close up for the night."

"I'm not famished or anything, but I wouldn't mind getting something." This was a good sign. It seemed like he was giving me an opening to indicate that I wanted to keep hanging. "But our options are going to be limited, especially around here. If we get an Uber right away, we can probably make it to Majestic Diner before they lock their doors, but we'll be cutting it pretty close. It's up to you whether you think it's worth the risk."

Alex hesitated. "Aw, you know what, fuck it. Let's go for it!" he laughed. "I'll order us an Uber right now. What did you say the restaurant was called, the Majestic? Our Uber is three minutes away. If we get there too late, then we can just find a Waffle House or a twenty-four hour McDonald's."

"Decisiveness like a boss," I grinned. "Okay, since it was my suggestion, if Majestic turns out to be a bust, then you have to let me treat you to all your heart's desires off the dollar menu."

"Ha! But only off the dollar menu!"

"Well, if we go to Waffle House, maybe I'll let you split my chocolate chip waffle with me too."

It was the kind of stupid banter that is only charming to two people who are crushing on each other, I know. But being with Alex was exciting. Even as we walked to the street to meet the Uber, I could tell that everyone in the bar was looking at us, looking at *me*, admiring what an attractive couple we were and wondering how I managed to snag a country music rockstar when he could have been with any other woman in the world. Being with him solidified my status as a star too. Maybe I would resurrect the deactivated social media accounts I had registered under my real name. He would want to be able to tag me in the pictures he took of us traveling the world and make me his recurring #wcw. All his female fans would stalk my profile, wanting to steal glimpses into my life, to copy my style and my attitude so that maybe they could attract a man like Alex too. And when you added in all the horny guys and lesbians who'd follow my account just to see my occasional bikini pics, I bet I could have a million followers by the end of the year and make six figures as a full-time influencer. Not that we'd need the extra income; Six Times Country was going to be huge and Alex was already a pretty savvy investor. I could manage our money so he could focus on his music. We could embody the ideal entertainment-industry power couple, and the best part was, Alex seemed to share my vision.

Chapter Seven

There was a surprising amount of activity when Alex and I walked out onto Poplar Street: two homeless gentlemen leaning against the adjacent storefront, having an animated but respectful conversation about the impact of modernization on the Catholic Church; a young patrol cop absentmindedly listening to some bloated former frat boy bloviating about the Georgia Bulldogs' prospects for next football season; a red-faced white guy trying to get his crying girlfriend into the passenger seat of his car, snarling, "For fuck's sake, Nicole, can we go one bloody weekend without having this fight?"; a short guy plodding toward us reeking of weed, who immediately changed direction and darted onto Forsyth Street when he spotted the police officer, who, incidentally, gave even less of a shit about the cannabisseur than Alex or I did; and three piss-drunk girls falling over each other and scream-singing the lyrics to some random song at the end of the street.

"What a shitshow," I said.

"I think they're shrieking the chorus to 'You're Bad For Me,'" Alex said. "Which, unfortunately, is one of ours. I don't blame you if you ditch me now."

I laughed. Alex grabbed my hand and kissed me. Those lips. He ran his left hand through my hair and kissed me again. Irrespective of what came to pass between us later, I will never deny that Alex Montalvo-Moore knows how to kiss a woman.

As much as I wanted to rip his shirt off on the streets of downtown Atlanta, however, I knew that I needed to play it cool.

I grabbed his other hand and nuzzled into his neck so he'd know that I was still interested, but I whispered into his ear, "We should probably behave in front of the Uber driver."

A car turned onto Poplar Street. Alex glanced at his phone.

"I guess you're right," he sighed and nodded his head toward the blue sedan. "I think that's our man."

We politely greeted the driver and cuddled up in the backseat. Fortunately the guy wasn't too chatty, but he also did not seem like the type who would take kindly to two twenty-somethings attempting to stealthily get each other off on his leather seats eighteen inches behind his head, so Alex and I managed to keep our hands mostly to ourselves. The tease was only heightening the anticipation, and when we tumbled out of the car at 2:10 a.m. in front of Majestic Diner, the sedan hadn't pulled away before we were causing an enviable spectacle of lips and tongues and hands for all of Poncey-Highlands.

"Come on," I said after a moment, gently pushing him away. He seemed to crave the chase. "We've made it this far. Let's see if we can still get a table."

Despite the late hour, the restaurant was almost at capacity and was buzzing with drunken banter. The hostess looked a little annoyed by our arrival (or perhaps she was just jealous), but she sat us at an empty booth toward the back.

"We'll be quick," Alex assured her. I arched an eyebrow; we'd be paying them good money for our food, and I certainly would not be rushed.

I ordered a veggie omelet and Alex got the house-special burger, which I remember mostly because of how delighted he was by it. I let him eat some of my grits, and he was disproportionately excited about that as well.

"Our quality of life on tour has improved so much in the past year or two," he explained. "The venues and the crowds, where we stay, our days off, how much we earn, all of it. We've been past those early days of sleeping on strangers' cockroach-infested floors and living off of five-dollar per diems for weeks at a time for a while now. But over the past year or two, it's like we've broken through to the next level, and the level above that is in sight. We just need to stay focused and stay the course. But for whatever reason, the past two weeks of this tour have been fucking brutal. We've had too many back-to-back shows, so we're all exhausted. In a couple of cities, we've gotten stuck with some incompetent audio engineer that the local venue insisted we use, and every single one of us has had our instrument or our gear or one of our mics malfunction at some point onstage during a performance. To be honest, in most of those cases the issue was minor enough that the majority of our fans probably couldn't tell the difference, but it's the principle of it. We're professionals and stupid shit like that should not keep happening.

"And then at our Austin show a few days ago, the sleazy fucking promoter shorted us a few thousand bucks. So Mark, our tour manager—you know, the cranky guy you thought was in his fifties? He had slept for about two hours total over the past four days and was running on nothing but his usual cocktail of cocaine and Adderall and rage. Mark starts threatening to kick the shit out of the promoter unless we get our full comp in cash as agreed, and the promoter pulls out a massive fucking hunting knife and chases Mark a half-mile down the road. Fucking Texas, man. We're lucky that asshole wasn't carrying a gun.

"Plus, the label forced our openers on us this tour. We had no say in it at all. They are a bunch of nineteen-year-old punks who think they're the modern-day incarnation of Lynyrd Skynyrd, and they act like it's acceptable to show up late and hungover to soundcheck and to parade a different set of the trashy groupies that they pick up outside the venue through our greenroom every night. You'd think they'd realize what a huge opportunity this is for them and show a little respect."

Alex paused. I looked at him wide-eyed. Most of our conversation had been light-hearted and silly up until that point. I had no idea how he wanted me to respond.

"Wow, I guess I needed to get that off my chest," he said. "I'm not complaining. Not really. This isn't my first rodeo, and I knew what I signed up for."

"And it's not the glamorous life of private jets and caviar and champagne that your fans probably assume it is?"

"Right. Not even close. Even the ones who realize that much... how can I explain this? For most of the people who came out to see us tonight, it's the most exciting thing that's happening to them all month. I don't mean that in a rude way. They get dressed up, they get drunk, they let loose with their buddies, they see their favorite band onstage after having saved up to buy the tickets, maybe they splurge and buy a t-shirt to commemorate the entire affair because the night is an adventure for them. And they assume that every single night on the road must be the same way for us. An adventure. A party. Exciting. But at this point? I hate to sound like an asshole, but it's not. It hasn't been for a long time. It's our job. It's the only job I can imagine doing, but it's still a job."

I nodded. To think, when Jana and I had gotten ready together earlier that night, I had momentarily considered dressing up in a country-western style outfit for fun. I'm sure I would have caught Alex's eye either way, but I doubted that we'd be having this conversation if I'd looked like another generic fan at first glance.

"Anyway, I really needed this night. I needed to sit down and have a delicious, hot burger with a beautiful woman, away from the rest of the guys. We're all on edge. But they're my brothers, all of them, and none of our fights stick, you know? Even Chip, who was our original bass player before Ezra, he quit mostly because he and his wife had twin daughters. The twins thing was a surprise, and they already had a two-year-old son, and Katie probably would have divorced him if he'd left her in Knoxville for months at a time to deal with all that on her own. Cutest kids ever, but Jesus. Three of them. We understood. There's no animosity there. Mark and Josh were being assholes tonight, which frankly was pissing me off, because y'all were our guests and for all they knew our biggest fans. And I don't give a fuck if they're 'just' the crew, because their behavior is a reflection of the band, and I'll be damned if I see some shitposts circulating the internet about how Six Times Country is full of pricks who think they're too good for their fans or who've lost touch with their roots or whatever. But it's the stress. It's the fact that we've all more than paid our dues, but this tour we've been dealing with more than our fair share of bullshit. I think you'll really get along once you get to know them."

"Once I get to know them?" I repeated.

Alex chuckled. "Yeah, if you want. They're as much a part of the band as me and Chris and Sean and Ezra. I'm hoping this isn't the last time I ever see you."

"I'm hoping that too," I admitted.

There was a comfortable silence. We smiled at each other. I peeled the crust off my toast. He took another bite of his burger. I felt a fleeting sense of contentment. If dating were comprised of moments exclusively like this, perhaps I wouldn't be so cynical.

But of course, we were promptly interrupted by Alex's phone, face down on the table, buzzing to indicate an incoming call.

"I better—" Alex started, and picked up his phone. I nodded. In fairness to him, if someone was calling rather than texting, especially at this time of night, it was probably important.

"Hey, what's going on?" Alex's voice dropped half an octave and his entire demeanor changed. "No, I'm in Atlanta tonight.... Eating at a diner, what does it matter?... Seriously? Don't ask me questions when you don't really want to know the answers.... We're not getting into this right now.... Hey, just stop. Is there something wrong with the loft?... Are you okay?... No, that's not fair. I thought we had an understanding. You should not be calling me like this.... Shannon, knock it off. Just stop it. We're not doing this tonight.... What? Fine. I will call you tomorrow when I'm at the venue, okay?... Okay, thank you. Yeah, that plant was about to die anyway, your green thumb is the only reason it lasted as long as it did. I'm not mad. But can you please remember to wait until Tuesday to take the garbage out?... Holy shit, I'm not berating you, I was just asking! Jesus, Shannon. The building manager called me on Thursday and warned me that if I left three bags of garbage sitting outside the door stinking up the hallway for four days straight again, I'd get a fifty dollar fine tacked onto the monthly HOA dues. Are you telling me he's making that up?... He's not conspiring against—... Okay, okay. I hope that's not—." Alex stopped short and looked up at me. "She hung up."

Mind you, for this entire six-minute trainwreck of a phone call, during which two-thirds of the diner had cleared out since it was now past closing time, I could hear the voice of a hysterical woman on the other end. Between the sobs and cusswords and mid-sentence screams, ninety-five percent of her side of the conversation was indiscernible, notwithstanding how obnoxiously loud it was even with the phone pressed against Alex's ear. But listening to Alex's side was enough. Clearly he was married to some psycho bitch. Of fucking course.

"I'm not married," Alex started, as if reading my mind. "Or engaged, or in a relationship, or anything like that. It's complicated."

This should be fucking good, I thought. I glared at him but didn't respond.

"Shannon and I were together for six years. We've been broken up for the past six months. She moved out right after, but I guess she got into a fistfight with one of her new roommates and they kicked her out of the house. I don't know the details. I told her she could stay in my loft while I was on tour. Maybe it was a stupid idea. It was definitely a stupid idea. I guess I felt bad for her and didn't like the idea of leaving her homeless. She hasn't taken the breakup well. She's always been troubled. She thrives on drama. I know she isn't my responsibility anymore, but I couldn't stand the thought of her bouncing between random guys' houses just so she'd have a place to sleep."

"Honestly, Alex, that mess is none of my business. We had a nice time together tonight. You don't owe me anything beyond that. It sounds like you still need to figure out your relationship with what's-her-name, Shannon." I paused and scoffed. "But I have zero interest in playing sideline spectator or guidance counselor or your priestly confessor, to any of it."

"No, please, Olivia, just listen." Alex looked panicked, and I'd be lying if I said I wasn't pleased to see it. "She's crazy, I mean it. But we are really, truly done this time. The only reason I let her back into my house at all is because I'm on tour. I literally changed the locks after we broke up and I had to have the building manager give her the spare key he keeps on file. And she knows!

She knows she needs to find a new place for herself by the time I'm back from tour. That's not negotiable. Please don't be mad at me. I didn't mention her before because there isn't anything to tell. She is an ex-girlfriend. She's taking care of my place while I'm away only because I pity her. I pity her! We were toxic for each other and I don't miss any of the fighting or the drama or the lies or the manipulation. You have to believe me, we are broken up for good. But she's mentally unwell. I'm just trying to have some compassion for her and help her get back on her feet."

"Okay," I said. I hadn't decided whether or not I believed him at this point. With the luxury of hindsight, I know that my instincts were screaming that something was off and I wasn't getting the whole story. But on the surface, the facts seemed to align. The way he spoke to her on the phone did sound much more like a beleaguered ex or an irritated roommate than a boyfriend or lover. And her rabid screeching and the few fragments of her side of the conversation that I had been able to discern seemed proof-positive that she was crazy and controlling and probably delusional. Back then, some small, pathetic part of me was probably still clinging to the vain illusion that happy, meaningful, empowering romantic relationships existed. And so I myself succumbed to the universal force that I would so often later use to my advantage: people will believe whatever you're saying if they want badly enough for it to be true.

"Okay?" Alex repeated. "Really?" He looked overcome with... relief, I guess, but also some other emotion that I couldn't decipher. "Thank you for believing me, Olivia. You have no idea how horrible Shannon is. We never should have been together for six years. We fell out of love a long, long time ago, but we couldn't give up making each other miserable. And I don't trust her not to, like, kill herself in my house just to spite me. She knows I'd never forgive myself for it if she did, which is why I haven't banished her completely."

"But your relationship is really over?" I confirmed. "If it's not, that's your business and that's fine. But we were making out in the parking lot when we got here, so I need you to hear me clearly when I tell you that I have no interest whatsoever in being your side piece. Or in having some crazy bitch with a switchblade come hunt me down in Atlanta."

"It's really, truly over this time," Alex assured me. "I'm so sorry you had to hear all that, and I'm furious with her for ruining our night."

"Okay," I said again. "It's whatever. It's really late anyway."

"Did you still want to go back to the bus together, though?"

I gave him my most disdainful look.

"Not to fuck!" he quickly added. I started laughing; I couldn't help myself. He really was sexy, and I had sufficiently scared the shit out of him. I had no intentions of sleeping with him that night—I still needed to punish him a little for Shannon's interference—but I didn't want to be so harsh that it ended up turning him off.

"I'm pretty sure that's what Jana and your drummer are doing right now," I said, rolling my eyes. "I need to go back and fetch her and our car anyway. If you want to hang out until they're done, I'm down. As long as you don't have any expectations."

"You're not like any other girl I've met, Olivia." The waitress had dropped off our check unsolicited, a not-too-subtle hint to pay up and get out. Alex fished through his pockets and dropped another wad of cash on the table, enough to cover both of our meals. "I genuinely want to spend time with you doing whatever you want, wherever you want. And besides, the bus is a Petri dish. You are ridiculously hot, but I'm kind of glad, in a weird way, that you don't want to get naked in there."

I groaned. "Is it so filthy that I shouldn't even get on for a nightcap? Do I need a tetanus booster first?"

"No! No, it's fine! Hell, I will wipe down your seat with a full bottle of Clorox for you before you sit down if you want. Just know that I keep my house in Knoxville in much better condition."

By the time we walked outside to wait for our Uber, I was smiling again. He was hot and charismatic and talented and passionate. He stood to be the rare man who was worthy of my affections and attention outright, without having to shower me with gifts and flattery and fancy meals to capture and keep my interest. He made it easy for me to look past the sin of having a former girlfriend who obsessively wanted him back. Who could blame her? But he was going to be mine instead. When the Uber dropped us off in front of the Tabernacle, I willingly followed him back to the parking lot and joined him on the tour bus.

Josh was sitting upfront playing a videogame with the volume turned down. He seemed in better spirits than when I'd seen him last.

"What's up, man?" Alex said. "Where is everyone?"

"Mark and Ezra are asleep." Josh paused the game. "Let's see, Sean took off with those sea donkeys who were all up on his dick after the show."

"Jesus, dude, come on!"

"What? You asked. Besides, your girl is fit, what do you care?" Josh straightened up and held out his hand. "I'm Josh. You're not some snowflake that's going to start crying because you're offended on their behalf, right?"

"I'm Olivia," I said coolly. "We met earlier. And no, I'm not offended. If anything, I'm honored to be in the presence of such an all-powerful edgelord."

Alex snorted back a laugh and Josh cracked a smile.

"But, I mean, you both saw those busted-ass slam pigs, right?" Josh backtracked nervously. "Even if Sean's trying to get his foursome-card checked, he can do better."

"He's going to need a two-week supply of penicillin, but as long as we don't have to fumigate the bunks for a crabs infestation, I'm going to mind my business," Alex shrugged.

"Naomi's going to the D.C. show and staying with us through Brooklyn, though. This tour has been enough of a clusterfuck without her grilling me for four days straight about where Sean's dick has been."

"Yeah, I know," Alex shrugged again. He turned to me. "Naomi is Sean's girlfriend. They have a 'don't ask, don't tell' policy when he's on the road."

"Naomi doesn't ask *him*," Josh clarified. "She has no qualms about pestering the fuck out of the rest of us."

"And where's everyone else?" Alex asked, eager to change the subject.

"What everyone else?" Josh replied. "Chris is in the back getting his dick wet. I've been listening to her friend's muffled moaning since I got back an hour ago. And I don't know where the fuck Carlos is. He still hasn't replied to anyone's texts. Mark is going to fire him, dude. I'm not kidding."

"That's not Mark's call to make," Alex said flatly. "I'll talk with Carlos and let him know he needs to pull it together and kiss Mark's ass for a few days. But bottom line is, he's my tech, and unless he gets himself left behind at a truck stop or he shits on the bus or something, he's not getting fired and he's not going anywhere."

"Alright, man," Josh threw up both arms in surrender. I guess he intuited that I'd be sticking around for a while, because he started to act more deferentially toward me. "We have vodka and rum, and I think Sprite, Coke, and orange juice for mixers, if you want to make yourself a drink," he offered. "Have you played Grand Theft Auto before? You can have a turn if you want."

"My brothers have this game but I suck at it. I'm content just watching you play," I replied sweetly. It seemed important to Alex that I get along with his crew, so if Josh was going to make an effort to be nice, I was willing to reciprocate. "I will take you up on the drink, though. Thanks. Alex, if you're pouring, I'll do a rum and Coke, light on the rum."

Alex made us each a rum and cola and handed Josh a beer.

"Thanks, bro," Josh said. "You read my mind."

Josh never seemed to catch on that he was the third wheel, but it ended up annoying me less than I would have thought. Alex and Josh mostly rotated the Xbox controller between themselves, although I took two turns at the game for fun. Jana and Chris emerged from Chris's bunk around 4:00 a.m. We all exchanged knowing smirks but no one hassled them too much about whatever naughty things they'd been doing to each other over the preceding four hours. (Incidentally, Jana later confessed to me that the sex was mediocre at best and ninety-five percent of their time together was spent smoking weed and napping.) More drinks were poured, more stories about life on the road were shared, more of the San

Andreas countryside was shot up by Josh's avatar. Sean returned just before 4:30 a.m., alone.

"I don't want to talk about it," was all he said, shaking his head as he walked back to his bed. "I'm going to sleep."

We devolved into laughter and speculated about the variety of outrageous scenarios that could have unfolded between him and his three homely groupie lovers. When I started chatting with Chris while Alex was taking his turn at GTA, Alex promptly blew the mission, handed the controller back to Josh, and put his arm around my waist. I was taken aback by his sudden possessiveness, but not angry about it. If circumstances were going to force me to share him with his bandmates and his fans, I was pleased that he wasn't interested in sharing me with anyone. I didn't want the night to end.

Then, at 5:04 a.m., all hell broke loose.

A muscular, attractive, six foot three guy, who I could only assume was Carlos, burst through the bus door, accompanied by six other people. Perhaps if his companions all had been females, it wouldn't have been as big of a deal. Perhaps if they all had been a little bit quieter, things wouldn't have combusted.

But that's not what happened.

"They're strippers, guys!" Carlos bellowed. "These are the hottest dancers at Tattletales!"

"Not Tattletales, dumbass!" one of the girls shrieked. "Tattle- tales girls don't get paid like we do!"

At this, the three other girls started screaming about how much they love money and how their club has the hottest bitches in Atlanta. Now, I'm not judging. Jana has been dancing at gentle- men's clubs since the day she turned eighteen, and a few nights a week on the pole have afforded her a lifestyle that she could never attain on her makeup artist's salary alone. She bought herself a Jeep Renegade in cash (it was certified pre-owned, but still in great shape), she gets her lashes and her extensions done at the best salons in Buckhead, and she's saving up to buy a condo someday. All of which is to say, I'm not a hater and I have no doubt that these girls had a very lucrative night. But they were losing their fucking minds. And this, in turn, was getting the two random dudes with them all riled up. They started growling and body-slamming into each other in some sort of bizarre impromptu pro wrestling match or homoerotic mating ritual, except there was absolutely no space for this shit. The whole bus was shaking. One of the stripper girls was suddenly topless. Someone hurled a handful of cash in Jana's direction, which Jana promptly pocketed. In the commotion, an unidentified culprit barfed all over the bus stairs. The whole thing would have been hilarious, but for the fact that I was pretty sure half of them were on PCP and there was a non-negligible chance that one of them was going to rob and kill us all.

"Would you assholes shut the fuck up?" Sean screamed from his bunk in the back. "I need to fucking rest my fucking vocal cords!"

"This is going to get really bad, really fast," Alex whispered to me.

"Everyone who is not in the band, get the fuck off this bus, RIGHT FUCKING NOW." Mark's voice reverberated from the other end of the bus. Something large and metallic clattered to the floor. "RIGHT FUCKING NOW!" he screamed again, stomping toward us.

"Or what, bro?" the shorter of the two random guys hollered back, chest puffed out.

"Come on," Alex said, grabbing my hand. I reached for Jana in an attempt to pull her along with me.

"My purse is with Chris's stuff," she whispered.

"This is fucking insane," I said to no one in particular. I honestly didn't know whether to be amused or terrified at this point. "Jana, get your shit and meet me outside."

Alex was already shoving his way through the mass of unwelcome strangers, dragging me along behind him, out the door. I turned back just in time to see Mark, tomato-faced and dripping with sweat, waving around a rifle.

"He has a fucking gun, Alex!" I said, as Alex yanked me a few feet away from the door. "What the hell is happening right now?"

"Mark does? Shit, I guess I should have known," Alex said. "He must have bought it at the Texas/Louisiana border after we got ripped off in Austin."

"You didn't realize?"

"We weren't sure. We stopped at a pawnshop. Mark said it was to find a stopgap replacement for Chris's backup hi-hat that had gotten cracked in transit. But he was being vague about the whole thing, so we kind of thought there might be more to it. What, did he get a pistol or something?"

"It was a shotgun!" I said. "Look, I'm a Georgia girl, born and raised. I'm not a gun nut, but I know how to shoot. I'm Team 'Stand Your Ground' all the way. But this is outrageous."

"Yeah, it is outrageous." Alex cracked a smile. "It is, indeed, outrageous." For the life of me, I don't know why—some twisted combination of nerves and adrenaline and lingering sexual tension, I suppose—but I started to giggle. Then Alex started to laugh, and I started to laugh harder.

"This is absurd!" I sputtered. "Why are we laughing? None of this is funny. We've both lost our damn minds."

"This entire tour has gone off the rails," Alex howled. "I promise, Mark is not going to shoot anyone. If for no other reason than because that cheap bastard doesn't want to lose the security deposit on the bus because of a bullet hole. The gun probably isn't loaded."

The hollering from inside the bus momentarily grew louder as the door opened again and four strippers—one of whom was still topless—went running off into predawn Atlanta.

"At least they had the sense to change out of their dancing heels before they got here," I muttered. Seconds later, the two guys bounded off the bus, screaming a stream of profanity at Mark and the band as they careened down the stairs.

"They went that way," I said, pointing in the direction the four half-naked girls had scattered.

"I'm speechless," Alex said, our laughter finally subsiding. "Would you believe me if I promised you that most nights on tour are not normally such a circus freak show?"

"I'd half-believe you," I teased. "But based on some of the stories you guys told me, I also think that this is nowhere close to your wildest night."

"I guess that's fair. But those days are mostly in the past. I hope none of that crap scares you off. I'm hoping you might be interested in coming to Greenville tomorrow."

"Greenville?"

"Yeah, Greenville, South Carolina. It's our next stop. I'd invite you to ride with us, but I don't know how you'd get back home. If you wanted to drive there yourself, though? I think Mark said it's only two or three hours away, and that's driving in this gas-guzzling monstrosity. No pressure. If you have to work, or if you have other plans..."

"I work some Saturdays, but I'm off tomorrow," I smiled. I had been waiting for an invitation like this for hours, but I didn't want to seem overeager. "I don't know. I guess I could get a hotel? For myself, I mean. I don't want to give you the wrong idea. Won't you be busy with band stuff all day though?"

"Only in the morning! And for a little while after lunch too. But by the time you get there, we'll probably be hanging out in the bus or wandering around the city. I don't know. It's been a while since we've played in Greenville and I'm not sure what's around the venue. But if you're there, then we can hang out until I have to play, and I'll give you an all-access pass so you can chill backstage or watch us side stage, whatever you want, and you won't have to worry about random dudes bothering you in general admission. And we don't have a Sunday show, so you and I can get brunch together and relax the next morning."

"You're making a good case for it," I said demurely. I'd seen girls dancing side stage at other shows, and it always pissed me off. Like, what made them so special? I was always hotter than any of them were, and a much better dancer. Alex was offering me the opportunity to watch the concert from my rightful spot. But he knew as well as I did that most girls would be prepared to blow him on the spot for the chance to hang backstage, and I needed to continue to distinguish myself from the pathetic masses. "What about Jana?"

"Well," Alex shifted uncomfortably, "is that a deal-breaker? If the only way you'll come is if she's there too, then I can talk to Chris and make it happen. But..."

"But he's planning on never seeing her again?" I interrupted.

"I wouldn't put it that harshly. He's not an asshole. But he's been exchanging messages with some South Carolina sorority girl he met on Tinder, and he already invited her to the show. It could get awkward."

"No, it's fine. I have my own car, and I'm pretty sure Jana has to work tomorrow anyway. I don't think she expects a marriage proposal after she took a swan dive into his crotch ten minutes after meeting him."

Alex laughed and I hid my irritation about having to play these idiotic games. The idea of being a rockstar's girlfriend had grown on me over the course of the night, and now it was clear that I'd need to forestall sleeping with Alex until we had spent several more evenings together. Strategically, this rendered accepting the Greenville offer my best option, even if I'd be forced—by virtue of the band's self-defeating, antiquated system of dividing women into slampieces and potential wifeys—to remain celibate the whole weekend. No one can claim that I'm unwilling to put in the work and make the necessary sacrifices to achieve my goals. Even as he and I were speaking, I had accepted my temporarily sexless lot and was considering whether I ought to purchase brownies or peanut butter cookies from Publix to saran-wrap and pass off as my own home-baked treats for Saturday night.

"So then you'll come? I can pitch in for your hotel. And no hidden meaning if you accept. I don't ever have to step foot in the room. As much as I would love to fall asleep with you in my arms."

And there it was. He had asked me three times to join him in Greenville, and now he had offered to pay. He was hooked. He would be invested, literally. We exchanged numbers as Jana tiptoed barefoot off the bus, her boots in hand.

"Girl, you're going to step on a needle in this parking lot, have some sense!" I yelled at her. I actually didn't give a shit what she did, but this was one last chance for me to present myself to Alex as the sensible one in the sea of floozies that had surrounded us all night. "Are you sober to drive?"

"I haven't had a drink in hours," Jana mumbled.

"You were drinking a screwdriver literally ten minutes ago."

"Oh yeah. But that was mostly orange juice, it doesn't really count." Jana plopped onto the cement to shove her cowboy boots back onto her swollen feet. It was a small miracle that we didn't get a full-frontal flash of her cooch.

"Okay, I better go handle this. And I need to make sure my brother found his way home too." I paused and kissed Alex on the cheek. "If I'm lucky, maybe I'll get some sleep before Greenville tonight. I'm in."

Alex grabbed my wrist firmly and kissed me. I let him grab my butt for a few seconds too, so that he'd have something to jerk off to after I left, and then I playfully squirmed away.

"More to come," I said.

"Good night, Olivia," he replied.

Chapter Eight

Jana insisted she hadn't had anything to drink other than a weak screwdriver or two since we left the concert, so I asked her to drive me home and let her figure out where and when to retrieve Milo. I suppose it would have been fine to sleep at her place for a few hours, but I didn't want to deal with the logistical nightmare of trying to get cars and bodies in the right location before I needed to leave for South Carolina. I also didn't want her to know about my plans with Alex yet. Part of me wanted to rub it in her face that I was the one getting asked to hang out with the band for another night, while she was nothing more than a fuck-and-chuck to them, but I didn't want to hurt her feelings or have her ask to come along so she could make Chris's night miserable (which is exactly what I would have done if I were in her position). I'd have plenty of time to brag about the experience after. Besides, this trip would be picayune in the scheme of things. My plan was to insert myself into Alex's world in a much more permanent way.

I slept for about five hours after Jana dropped me off. I didn't want to look sleep-deprived—if the previous night were any indication, Alex was forced to look at more than enough haggard women each day—but I also couldn't afford to lose any more of the time I needed to solidify my strategy. And while it was important that I not show up in South Carolina *too* early, I didn't want Alex hanging out with whatever sorostitutes Chris's Tinder match brought along with her while he was waiting for me. Perhaps I was being overly cautious, though, because by the time I woke up, Alex already had texted me three times to give me the information for the band's hotel, remind me that he was willing to pay for my room, and tell me how excited he was to see me again.

The hotel that the band was staying at wasn't a total dump, but it wasn't up to my standards, so I found myself a much nicer spot a few blocks away (but still under $250 per night, God bless South Carolina) and texted Alex back to let him know that I had reserved my own room down the street. This served a few purposes: I needed to set expectations early about the high standard of living I intended to maintain, of which accommodations were only one small component, but by paying for the hotel myself, I was underscoring my self-sufficiency. I also was creating an illusion of independence, which would give me leeway to be more possessive and aggressive when other women were around, if the situation so required. Plus, I didn't want to worry about Alex or his bandmates seeing me waiting around in the lobby or dragging in a suitcase from my car before I had a chance to change into the right outfit and freshen up my makeup. As a rule, a bit of mystery and physical distance will make you all the more desirable.

Being a "rocker chick" in a sea of country clones had worked swimmingly the night before, so I decided to stick with a similar vibe for the rest of the weekend. I packed a few outfit options for the concert, some cute-but-sexy pajamas (not lingerie, which would've been way too obvious), and some casual clothes that would show off my physique for Alex's day off in Greenville on Sunday. I looked up Six Times Country's tour schedule and saw that their next stop, on Monday, was Chapel Hill, North Carolina, which was a three and a half hour drive from Greenville. I tossed extra socks, underwear, and pajama bottoms into my suitcase just in case. I didn't want to get ahead of myself, but if Alex asked me to accompany him to another city, I wanted to be prepared. I would gladly call in sick from my bullshit job at The Roosevelt for this.

Before I left my apartment, I found Shannon on social media. Alex hadn't given me her last name, but since he had said that they had been together for six years, I figured that if I scrolled back far enough on his Instagram account, she would be tagged in one of his posts. And although his most recent twenty or so photos were action shots of him with his guitar onstage and promos for their ongoing tour, I didn't have to scroll far to find her, sitting next to him and gazing up at him at a brewery geo-tagged as the Elkmont Exchange. Friends on each side of them were leaning into the picture, and the table was filled with pint glasses and appetizers. So, I thought, it was a group outing, and she probably forced herself into the seat next to him. All Alex's caption said was, "Last night in Knoxville before tour starts," followed by details about where his fans could purchase tickets for the band's upcoming shows.

A quick glimpse down the rest of his page, where the same chick appeared in every third or fourth photo except for stretches when he was on tour, validated my assumption that she was Shannon. He hadn't tagged her in the brewery pic, but she was tagged in a photo of them holding hands amidst a crowded Pike Place Market in Seattle from a year before. Naturally, I clicked through to her profile, which was (small blessings) set to public.

Her bio lines identified her as a "medicine woman" and an "energy muse." She pronounced herself a "dreamer" and a "seeker" and a "mindful mover." Her posts primarily consisted of videos of her belly dancing in a sparsely decorated bedroom, close-ups of her face decorated with rhinestones and her hands decorated with henna, high-angle shots of crystals and burning incense, and screengrabs of the musings of self-quoting, self-proclaimed "modern-day philosophers" on love, the cosmos, and the power of femininity. She was tiny, with long dark hair and dark eyes, and not entirely unattractive. She was probably pretty decent in bed. And yet, I wasn't jealous or concerned. Her absurd desperation to demonstrate her spiritual awakening to the world via this collection of clichéd Instagram posts—notwithstanding that she had just been booted from her old apartment for punching out her former roommate—negated whatever threat she otherwise might have posed to me. Her particular brand of bullshit must have been insufferable once the ayahuasca wore off.

Look, the fact that Alex had posted a photo with her right before he left for tour, several months after they purportedly had broken up... well, it wasn't great. But it wasn't determinative either. He had admitted that he was still in her life, mostly because he was worried about her. He hadn't been posting any late-night "missing this girl" pics of her while he was on the road. Shannon's Instagram profile was a shitshow, and although the allusions to her "twin flame," to her "mirror soul," to her "divine connection" with a conspicuously absent "warrior king," were clearly references to Alex, Alex himself had conceded that she was having trouble letting go. All any of this proved was that she was batshit crazy and delusional, albeit a version dressed up in New Age, pseudo-spiritual packaging that someone like Alex could find appealing for a little while.

To be clear, any fleeting concern I may have had about Alex's potentially ongoing relationship with Shannon didn't stem from some misguided sense of feminine solidarity with this neo-hippie lunatic. I don't owe her or any other woman some nebulous duty of loyalty just because we both possess vaginas. Rather, I don't like squandering my money or my time, and her existence had the potential to render the previous night and the forthcoming trip to South Carolina a wasted investment. Six Times Country had decent name-recognition and their fanbase was growing, but back then they weren't quite so huge that it merited pursuing Alex simply for the cachet of occasionally being seen with the band without having Official Girlfriend status too.

Besides, having restricted my use of social media since high school in order to more effectively run certain scams and to keep my bosses, boyfriends, and haters out of my day-to-day affairs, I didn't currently have a suitable platform from which to brag about our time together anyway. Being a country music star's girlfriend could open up the path to a lucrative career as an influencer and entrepreneur in my own right, and Alex's aspirations to build a real estate empire throughout Tennessee and beyond heightened his appeal, but my machinations were a moot point if Shannon were still in the picture in any significant way. Properly executing the weekend road trip to Greenville would set me back a few hundred bucks, which would be a worthwhile expenditure if everything went according to plan, but a disaster (with no readily apparent means of exacting suitable revenge) if it didn't.

I've never shied away from calculated risk, but I think the deciding factor that impelled me to toss my suitcase into my trunk and head east was that I genuinely liked Alex. He was smokin' hot and easy to talk to, and I'd had fun with him the night before. I know now that's not a good enough reason to drive across state lines, but I was younger and—Lord knows why, given how consistently shitty they were—I still had some shred of naïve optimism about men and love.

As it turned out, Greenville couldn't have gone any better, which only reinforced my reckless hopes. By the time I checked into my hotel, changed my outfit, flat-ironed my hair, fixed my eyeliner, and took an Uber to the venue, it was a little after 5:30 p.m. Chris was backstage giving a private drum lesson to a handful of aspiring percussionists, but the rest of the guys were hanging out on or around their bus. Sean was resting his voice before the show, but I suspected from the way he greeted me that he was jealous that Alex had snagged me first. Mark had put away the shotgun and was clunkily typing out emails, his laptop pressed against the front right window in an effort to mooch off the venue's wifi signal without having to go inside. Josh had showered, shaved, slept, and eaten in the interim since I had last seen him, and even as he lugged boxes of t-shirts into the venue, he was in a surprisingly jolly mood.

"Chris's Tinder date is bringing two friends to the show tonight, and one of them said she thinks Josh is kind of cute," Alex whispered by way of explanation. He had pulled me next to him on the cushioned bench at the front of the bus, the designated social area, but the TV was off and the stereo was turned down while Carlos, Sean, and Ezra napped in the back. "You have to be over eighteen to get a boob job, right? These girls say they're sophomores, which is too young for my taste, but I don't care if they hang around as long as they meant sophomores at USC-Greenville, and not at the local high school."

"I have no idea what the rules for fake tits are. Mine are real," I whispered back. "Regardless of whether these chicks are legal, doesn't Josh have a girlfriend? Not that I'm judging, but..."

"You mean the girl from Knoxville he was telling you about on the bus last night? You'd have to ask him, but I'm pretty sure 'girlfriend' is too strong of a label. She's more like his recurring friend with benefits while we're home."

"Okay," I shrugged.

"Besides, nothing is going to happen with the jailbait. He could be meeting up with his favorite pornstar later, and he'd still be more excited about the prospect of having a real bed all to himself tonight." Alex paused and started laughing. "Trust me, you can't imagine how nice it is to be around a normal, clean female, with soft skin, who smells good, after being cooped up with a bunch of other filthy dudes for weeks on end. It's not even sexual, not in the way you think. Well, at least not always. But I know Josh. After he spends a few hours with this girl, he's going to want to sleep alone, in total quiet and darkness."

Alex stood up to grab two beers from the bus's refrigerator, which gave me a second to reflect. It was a weird thing for him to say. I'd assumed that the reason he had been chill about not hooking up the night before and had been so enthusiastic about inviting me to spend time with him in South Carolina was because he recognized my high value and saw the potential for a meaningful relationship with me. But if Shannon had exercised her (culturally appropriated) brujería on Alex and a part of him remained trapped under her spell of tantalizing crazy, then there was a chance that I was nothing more to him than ambulatory potpourri, a source of pleasant-but-temporary feminine companionship to tide him over until he returned to the chaos and ardor and "ethereal soul-merging" (or whatever horseshit phrase she would use to describe it) of his life with Shannon in Tennessee.

It was unacceptable. I repressed the urge to call him out on the spot, to demand that he clarify his relationship with his purported ex, and to question his motivations for inviting me to Greenville and acting like there was something special between us. I'm not some whiny, insecure little bitch-ass. Shannon's "feminine divinity" was a piece of shitty performance art; mine is the real fucking deal. The only question was whether I should dethrone her by emphasizing my naturally regal, sophisticated demeanor and appearance, thereby placing myself in stark contrast to her unrefined, spiritual-babble inanity, or by beating her at her own game and unleashing my worst impulses in the name of inflaming Alex's passions.

"I typically don't drink before we play, but we have a meet-and-greet at 6:30," Alex said as he handed me a Coors Light and sat back down. "We've done promo events with this radio station before. They're a couple of shock-jock buffoons in their late-forties. As soon as we're off the air, they'll start grilling us about all the 'hot young pussy' they think we get on the road. I give Chris shit about swiping right on college-age girls, but these assholes are fucking creepy. I'm not letting them anywhere near you, Liv. No joke. If I had a daughter of my own, I'd take Mark's shotgun with me."

"So you're, what? Drinking now so that you can tolerate their presence later?"

"Yep," Alex said with a huff. "I'm sorry I didn't tell you about it before. I didn't know it was on our agenda until we did a live interview with them this morning. Usually we charge extra for VIP tickets that include a photo op, but this is a sponsored fan event that was orchestrated by the label. Pretty much everyone attending will be the winners of some call-in contest put on by the radio station over the past week or two. I know I shouldn't bitch about it. It's good publicity and it won't take more than a half hour or so."

"What am I supposed to do by myself all that time?" I snapped. Although I wasn't thrilled about the thought of waiting around on a folding chair while a bunch of bucktoothed, zit-faced dorks who couldn't afford a subscription to satellite radio fawned over Alex and his bandmates, I wasn't nearly as annoyed as I was pretending to be. If Shannon were any indication, Alex craved someone unpredictable and unstable, whose volatile tempera-ment would keep him on his toes.

"I know, babe, I really am sorry," Alex pleaded. "I don't like it either. You can wait on the bus if you want, or I can find you an extra chair and you can sit close by wherever we are, or I can get you situated backstage where you'll probably be the most comfortable. The set-up here is pretty good. It's clean and they have free wifi. You can help yourself to our food and drinks all night. If you want, I'm sure I can score you some cocaine or weed."

"Are your openers back there? I guess I can chill with them while I wait. That doesn't sound so bad."

The look that flashed on Alex's face told me that I had said exactly the wrong thing, which was exactly the right thing to do.

"I'm going to tell those little shits to get lost," Alex grumbled. "They need to stay the fuck out of our dressing room anyway. They're pests. If you're around them for more than five minutes, you'll probably get so pissed off that you drive back to Atlanta."

I said nothing.

"And that's the last thing I want," Alex said, cupping my face with both his hands and kissing me. Mark, who had been laser-focused on his emails since I'd arrived, yanked off his headphones, slammed his laptop closed, and stood up just as Alex was pulling away.

"Be out there in ten minutes," Mark said to Alex. "We let them in at 6:30 on the dot, with a hard stop at 7:00. Don't give me that look. And don't scowl like that in the fan photos either. I'm not the one who arranged this shit."

"Ezra and Sean are in the back," Alex responded.

"Do me a favor and wake them up in five minutes? The venue's in-house lighting tech finally showed up, and I need to find him. And you, Olivia? I'm going to put you to work."

The hell you are, I thought.

"How do you feel about manning the merch booth with Josh?" Mark continued. "He'll do all the heavy lifting. Literally. He's finishing setting up. We just need you to be there to take cash and hand back shirts and posters and other shit for the fans that got early access. They prefer to see a pretty girl there anyway."

"I thought my retail days were behind me," I said with a pout. I was half-joking.

"You don't have to if you don't want to," Alex said.

"Find Josh out front!" Mark called as he exited the bus.

I rolled my eyes, but as long as I didn't have to get sweaty or put down my beer, I didn't mind obliging. There wasn't much else to do anyway.

Alex sighed and walked toward the bunks in the back of the bus, banging on any available hard surface along his way. "Wake up, assholes! Meet-and-greet in eight minutes with our favorite shitheads at 97.7 'The Spur.'"

"But I need more young pussy," Ezra moaned, still half-asleep.

"So much wet, tight, young pussy," Sean mumbled with a laugh.

"For fuck's sake," Alex muttered as he returned to me up front. "Sorry about them. But see, I wasn't kidding about those radio station guys being pervs. We all think so." He banged on the side of the bus again and added more loudly, "Eight minutes! Mark is already out there. This one is only thirty minutes, let's just get it over with. Yo, Carlos, you too, dude. I need you to check the tubes and cables on my amp again before we play tonight. It seemed okay at soundcheck, but there was a weird humming noise the whole time we played 'She's Trouble' last night. It threw me off. That can't happen again."

"Yeah, man, I'll get on it right now," Carlos shouted. He was squeezing past us before Ezra or Sean had so much as sat up.

Alex didn't want to wait for them, so I followed him off the bus and to the front of the venue, where Josh had set up an elaborate display of men's and women's apparel, CDs and vinyl, and posters, pins, and other vendibles, all emblazoned with the Six Times Country logo in various colors and styles. Notwithstanding my aversion to manual labor, it was the best place for me to be. I was able to surreptitiously keep an eye on Alex and ensure that none of the contest winners posed a threat, plus I was earning bonus points with the cantankerous Mark and mercurial Josh, which would be useful to my long-term strategic approach. Besides, as the fanboys and groupies were shuffled past me single-file for the privilege of spending twenty-five seconds with the band, collecting as many absentminded autographs and crappy selfies as they could muster before being escorted away, I got to bask in the satisfaction of knowing that I was now an unofficial part of the

Six Times Country team, living out those losers' fantasies, and everyone who saw me next to Josh in that merch booth must have been wishing they could trade their life with mine.

The show itself was uneventful. I stood in the wings while they played, chatting with Mark, looking out at the fans (especially the ones standing toward the front of the opposite side of the stage, exactly where I had been the night before), and trying to ignore Chris's college bimbos, who had arrived at the venue ten minutes after doors, all three of them already totally shitfaced. Unfortunately for everyone, their pregaming hadn't curtailed their thirst for the two bottles of Captain Morgan floating around the greenroom, both of which they had obliterated, with a bit of help from the openers, in the three hours before Six Times Country got on stage. Mark looked disgusted as they spasmodically twerked and jerked off-beat, falling over each other two feet from the stage. Even Chris, who was oblivious to their antics for most of his set, looked vaguely horrified when he glanced over during the band's second-to-last song and saw his date sloppily dry-humping the uglier of her two friends in what she clearly assumed was a sultry and seductive dance. I remembering thinking, if these are the kind of chicks that country music stars pull, it's no wonder that Alex is so captivated by me.

We all hung around the venue for another anticlimactic hour or two after the concert was over. There were no wild parties or hard drugs or orgies backstage. I had read Pamela Des Barres' memoirs and Mötley Crüe's *The Dirt* long before I set my sights on Alex, so maybe my expectations were a little skewed, but all we got was Chris's trio of imbeciles doing a clumsy sapphic triple-kiss, which would constitute a disappointment under any circumstances. It was risible, not sexy. Alex helped a little with load-out and signed some autographs for the two dozen superfans who were still lingering forty-five minutes after the lights went out and everyone else had left, then finally joined me on a couch where Ezra was cuddled up with some random brunette (not his girlfriend, who was waiting for him at the next tour stop) on the other end.

A big group of us walked to a dive bar five blocks away to play pool and have a few beers. Almost everyone left before last call, either to maximize the time spent enjoying a cushy hotel bed, or to follow a local girl back to her shitty apartment for a shitty blowjob, as the band had come to a consensus agreement that townies were prohibited from entering their shared hotel rooms. Objectively, it was a boring night spent waiting around, punctuated by a few exciting moments of stardom-by-proxy.

If you're wondering why I would put up with it, bear in mind that I was just starting to develop a realistic picture of how much better the life I deserved could be. I always knew that I was destined for greatness beyond Snellville, but it's hard to grasp what that kind of greatness entails until you've left. At the time, I owned my car outright, I had my associate degree, hell, I even had a steady job in Buckhead. I had been told that this was the pinnacle of achievement for someone like me, and it took me a while to realize that these were lies I was being fed to keep me complacent and to stop me from aspiring to more. The system doesn't want someone like me to realize that "more" exists at all. I'd had glimpses of a grander reality through the books I read and the higher-status older men I occasionally agreed to date, and it contained a lot more than fancier cars and more expensive shoes. The reason why I'm different is because I had the balls to stop passively admiring and envying and instead to ask, why not me too?

So yes, I stoically tolerated the tedium. And I approached the "wow" moments with the same calculated nonchalance. I made Alex feel like he'd need to win me over with something other than his burgeoning celebrity. I hadn't yet fully mapped out my endgame, but the experiences to which and individuals to whom Alex could expose and introduce me stood to benefit any number of my coalescing aspirations, and my façade of indifference to it all made Alex that much more eager to impress.

I sent Alex back to his room alone that night in Greenville, but we met in the lobby of my hotel the next morning. We spent the day together, mostly sampling the extravagant bloody mary offerings at several bars downtown and messing around on the outdoor gym equipment in and around Falls Park on the Reedy. He convinced me to join them in Chapel Hill, North Carolina, the next day. I cringe to admit it now, but it was the happiest I had felt around a guy since Manny.

Bus call was a relatively early 3:00 a.m. in North Carolina, since the band was scheduled for several live interviews with college and local radio stations in Charlottesville, Virginia, the next morning, but Alex and I spent enough time together before and after the Chapel Hill show that I was happy that I had joined for an extra stop on the trip. I ended up hanging out with Ezra's girlfriend, Alyssa, while the boys were busy with band duties. Alyssa was surprisingly cool. After spending thirty minutes with the petite, sultry hairstylist with a wicked sense of humor, sleeve tattoos, and impeccable makeup, I couldn't help thinking about the slag Ezra had hooked up with less than twenty-four hours prior. Alyssa would have been too good for him even if he actually did stay faithful to her.

Despite the fact that I liked Alyssa and thought Ezra was a moron, I had no intention of ratting out his misbehavior. Nevertheless, both Mark and Alex took it upon themselves, apropos of nothing, to warn me against mentioning anything to her. "What happens on tour, stays on tour," they both told me, verbatim. For all my book smarts and all my street smarts, back then I wasn't able to recognize this for the flaming dumpster fire of red flags that it was. Their bro-code of honor was unbreakable, and their duty of loyalty to each other was so strong that, from their vantage point, groupies and wifeys were rendered almost indistinguishable. Perhaps all WAGs implicitly understand and have made their peace with this truth. It is, of course, both unacceptable and inapplicable to someone like me—no matter who I'm dating, I'm the fucking star—but I thought I had a future with Alex and wasn't prepared to acknowledge reality.

Alex and I had fooled around some but still hadn't slept together by the time I started the drive back to Atlanta before dawn on Tuesday morning. I made it to The Roosevelt apartment building just before twelve noon, looking sufficiently worn down that Bradford didn't question the veracity of my "forty-eight hour stomach flu" fib. In retrospect, I was luckier than I realized at the time; I was so giddy over Alex that if Bradford had fired me for skipping work on Monday or for my tardiness on Tuesday, I probably would have shrugged it off and started applying for office manager jobs in Knoxville.

Instead, Alex and I spent the whole week texting and sending each other memes. He FaceTimed me twice from the bus and called me once from a venue before he got onstage. I knew that the band had a lot of downtime traveling between shows and waiting around at venues, leaving Alex ample opportunity to swipe through girls on Tinder and DM or text the best ones throughout the day, but it didn't seem wildly unreasonable to think that I must have been special for him to put forth all this effort consistently throughout the week.

Chapter Nine

Six Times Country was playing in Worcester, Massachusetts, on a Sunday night, with Monday to be used as a half-day of rest and a half-day of travel across the northern border. The expectation was that every member of the band would be refreshed and ready to go for a full day of Canadian press starting at 8:00 a.m. on Tuesday morning, followed by a sold-out show in Montreal that night.

"Mark tour manages a couple of other bands," Alex explained over the phone, "and he says he's been catching shit from the border patrol agents coming and going in both directions. If you look up the tweets from the guys in Manic Architects from a year ago, you can read the whole story. Border patrol detained them and brought out a drug-sniffing dog, all because one of their roadies had a half-ounce of cannabis in his backpack. The dude was from California, he had a prescription! All they did was confiscate his stash and I think they might have given him a small fine, but the whole thing ended up taking so long that the band missed their show in Detroit. Mark says that he had a bunch of Adderall and cocaine on him at the time too, as usual, but he knew how to hide it in a way that disguised the scent from the dogs. So he couldn't really get too mad at the kid for having a little weed without being a hypocrite. But between that and some other situation he had with the drummer from the Zodiac Chocolates getting a hard time about his UK passport, Mark builds in an extra buffer of, like, six fucking hours to get through the border."

It has always been funny to me how women are accused of being "chatty," when every guy I've dated has dominated our conversations with an endless stream of personal anecdotes like this, and has expected me to pay rapt attention. I already knew better than to try to share a story of my own. They simply don't care.

"Wow, that's totally wild," I cooed. "Then what happened?"

"What, with the Manic Architects' tour? They had to refund tickets for the Detroit show, but the roadie didn't get fired or anything. Like I said, Mark had a bunch of drugs on him too, he just knew how to not get caught. Anyway, Mark's paranoia is why our bus call is at noon on Monday, even though Montreal is only a six- or seven-hour drive for us. I doubt we'll get hassled or delayed, and we'll end up sleeping in the bus in a Canadian Walmart parking lot, guaranteed."

"Wow, that really sucks."

"Nah, I'm used to it at this point, especially on this cluster-fuck of a tour. Although I'd much rather wake up in bed next to you. Oh, right, that's what I wanted to ask. What if I flew you to Worcester on Sunday morning? The Atlanta airport is a hub for Delta, right? I bet I can get you a direct flight."

While we were talking, I was hiding in the public bathroom in the lobby of The Roosevelt, the only restroom option available to staff other than Bradford, who had his own pristine personal toilet secured by lock and key. This was the same bathroom where I'd twice stumbled upon methed-out vagrants trying to bathe themselves in the sink. At the same apartment complex where, on a daily basis, I was subjected to a parade of ugly, stupid, spoiled women who nevertheless managed to have their jobs or their fathers or their sugar daddies fund their travels around the world. The monotony of waiting around backstage or on a tour bus for Alex to finish with his band responsibilities and pay attention to me was a delight compared to the monotony of my crappy job, the only benefit of which was that it gave me enough time to steal identities and run my trivial online scams, generating enough extra cash to make an adventure like this financially feasible even without Alex's beneficence. How can I be faulted for accepting his offer?

By Sunday morning, I had pulled together a set of twelve photos (selected out of hundreds) that I planned to use as the foundation of my new Instagram profile before I started to post pics of me and Alex together. Film clips would follow as soon as I had mastered the video editing app that I had added to my phone before boarding my flight to Massachusetts. Whatever unease I may have felt about flying three hours north to rendezvous with professional musician whom I barely knew was easily attributed to the fact that I had been on an airplane only a handful of times before. Alex hadn't gotten me a first-class ticket, but one of the cute female flight attendants in coach had short hair, short fingernails, multiple ear piercings, and hardly any makeup on, so I consciously deferred to the stereotypes and decided to assume she was gay. With a bit of flirting and a few vague references to an ex-girlfriend, I managed to score myself two free mini-bottles of vodka on top of the two that I purchased for myself, and she snuck me a pack of apple chips to boot. I was pretty tipsy by the time I met Alex outside the back entrance to the Palladium in Worcester, but the flight had passed quickly thanks to my adorable, muff-diving new friend, and at least my nerves were settled.

I'm a little skeptical about astrology, but the planets must have been aligned in a peculiar way that day, because Alex was already visibly drunk too. Indeed, the entire band appeared to have reached some sort of détente with their openers over the preceding week, because all of the guys were rotating through each others' buses and dressing rooms without incident and freely sharing their liquor and drugs.

"All of us went to a strip club together last night," Alex said. He was having trouble focusing his eyes on me, but at least he wasn't slurring his words. "You have nothing to worry about. The girls were disgusting. It was hilarious. We're like soldiers bonded by battle after surviving that hellhole. Atlanta has a place kind of similar, I think. Like, it's famous for being a disaster?"

"The Clermont Lounge?" I offered.

"Right! Except that place is fun. You get the sense that it's proud to be a dive and everyone working there is in on the gag. It still has a good vibe, and those ladies are probably making bank off of being stripper-misfits. That's not what last night was. Last night was a horror show of desperation and battered pussy, rotting in a dump twenty minutes outside Hartford, Connecticut. We might have felt sorry for the bitches if they didn't have such nasty attitudes. I don't think I've ever been so drunk in my life. Carlos scored some really good blow from the bouncer before we left, thank God, and all of us took a couple bumps this morning and decided to keep drinking. We'd have to cancel the show tonight otherwise."

Alex mistook my appalled silence for jealousy.

"I'm telling you, don't worry, I didn't touch any of them. You are much hotter, and I'm not trying to catch their chlamydi-herp-orrhea. I had to spend over a hundred fifty bucks on Patrón alone just so I could look at them without dry-heaving."

"And now you'll be spending the duration of my visit dry-heaving through your waking hangover instead," I muttered.

It took him a second to process my remark. "Yeah, I guess so," he chuckled. "I mean, no, not really. I'll be fine. Just don't let me have any tequila tonight." He paused and his face darkened. "I mean it, Liv. Don't bring that stuff near me. I don't want to see it or smell it again. Maybe not ever, but especially not tonight. I'm drinking rum and vodka only. And gin is fine too, I guess. And weed, to help with the nausea."

"And cocaine," I added, rolling my eyes. His attitude was borderline aggressive and it was pissing me off. I hadn't forced half a bottle of tequila down his throat the previous night.

"Maybe another line before we get onstage, but otherwise I'm done with that shit for a while too. Those fucking strippers, man. They ruin everything." Alex shook his head and then, abruptly, seemed to snap out of his trance and started swooning. "Have I told you yet how beautiful you look today? And how happy I am that you came to see me? How was your flight?"

"It was okay. The guy in the middle seat smelled like stale cheese, but the lesbian stewardess was cool. She gave me a couple extra mini-bottles on the house. I almost invited her to join me here tonight."

"Hot."

"Meh. Maybe. I've never been that into girls though."

"I'd rather have you all to myself anyway."

There was a long beat as we both looked at each other. After our time together in Georgia and North and South Carolina, after a week of him wooing me via text and phone, after he flew me all the way to Massachusetts on his own dime, what was I supposed to do? Storm off because his initial welcome failed to live up to my expectations? On the rare occasions I'm willing to put up with that kind of shit now, it's because I've recognized it for what it is and I'm biding my time until I can maximize my vengeance. When I was with Alex, though... well, he had reverted so quickly to his usual charming self that I chalked up his initially crude and obnoxious demeanor to his hangover and exhaustion and to too much time spent around the bad influence of his bandmates. I hate feminism, but even I have to acknowledge that every guy associated with Six Times Country used his good looks and musical talent to get away with being a sexist pig. They were bringing out Alex's worst impulses, whereas I would bring out his best.

I stayed. As long as Alex and the rest of them behaved themselves around me, I didn't care how disrespectful they were to other women. Throughout the night, whenever they made offhand comments that made me cringe—about their fans, their groupies, their girlfriends, the strippers from the night before, even a female attorney who worked at their label wasn't spared—I told myself that it was a sign that they were comfortable with me, and that since I was destined to be around for the long term, there was no point in maintaining a façade of polite restraint. Besides, they were all drunk, and although I normally cut myself off long before I'm intoxicated, I'll admit that by the time the opening act went on, I was well over my limit too.

Although the band had sold out the main room of the Palladium, the staff promptly ushered everyone out of the venue after the last song and hardly anyone lingered around the building for autographs. Load-out was quicker than expected. Six Times

Country, their openers, and the roadies had fallen into a rhythm of drug- and alcohol-induced efficiency and cooperation, and by twenty minutes until midnight, a pack consisting of me, nine guys (including members of both bands and their respective crews), and some random local girls had gathered to wander the streets of Worcester.

I'm hazy on what happened next, not because I was blackout drunk, but rather because the ensuing succession of events after the fifteen of us rolled into some random bar on Main Street defies my comprehension to this day. The bar was rowdy when we entered, and our presence magnified the energy tenfold. Alex and I alternated between shamelessly making out with each other and socializing with the rest of the group and with the miscellaneous fans who approached bearing offers to buy us rounds and share their weed.

At one point, about an hour after we got there, I was seated on a barstool between Chris and Alex. Someone bought ten shots for whoever wanted them. I was chatting with Chris about some trifling nonsense; despite his being a horndog and a womanizer and the guy who banged my cousin, his mischievous smile and cocky self-assurance were starting to grow on me. Four of the shots materialized, unsolicited, on the bar top in front of Chris. He took two for himself and slid the other two to me, one of which I promptly passed along to Alex.

By the time I had thrown mine back with a giddy shudder, Alex had lost his damn mind.

Apparently, the shot had tequila in it. Apparently, I should have known this. Apparently, I was intentionally ignoring his specific requests about abstaining from tequila that night, and indeed was trying to trick him into drinking it... to provoke him? To make him sick? To spite him? That part was never made clear.

"This is the same fucking shit Shannon does to me," he screamed before storming out of the bar, teary-eyed and purple with fury.

I looked at Chris for some sort of validation that Alex's reaction was bizarre, unmerited, disproportionate, anything. Chris threw up his hands in defense and shook his head. "You're the one fucking him," he shrugged.

I didn't bother to clarify that I was not, in fact, fucking him. Not yet and, after this insane temper tantrum, maybe not ever. But not knowing what else to do, I got up and followed Alex out the door and into the chilly New England night.

Alex was standing half a block down the street, leaning against a trash can with his arms crossed, huffy and glaring at the barroom door. If he were truly as pissed off or hurt as he's pretending to be, I thought, wouldn't he have fled back to his tour bus and locked the door? He wouldn't be standing in the cold, waiting for me to follow him in order to have an audience for his absurd caterwauling and public histrionics.

The booze and the few puffs I had taken from Josh's joint ninety minutes earlier must have mellowed me out, however, because I began by approaching Alex apologetically and with a hint of good humor. Like, this was just a silly misunderstanding and we could get past it, right?

"I'm sorry, Alex," I started. "I swear, I had no idea what was in those shots. Chris gave one to me and I slid the other one down to you. That's it."

"You're a bully," he pouted. And then, more loudly, "You think you can gang up on me with Chris and make a fool of me?"

He stuck his finger in my face for emphasis. My patience was immediately exhausted. "What the fuck are you talking about, Alex? Neither of us ordered those shots, and I certainly didn't give a shit whether or not you drank yours. What is wrong with you? Nothing that happened in that bar remotely justifies your behavior right now."

"You made me drink tequila after I told you I didn't want to!"

"I didn't make you do anything! I gave you a drink that someone else purchased for you and said 'cheers,' and you're acting like I was trying to poison you. This is fucking ridiculous."

"It's not ridiculous! You don't respect my feelings and you don't respect me. After everything I've done for you?"

"Everything you've done for me? You bought me one fucking plane ticket. A crappy seat in coach, for God's sake. Holy shit, if I had known you were going to lord it over me, I never would have accepted it. What, do you want me to reimburse you for the cost? Do I owe you two hundred dollars? Three hundred? I will go to an ATM right fucking now and go back to Georgia right fucking after, I don't care."

"I don't want you to go! Damn it! But I don't know why you're acting like this."

"Acting like what?"

"You know like what!"

Well, the truth is, I did know like what. Or rather, like whom. I was acting like Shannon. Like the type of crazy bitch who, rather than deleting Alex's number and walking away from him permanently like any sane person would do in this situation, would instead engage with him in some asinine fight in the streets of a random New England town, drawing the attention of concerned passersby and, if both of us didn't tone down this nonsense immediately, probably the cops. And the thing is, I could tell he was into it. The angrier that I got in response to his irrational outbursts, the more I could see his rage morphing into excitement. The fool was getting turned on by this petty, self-inflicted melodrama.

After another minute of back-and-forth, each of us spewing curse-laden rubbish at the other, he lunged at me. I should have been terrified that he was going to hit me or throw me to the ground, but I stood there motionless, steadfast and imperturbable. And instead of taking a swing, he kissed me with ferocious passion. I was so unsettled by the fact that I hadn't instinctively reacted with either fear or force to him pouncing toward me that I barely noticed his tongue halfway down my throat. Then, he pulled away. For a moment, he looked sheepish.

"I don't want to fight with you, Olivia," he whispered. "All Shannon and I ever did was fight. You wouldn't believe how she manipulated me. I didn't mean to overreact. It's because of the psychological trauma she inflicted on me over the years. It makes it hard for me to know how to act in a normal, healthy relationship anymore."

I wanted to suggest that he seek the services of a licensed therapist, or perhaps a daycare teacher with extensive experience in dealing with temper tantrums, to better address his emotional baggage and major personality disorders, but I restrained myself. Had he just said that we were in a relationship?

"Okay," I grumbled. "Whatever. I don't want to fight with you either."

And thus, idiotically, we walked back into the bar together holding hands.

Despite our tentative reconciliation, we both were still upset, and we both drank heavily to suppress it. Last call came and went, and for reasons that remain unclear to this day, Josh and Chris walked back to my hotel with me and Alex. All four of us were drunk, the three guys obnoxiously so. Indeed, the front desk clerk told me through pursed lips that we needed to quiet down or else she would phone the police. I didn't blame her.

Josh wandered outside in order to, as he explained at full volume, "take a fucking piss, motherfuckers." Chris was pacing and sporadically cussing at nothing in particular; he paused only to loudly, shamelessly, and crudely proposition me directly in front of Alex. Alex responded with words so garbled that I still don't know if he was defending me or offering me up for a devil's threesome. Then he toppled into a lamp, which shattered onto the lobby floor alongside his now totally limp body.

"That's it, I'm calling the cops!" the front desk clerk hollered.

"No, just hold on, we're going up to my room right now," I yelled back. "Chris, would you please stop fucking around with that fucking vase and help me with him?"

I started to try to drag Alex's passed-out ass to the elevators, which were situated about a hundred feet away. At this point, Josh wandered back into the lobby with two huge guys, both at least six foot four and jacked, who introduced themselves as Russian air defense contractors, visiting this trainwreck of a U.S. city for some military conference.

"They can score us some more coke," Josh explained.

"Would you idiots help me get Alex to my hotel room before we all get arrested?" I fumed.

The slightly taller, noticeably hotter Russian lifted Alex off the ground and tossed him over his shoulder. I probably swooned.

"Thank you," I said. "You are my savior. Can you take him all the way to my room? It's on the fourth floor, down the hall."

Happy to be the hero to a damsel in distress, the Russian smiled and hauled Alex into the elevator. I dutifully followed, with Chris trailing behind. Josh and the other Russian remained in the lobby.

I chatted pleasantly with the Russian on the way up, just superficial things like whether he was planning to see any of the United States outside of Worcester during this trip, what other countries he'd traveled to for work, and how Russia was different from here. He was flattered by the attention and I was grateful for his assistance, particularly as Chris and Josh had proven themselves utterly useless. We arrived at my hotel door.

"Can you dump him into my bed for me?" I asked. "I'll take his shoes off and make sure he doesn't choke to death on his own puke in the middle of the night."

Again, the Russian happily obliged. Chris insisted on waiting in the hallway. We could have used his help, but I wasn't about to get into it with him at that point. The Russian helped me tuck Alex in and got him a drink of water while I put a wastebasket by Alex's side of the bed.

"He will feel miserable tomorrow. Do you have ibuprofen for him?" the Russian asked.

"I have some in my purse. I'll leave it on the nightstand for him. Your English is flawless, by the way. I wish I were bilingual."

"I speak a bit of Turkish too, but not as good as English," he boasted. "Is this little man your husband?"

"No. He's not even officially my boyfriend."

"Would you ever date a Russian man?"

I laughed. "After tonight, probably yes!"

I gave him a hug, thanked him again, and walked him to my door. Chris was sitting on the floor across the hall waiting for us.

"Are you finally done in there?" Chris asked.

"No thanks to you, dude," I snapped.

"My colleague is texting me from the lobby," the Russian said. "It is nice to meet you. We will be down there for a while and I will be pleased if you join us."

With that, he strolled off to the elevator, leaving me to deal with Chris.

"Alex is sleeping it off in there," I told him. "I'm taking the other half of the bed, but you're free to sleep on the couch if you want."

"No, it's fine," Chris mumbled. "Just give me a second and I'll get up. Your new Russian friend isn't staying the night?"

"What? No, of course not. I obviously don't care if you go party with him, but I'm done. I don't want any cocaine or whatever other shit you guys are getting into with them. This night was a disaster. I just want to go to bed."

Chris looked up at me dubiously.

"I'm not messing around, Chris. I'm over it. You can crash on the couch, or you can sleep in the hallway for all I care, but I'm going to bed."

In response, Chris held out his hand for assistance getting up. I obliged and he nearly barreled me over.

"Can you hold your shit together well enough to make it to the elevator?" I asked.

"Walk me there," he insisted, dragging me along. "You are trouble, Olivia. You are beautiful, but you are nothing but trouble."

"I'm not sure where you get off saying that when I'm the only one that's not acting like a complete asshole tonight, but whatever." I shoved him into the elevator and hit the button for the lobby. "Good night."

The doors closed and I stomped back to my room. My buzz was gone. I changed into an oversized t-shirt and basketball shorts (Alex didn't deserve to see me in my sexy booty-shorts pajamas), and climbed into bed without bothering to wash off my makeup. The sooner I fell asleep, the better.

Alex mumbled incoherently when he felt my presence next to him. At least he wasn't dead. When I didn't respond, he rolled over and sloppily attempted to caress my cheek.

"So help me God," I seethed, "if you don't keep your hands to yourself and go back to sleep, you can spend the night on the floor."

After a few more nonsensical noises, Alex finally rolled back to his half of the bed and I was able to sleep in peace.

We both woke up at the same time the next morning, a little before 10:00. Almost immediately, we had sex. It wasn't part of my plan, especially after the debacle that was the preceding night. I won't justify my terrible decision-making, and can only concede that I was blinded by my emotions. He was a messy pain in the ass, but for some twisted reason—a twisted reason that extended beyond the fact that he was hot and semi-famous—I was still into him.

Then, ten minutes after our reasonably decent first time came to a satisfying end (for him, at least), Shannon sent him a flurry of text messages.

"Don't you so much as think about replying to her while you're in this room," I said.

Alex put his phone facedown on the nightstand.

"Okay." Alex scooped up his phone, longingly gazed at the screen, and put it down again. "Okay. I won't. But I have to text her back later when I'm on the tour bus."

"Why, though? Why do you 'have' to?"

"Would you rather I lied to you about it?"

"No, but that's not what I asked. What is so urgent that she needs to text you a dozen times first thing in the morning? And I can see that it's killing you not to respond to her immediately! Are you this frantic when I text you?"

"It's not the same thing." He looked so guilty that for a moment I wondered if they had broken up at all. Or was he feeling guilty that he was still dragging Shannon along, keeping her hopes up, even though he had moved on completely and was falling in love with me?

"So what is it, then? Did her shaman bless her kombucha with the wrong wind chimes? Did someone eat non-vegan chili out of one of her Tibetan sound bowls?"

I had, by implication, just confessed to stalking Shannon's social media, but Alex didn't seem to notice.

"She's struggling and I can't abandon her," he explained. "She has been through so much pain in her life. She was abused when she was a kid. She keeps having to change jobs because her coworkers get jealous of her and they try to undermine her and make her look bad in front of their bosses. Her closest friends have betrayed her and deserted her. We both feel things so much more strongly and deeply than other people. It's hard for anyone else to understand."

"I feel pretty strongly and deeply that this conversation is pissing me the fuck off," I muttered.

"You're the most beautiful girl I've ever met," he continued, ignoring my remark. "Shannon is my past, and you are my future. But I can't cast her out completely, especially not while I'm on the road. She'd end her life. All I'm asking is for you to be patient. I'm crazy about you, Olivia."

We ended up having sex again, and then stayed in my bed cuddling until 11:40 a.m., at which point he had to throw on his clothes from the night before and jog back to the lot where the tour bus was parked before their noon departure time.

"I'll call you and text you and we will figure out the next stop for you to come see me," he said as he left. "We still have another two weeks of tour, and I'll only be in Knoxville for a few days before we have to fly to Europe for a couple of small festivals. What you and I have, this is going somewhere. I don't want to wait."

I attributed the creeping sense of malaise I felt upon his departure to an emerging hangover and to missing him already. Rather than analyze it any further, I called the front desk, asked for a late checkout, and slept for another two hours before I had to stuff my clothes and cosmetics back into my suitcase and catch my 4:00 p.m. flight back home.

I had a middle seat toward the back of the plane, but fortunately the people on each side of me were relatively inoffensive: to my right, a gaunt old dude, probably in his seventies, who emitted a light odor of mothballs and who spent the duration of the three-hour flight looking out the window without so much as shifting his weight, and to my left, a haggard woman who must have been at least in her late forties (God help her if she were any younger than that) who clicked away on her laptop with unjustified self-importance, but who didn't fight me for the armrest, leaned her body away from me into the aisle, and was as uninterested in engaging in banal pleasantries as I.

By the time the plane landed in Atlanta, I had resolved a couple of things. First, I decided to apply for a passport; I wasn't sure if I'd be approved quickly enough to join Six Times Country in Canada this tour, but I wanted to be prepared if Alex invited me to the European festival circuit with him in a few weeks. Second, as you may have inferred, I decided that I was willing to give Alex another chance, irrespective of whatever his relationship status with Shannon was. Even if they weren't fully broken up—and I was starting to accept that I needed to brace myself for that possibility—their relationship was clearly a codependent, toxic disaster, and with a little time, Alex would come to realize how much better I was for him. And third, to that end, I realized that if I were serious about winning, I needed to play the game more strategically than I had thus far. Alex seemed most infatuated with me when I challenged him and fought with him and made his life exciting, as if this déclassé mimicry of Sid and Nancy's shtick could give his country-twanging ass some punk rock cred. It was an asinine burlesque, fueled by insecurity and cliché, but it was something I could use to my advantage.

We spent another week exchanging messages while he was in Canada, mostly on WhatsApp, ostensibly because neither of us was sure about what international rates would apply under my mobile plan if I called or FaceTimed him. We decided to meet in Chicago on Sunday, where the band would spend the night and have most of Monday off before driving to Bloomington, Minnesota, for a Tuesday show. He offered to pay for my plane ticket again, but this time I refused. In retrospect, that was foolish. I was the one burdened with the hassle and expense of visiting him. You'd think that with all the economics and psychology books I've read over the years, I would have recognized the marginal impact of each additional expenditure I was making. I subconsciously needed to justify the sunk costs I was incurring in pursuit of Alex's affection, which took the form of me over-valuing him as a partner and becoming more committed to making our budding relationship work. You'd think that I would have realized that I should accept, and indeed demand, as much as possible from him instead, so that he'd be the one becoming more attached to me. I have learned from my mistakes, at least. Lord knows, I have learned.

Chapter Ten

Originally the plan was for Alex to meet me at Chicago O'Hare airport and accompany me back to the hotel, which was a ten-minute walk from the venue. When I landed, however, I had a dozen missed texts messages from him, in which he apologized profusely for forgetting about a midday in-store signing session and live acoustic performance for which the band was scheduled at some indie record shop. There was no way he was going to be able to meet me at the airport.

I should have been furious, but it was an early-morning flight and I hadn't had the chance to properly do my hair and makeup. I'm a natural beauty, but my strategy for this trip required that I look especially glamorous and spectacular and unobtainable. So truthfully, I was kind of relieved. I got an Uber, checked into my room, and by the time I had finished freshening up and changing my outfit, I had missed two calls and several texts from Alex letting me know that their little celebrity appearance was over and he was anxious to see me.

We met at a restaurant between the venue and the hotel. Alex was already waiting for me in the open-air seating section when I arrived, wearing a grey Chevelle band t-shirt and drinking a margarita. Even though it was chilly, the sun was bright that afternoon and I looked like a rock goddess in my gold-rimmed aviator sunglasses, so I greeted him with a kiss on the cheek and sat across from him without complaining about the temperature outside and without remarking on how the primary ingredient in margaritas is tequila.

"I dig the shirt," I said.

"I figured you would. They gave it to me at the record store appearance. I didn't know that Chevelle is from Chicago."

"I didn't know that either. I only know a few of their songs, to be honest. 'Joyride.' 'Face to the Floor.' What's that other one? 'Send the Pain Below,' I like that one."

"Yeah, me too. Our fans find it hard to wrap their heads around it, but everyone in the band listens mostly to rock music and rap. Sean is the only one who listens to country music semi-regularly, but it's not his favorite genre either."

There was an awkward pause. If the wait staff was watching us, they probably assumed this was a terrible first date arranged by our respective meddling aunts.

"A bunch of my clothes got ripped off in Toronto," Alex continued, his face brightening with the pleasure of telling tales of his travails on the road. "Or Josh dropped them or lost them, or he pawned them off, or something else happened that he won't admit to. All I know is, he went to the Laundromat with a duffel bag filled with my shit and returned with about half of it. He swears that he left my stuff alone for five minutes max to get a coffee across the street while the clothes were in the washer, and according to him the only other person in there was some cute old lady who was folding her husband's shirts and minding her own business. Whatever. I'm so ready for this fucking tour to be over. The store manager today heard what happened and gave me this shirt, plus one from Rise Against and one from some instrumental metal band that's based out of Chicago too. No joke, they're called Russian Circles." Alex snorted. "I bet you'd like that."

"Hmm, maybe. I haven't heard of them. I'm not that into metal music. No hate. It's just not my thing. That really sucks about all your clothes, though. That's crazy. I thought Canadians were supposed to be really honest and boring. Like, even snatching a bunch of soaking-wet clothes from a Laundromat would be too edgy for them."

"Yeah. I mean, there are thieves and assholes everywhere, including Canada, but I don't think Josh is telling me the full story.

For all I know, he traded my stuff for drugs. But it's not worth it to get into it anymore with him. Once again, I'm the one who has to make all the thankless sacrifices to maintain group cohesion."

At this point, the waitress approached to check if I wanted anything to drink and to see if we would be ordering any food. I was grateful for the intrusion. Alex's biceps looked amazing in that grey t-shirt and he had grown in just the right amount of sexy stubble, but this self-pitying monologue was intolerable, particularly since I had witnessed firsthand Alex's bandmates putting up with Alex's own special brand of bullshit to keep the peace. I'll never understand why people these days happily embrace victimhood as a core component of their personal identity.

I hadn't eaten yet and Alex's behavior was so bizarre that I wasn't sure if I'd be letting him see me naked again, so at the waitress's recommendation, I ordered a gourmet Chicago-style hotdog. It was spicy and salty and I was running a risk that my tiny waist might bloat a little, but hey, at least it was phallic. Alex got a foodie twist on cheesy fries and onion rings.

"Have as much as you want," he offered when the waitress set down our food. "We don't go on stage for another six or seven hours, but I don't want this bouncing around my stomach. And I don't have much of an appetite right now anyway. Something is making me nauseous."

We both busied ourselves with our food in silence for several minutes. Alex had ordered another drink, this time a tequila sunrise, thereby verifying his intention to fuck with my head, although this was a moronic way to go about it. I ordered a long island iced tea in the hopes that the drink would give me enough of a buzz that he'd stop pissing me off.

As it turned out, a single drink wasn't quite sufficient, but the second one did the trick. Alex finished his tequila sunrise and ordered a long island for himself as well, and within an hour, we were talking and laughing the way we had on the first night we met. Alex paid the check and, leaving behind a half-eaten hotdog and a basically untouched basket of appetizers, we walked back to my hotel room. We were both half-undressed before the door clicked into place.

Alex didn't bother with foreplay and he came relatively quickly, which was annoying but not a deal-breaker per se. I figured that round one was a bust, but if I gave him fifteen minutes to recover, we'd have a more mutually satisfying round two. That was more or less how our previous time together had unfolded. Besides, the overwhelming majority of men are comically awful in bed. On some level they all must know this, and yet somehow each of these clowns convinces himself that he alone is different, that he is the lone stallion, that his particular dick possesses magical powers that bring women to ecstasy. A few cursory moans, or indeed just a lack of outright complaints, from an obliging woman is enough to persuade them that their puny pecker is a golden chalice and their putrid jizz contains the elixir of life.

Alex was oblivious and, like most guys in their twenties or thirties, he readily accepted my affirmative answer with a look of stupid, smug satisfaction when, as an afterthought, he asked if I came too. But I'd already had enough exposure to the men in their forties and beyond, who bragged to me about their "expert tongues" and their "endless stamina," who made bone-chillingly creepy offers to "draw me a bath" or "massage me in lavender oil from head to toe," and who refused (or who were too jacked up on Viagra) to wrap up their vile performance in their aged, failing, flailing bodies, all of which ultimately required that I execute a meticulous performance of faking it. Their ex-wives deserve handwritten thank you notes for keeping these buffoons out of the dating pool for as long as they did. Some part of me back then must have already accepted that sex is just a means to an end and lasting romantic love is a myth, so Alex's indifference, while not exactly endearing, seemed to be perhaps the best alternative I could hope for.

Two minutes after he had finished, however, Alex jolted upright in bed.

"Holy shit, what time is it?" he asked.

"I don't know, my phone is over by the TV. The clock is on your side of the bed."

"Is this thing right? Is it 5:30 already?"

"Alex, I just said I don't know. It might be fast. Where is your phone?"

"It's in my pants." He sprung out of bed and started digging through his pockets. "How did it get this late? Doors are at 6:30 and they have some fucking local opener going on at 7:00. I had to pick up another new cable earlier this afternoon and I still need to do a line check."

"Shouldn't that be Carlos's job?"

"Well, sort of." Alex looked surprised that I knew to ask. "But it would be unprofessional for me to punt the full responsibility to him. I'm the one on stage, so I need to be there. Like, right now."

"So you're bolting?" I asked. I was feigning more disappointment than I felt. I needed the extra time without him pestering me to do a wardrobe change and fix my hair.

"Yes. I'm going to run there, literally, as soon as my shoes are on."

I chucked one of his rolled-up socks in his direction. "Do what you need to do."

Alex tied his laces and bent over the bed to kiss me on the cheek. "Come to the back entrance of the venue and text me if security hassles you about getting in. I wouldn't want you to have to blow a bouncer to get through the doors."

"Don't be a fucking pig, Alex," I snapped.

"I was just kidding. I'll give you an all-access pass when you get there. Sorry I don't have an extra one with me now."

"It's fine. I'll be there in an hour or so."

"Okay. I really have to run now. See you tonight, gorgeous." He gave me another kiss and hustled out the door.

As soon as I heard it slam shut behind him, I got out of bed and looked at myself in the bathroom mirror. My makeup was a mess and I felt drunker than I wanted to, so I decided that it was worth it to take a hot shower even though I'd have to blow-dry my hair again. Alex was getting on my nerves, so if it took me longer than an hour to get to his show, so be it.

I had brought along a skintight lime green dress as one of my outfit options for the trip. It was a bit much for a country show and I almost didn't pack it, but now it seemed perfect. I wore my hair down with the ends slightly flipped out and emphasized my eyes with violet and bronze tones and a nude lipstick. No jewelry other than a pair of big black hoop earrings, and simple black heels on my feet. I looked like a fucking movie star. Alex should count his blessings if I made it to the venue without getting scooped up by a Chicago Bulls player or a famous politician or a mob boss first.

I decided to stop at the hotel bar for a cocktail, and after watching every man in the place practically fall off his barstool admiring me, I finally wandered over to the venue. It was after 7:30 by then, and I could hear an amateurish-sounding bluesy band playing inside as I approached. I went to the back entrance as Alex had directed and the security guard waved me past. The tour buses were parked in a private lot to the left, and since I didn't think Alex would want to watch some random local band from the wings, I decided to walk that way first.

The Six Times Country bus door was locked, so I knocked twice and started to text Alex. Mark opened the door before I had a chance to hit send.

"Olivia! Hey, I wasn't expecting to see you again. So soon, I mean. You look amazing tonight." Rather than let me past, Mark turned his head and shouted back onto the bus. "Yo, Alex. You have a visitor. It's Olivia."

A few muffled words were spoken and Alex appeared behind Mark.

"Hey, Liv. Where've you been?"

"Where have I been? At the hotel since you left me there, obviously. I didn't want to show up too early while you were taking care of shit here."

"Yeah, okay." Alex pulled on Mark's shoulder, indicating he should move aside and let me on the bus. "You really do look smoking hot tonight."

"Thanks," I said, as I climbed up the stairs. Something strange was going on. I almost excused myself, thinking that perhaps the band was having a serious group discussion or working through an internal fight, but when I poked my head around the corner there were three random girls hanging around up front. Had Alex been flirting with one of them? Hooking up with one of them?

Chris and Ezra appeared to have laid their respective claims to the two generic bleached-blondes, but the third—a brunette and the oldest by a few years, who was wearing an unfortunate pair of thick black-rimmed glasses, but who was otherwise the prettiest and fittest of the trio—didn't seem to be attached to any of the guys. I certainly wasn't about to lose Alex to her.

"I'm Olivia, nice to meet you," I said to her with a saccharine sweetness as I sat down to her left. "How do you know these guys?"

"Pretty dress," she said. "I'm Clara, it's nice to meet you. My sister is the band's attorney."

"Technically, she's counsel for the label," Mark interrupted.

"Oh, right," Clara giggled. "My bad. Legal stuff makes my brain go numb."

"That's why we like you," Mark chuckled.

"Yeah, Kaisa—that's my sister—she lives in L.A. and we don't talk much about work stuff. But she's the lawyer. She got us the tickets and backstage passes tonight."

"That's cool," I said.

"Yeah, we're stoked. All three of us are pediatric critical care nurses at Comer Children's Hospital. My girlfriend works in the NICU, but she couldn't switch her shift tonight."

"Zaria hates country music anyway," said the girl with her hand on Chris's upper thigh. "I mean, no offense to you guys! We disagree! But she's into, like, jazz music. Like, the stuff your grandparents listen to."

"Yeah, Zaria would have offered to come to make me happy if she didn't have to work, but I could tell she was relieved to give away her ticket," Clara laughed. "All three of us are huge Six Times Country fans."

"And all three of us are ready for a girls' night out!" the one next to Ezra shrieked. This was promptly followed by an eardrum-shattering round of whooos and squeals. At least I had an explanation for the weird vibes I was getting. If I were forced to listen to this shit because the lesbian sister of my boss's attorney invaded my personal space with two of her annoying friends, I'd be irritated too.

After half an hour of hanging around on the bus, most of the group started moving inside to the greenroom. Eventually, it was just me, Alex, and Sean, all of us avoiding eye contact and silently fiddling on our phones. When Sean stood, I got up too; I looked too damn good in my dress to waste the night pointlessly trapped on a bus waiting for Alex's mood to swing back to happy. At that point, I didn't care whether I followed Sean backstage or ended up hanging out in the audience. But Alex grabbed my wrist and shook his head, and Sean left us on the bus alone.

"What the hell is going on, Alex?" I asked. "You're the one who invited me out here, and you've been acting strange all day."

"Honestly, Olivia, I can't even look at you right now," Alex huffed.

"Would you care to explain why?"

"If you don't think you've done anything wrong, then you are more morally bankrupt than I thought."

"Because I accepted your offer to pay for my plane ticket last time? Or because I didn't accept this time?"

"What? No. Come on, Olivia. Did you think I wouldn't find out?"

"Find out what?" Now I was getting angry. "Fuck, Alex! Maybe this bullshit melodrama is how you and Shannon used to get each other off, but I have no patience for it. If you have justifiable beef with me, then fucking spit it out already. Otherwise, stop pouting like a petulant toddler. You're a grown-ass man. Act like it!"

"You're going to make me say it? It makes me fucking sick to my stomach to even think about it."

"Fucking say what you have to say, and say it now, or else I'm leaving."

"You fucked some Russian guy in the hotel room bathroom and then climbed into bed with me, you slut. You didn't think I'd find out?"

"Holy shit, Alex. Holy shit. How in God's name am I supposed to respond to something like that? You're delusional. Like, I honestly think you might need to be institutionalized."

"You're going to deny it? Right to my face, you're going to lie to me and act like it didn't happen?"

"The Russian at the hotel in Worcester? Is that who you are talking about? The guy who helped me drag your half-dead ass up to my hotel room while your dickhead bandmates were busy trying to score cocaine and causing such a scene in the lobby that the hotel staff almost had all of us arrested?"

"Yes, of course the Russian in Worcester. Or are you fucking so many other guys that you can't keep track? You make me sick."

"This is literally the most insane argument I've ever had with anyone in my life. You are beyond hope. That guy was the only reason the cops weren't called."

"And you thanked him by giving him your pussy. Nice."

"I thanked him by saying fucking 'thank you' to him. Did you dream this? Or is it because you have some vague recollection of him being in the room with us from when he was carrying you into bed, and you've created a whole fucked-up story in your mind about what happened next? I can't believe I'm defending myself over this idiotic accusation, but I'm genuinely curious as to how you came to the conclusion that sometime between taking care of your incoherent ass and trying to keep hotel management from throwing us onto the streets, I decided to fuck a total stranger."

"Chris saw it happen."

"Chris! That's your source? Lord, this entire band is deranged."

"Are you saying he's lying to me?"

"Yes! That's exactly what I'm saying. It's an outrageous lie. He was right there the whole time."

"That's exactly what he said! He was right there with you when it happened. So yeah, I believe him over you."

"Your boy Chris was almost as useless as you were at that point. He followed me and that Russian guy all the way up to my floor and down the hall without saying a word and without helping to carry you at all. And then he refused to come into the room."

"So you and the Russian could fuck."

"No! So we could dump you into bed and get you water and a barf bucket. He was in the room with me for five minutes, and the whole time we were taking care of you. What the fuck did Chris say?"

"That he could hear you two banging for fifteen minutes straight."

"I'm done. I'm fucking done with this conversation. Chris's drunk ass was slumped against the door across the hall when the Russian guy left, and then *he* hit on me! He had been propositioning me all night and I turned him down because I am loyal to *you*. I left Chris with blue balls at the elevator, and if he's lying to you, it's because he's bitter and jealous that I refused to bail on you to go hook up with him. And then I went back to the room and checked on you, and we both went to sleep."

Alex opened his mouth as if to respond, and then stopped himself. He seemed to be thinking over what I had said.

"So you didn't fuck the Russian?" he asked, finally subdued.

"No! I don't know how many different ways I can say it. It's ridiculous that you would think so. I was nice to that guy because he was the only person who was man enough to actually help me. He literally carried you over his shoulder, and I was grateful and sweet to him because I never would have been able to move you all by myself. Your 'bros' certainly didn't give a shit. I'd like to say that Chris was just mistaken and this was all a big misunderstanding, but frankly it seems malicious, especially given the way he was flirting with me that whole night when you were too hammered to realize what he was up to. And I'm fucking pissed that you would believe such an absurd story with no evidence that it had any basis in reality, and then proceed to act like such a dick to me all day without asking me about it first. And if you actually believed a word of it, then why the fuck did you have sex with me earlier today?"

"I dunno," he shrugged. "I figured that if you give it up that easily..."

"You know what? Fuck you, Alex. You're mentally ill. You need professional psychiatric help." I picked up my bag. "And so does Chris. You're both narcissistic sociopaths and at this point I don't give a shit what you think happened. You and Shannon deserve each other. Go back to her. Go back to making each other miserable. It's the best you can hope for, and it's more than you deserve."

"You're a slut," he screamed back. He was practically in tears. "Now I know for sure that you did it. You're a slut and a liar. I can't believe that someone like me was starting to fall for someone like you."

"Someone like you? Who do you think you are? Truly? You're not Jimmy Page. You're not Axl fucking Rose. You're a dipshit guitarist in a shitty country band. You'd be lucky to be with me."

"I *have* been with you, you bitch. And now I'm done with you."

"No, now I'm done with *you*, you dickless prick. You are a fucking disaster, Alex. Seriously, just go fuck yourself."

And with that, I shoved open the bus door and left. In retrospect, I wish I had said something more clever and cutting as my parting words, but the entire fight was so ludicrous that this was the best I could muster, and I needed to get away from him as quickly as possible. I considered going into the venue and smacking Chris squarely across his conniving face, but he wasn't worth it. How dare either of them. How dare Chris make up such a flagrant lie, and how dare Alex believe him. How dare they waste my time and money and toy with my emotions like I was another one of their disposable, interchangeable groupies. This lot of middling musicians? Please.

Feeling fortunate to not have to sit through another one of Six Times Country's horrible concerts, I walked a block down the street and into a hipster bar, where a group of three hot guys in their early thirties promptly invited me to join them for a drink. The next morning, I got on standby for an earlier flight and happily got the hell out of Chicago.

This wasn't quite the end of Alex, however. Ten days later, the maniac called me from Knoxville. He left me a gem of a voicemail: tour was over and he missed me and he wished we hadn't left things the way we did in Chicago. He didn't think that Chris would lie to him, but maybe the Russian and I had just fooled around a bit or something and Chris thought it went further than it actually did. He had messed around with other girls on tour, but I was the only one he had slept with, and that meant something to him after his heartbreak over his relationship with Shannon ending for good. We could leave all that behind us and try again. Would I want to come visit him in Knoxville? He'd be there for a few more days before the European tour.

His soliloquy lasted three minutes before my phone's voicemail automatically cut him off mid-sentence. I listened to it at 6:00 p.m. after work and decided that I should sleep on it before responding. By the time I woke up the next morning, I had seventeen missed texts from him wherein he retracted the Knoxville invitation and informed me that he couldn't get past my affair with the Russian. I blocked his number.

A week or so after, out of morbid curiosity, I checked Shannon's Instagram account. She was posting ten pictures a day from the same European cities where Six Times Country just happened to be scheduled to perform. Whatever. They can both get fucked. At least no one else will be subjected to their schizophrenic madness if they are monogamously terrorizing each other.

I told you about Alex because that was basically the last time I bothered trying to date anyone for real, but I could have told you about any of the attempts before him and they wouldn't have been much different. At least with Alex, the betrayal and mind games were peppered with the excitement of traveling to new places and being seen with the band. Alex was self-absorbed and emotionally unstable, and I'm still unsure whether he and Shannon were ever truly broken up, but at least our affair was a respite from the mind-numbing monotony of my job at The Roosevelt. That's more than I can say for the so-called "normal guys" I've gone out with, who felt equally entitled to my time and attention on their terms, but who had nothing to offer me but (at most!) a wasted decade or two popping out their kids and prioritizing their career and ambitions over my own before they would move on to a younger girl "without all the baggage." Hell, in some cases, the fool already had the embittered ex-wife and the three resentful kids living in a mansion for which he still paid the mortgage but at which he was no longer welcome, together with the woe-is-me tale about how unfair to men the divorce court judges are in Fulton County (or in Forsyth County or in Cobb County, et cetera) and the lamentations about how alimony and child support payments now consume half his base salary. Each of those jackasses envisioned me as round two of three or more. For each, I was supposed to be sympathetic about his past and excited about him repeating the same future with me. Screw that.

I had known since my revelation in my sophomore year English class that I shouldn't *depend* on a man for my survival, but I suppose that, up until Alex, I had held out some hope that maybe I could enjoy a version of... honestly, I'm not sure anymore what I wanted from any of those men. I knew what I didn't want: I didn't want the shackles of being a wife, I didn't want the burden of children, I didn't want to be poor, I didn't want my life to be boring. I didn't want what these fools were offering me, which wasn't much beyond the dubious privilege of being able to claim them as my steady, stable boyfriend and to receive the social validation attendant to such "coupled" status.

So, I stopped. It really was that simple. I consider it my second epiphany, and there were no tears, no resistance, no internal negotiations. It was a realization that I'd always had within me, and now it was clear to me in a way that left me calm: not only should I not rely on a man for my financial or emotional wellbeing, but I ought to take as much as I could from him, otherwise he would take much, much more from me. He'd take my time, energy, emotional labor, self-esteem, youth, status, care, and love, unreciprocated and for his own ends, and leave me with nothing, because that's what men do. All I'd be trying to do was take some of his money first. I certainly don't want your pity, but I'm not the bad guy either.

Chapter Eleven

Despite the success I had ripping off Marissa, I never developed a true passion for traditional identity theft. It was a useful backstop when I needed to punish someone or had unusually high lifestyle expenses in a particular month, but beyond that, it bored me. I have my reasons for describing these little side jobs to you anyway—reasons that I'll explain to you later, because it has become clear that you won't be able to figure it out for yourself—but I don't want to drag out this part of my story beyond mentioning my experience with one particularly heinous bitch, Arlene. The only reason I would ever wish anything good on her, is so that I could be there to take it away.

I met Arlene while I was working as the receptionist at a law firm in Dunwoody, right after Bradford did me the favor of arbitrarily firing me from the prison of tedium that was The Roosevelt's front office, and giving me an excuse to upgrade from my shitty East Point apartment to more suitable accommodations in Sandy Springs, just north of Buckhead. By then, all the petty nonsense with that hack guitarist Alex Montalvo-Moore was fading from my memory, and the new job at Assface, Douchebag & Child Molester LLP was supposed to be another step up for me. I had made it through a brief period of unemployment without having to move back to Lillian and Raymond's house in Snellville (thanks in no small part to Marissa's "contributions" to my financial welfare), and I convinced myself that this new position would be a fresh start. My optimism was, of course, wildly misguided.

What an utterly miserable group of self-involved shitheads they were, attorneys and staff alike, to the last person.

Despite the fact that I could have opened credit cards or applied for loans with much higher limits if I had utilized an attorney's name and social security number, no one was more deserving of the hassle, and hopefully at least some personal financial loss, of a well-executed identity theft operation than the firm's second-most senior paralegal, Arlene. I was astonished when I learned how much money she was making. I didn't come across that information intentionally, by the way. Arlene found it necessary to drop her pay stubs in the trashcan next to my desk every other Tuesday when she was leaving the office, clearly her way of rubbing my face in the fact that her salary was three and a half times larger than mine.

It was ridiculous. She lounged at her desk all day, constantly eating the most rancid-smelling foods imaginable, constantly blabbering on the phone to hometown friends about inane local gossip, and occasionally lumbering to a conference room to bark out orders at the other paralegals and secretaries, without ever accomplishing anything remotely productive herself. The attorneys were able to shut their office doors so that they wouldn't have to see her filth or be distracted by her asinine blather, but no one on the staff enjoyed the luxury of privacy and so none of us were spared.

She was a lazy, incompetent bully, but she went to the same random revivalist church in Dawsonville as Ms. Jessica Fitzgerald, the pretty-for-her-age, blond-haired female junior partner whom the clients and senior partners (all older hetero men, of course) adored. Jessica's protection, grounded in their shared religious faith, gave Arlene a measure of job security that none of the rest of us enjoyed. And beyond Jessica, with the exception of a third-year associate whom Arlene seemed to think she could get away with harassing and haranguing the same way she did the secretaries—he was a twenty-seven-year-old Howard University law school grad, and the firm's only Black male attorney at the time, which I do not think was a coincidence—Arlene knew how to butter up all the lawyers who had any say in the firm's employment decisions.

Rumor had it that Arlene's only real responsibility was to help one of the senior partners, Mr. Wheeler, cover up his chronic infidelity from his unsuspecting wife. Since Arlene was brilliant at manipulating Mr. Wheeler's mistresses and his spouse—and Wheeler himself, for that matter—she was able to regularly show up to the office two hours late, screw around all day, and nevertheless retain her job despite two previous economic downturns, including a particularly brutal year in which half the staff was laid off.

I might have respected the scam, and probably should have had the sense to start banging Mr. Wheeler myself—although the office gossip also suggested that, after a blighted former lover caused an epic scene in the lobby when Wheeler was a senior associate fifteen years earlier, he had learned that it was best to safely store his dick in his pants around anyone who worked in the building—but Arlene was an insufferable cow. The pay stubs in my trashcan, always deposited with a knowing smirk, daring me to look, were the last straw. The fourth or fifth time she did it, I swiped the stub and put it in my purse. I dumped a soggy Styrofoam bowl of cereal into the bin immediately after, on the off chance that she might return to retrieve it (or rather, to catch me having taken it first).

That one perforated half-sheet of paper was a godsend: a portion of her SunTrust Bank account and routing numbers for her direct deposit. Full social security number. Pay rate and total annual pay to-date. All for Ms. Arlene H. Winslow, 1438 Arrowhead Terrace, Ellijay, Georgia 30540.

I had to commend that fat bitch on one thing: she was driving an hour and a half each way, every day, from her house to our office. Presumably she realized that, without Jessica's and Mr. Wheeler's protection, she was unemployable anywhere else. Then I looked up her address on Zillow and nearly gagged. She lived in a mansion! A failure to act on this unexpected blessing, bestowed upon me in her inane attempt to slight me, would be unforgivable.

After duly considering the potential merits of a three-hour round trip to burn 1438 Arrowhead Terrace to the ground, I decided it would be simpler to repeat everything I had done with Marissa's information. By then, Marissa had long-since cancelled all the credit cards I had opened (which were maxed out anyway) and shut down the other fraudulent services accounts I had created (which had been tied to my old address and were no longer useful), and I needed to transfer all those expenses somewhere new. Arlene had gone out of her way to make me miserable and flaunt her undeserved wealth to spite me, and now the punishment would truly fit the crime.

The wildest part is, observing the attorneys' shady business practices on behalf of the firm's scumbag clients was how I figured out how to get away with it, in a way that was far more sophisticated than the improvised, relatively haphazard process I had strung together when using Marissa's info. For example, I had to process the paperwork for sleazy businessmen who wanted to set up dummy corporations but who, under state law, needed to file a physical address for the company with the Georgia Secretary of State. As with the credit card companies, an anonymous P.O. box would not suffice. The firm had found clever ways around these rules, of which I promptly availed myself in applying for six new credit cards under Arlene Winslow's name. Within two weeks, I had twenty-eight thousand dollars of credit to play with. I was about four months into my tenure at the firm at this point and I knew I wouldn't be sticking around much longer, but I wanted to observe at least some of the aftermath of my scam in person, so I maxed out all six credit cards immediately on untraceable prepaid gift cards and never bothered to pay the minimum on any of the accounts.

Arlene must have been more diligent about checking her credit report than Marissa was, because she caught on to what happened shockingly quickly. Barely a few weeks had passed before the entire office heard about how her FICO score had tanked over 160 points overnight. For a full month thereafter, we were subjected to her incessant moaning about how unfair it was that something so awful would happen to a good Christian woman like her, although she was quite content to use the ordeal as an excuse to push all of her work duties onto the secretaries and other paralegals while she was "busy dealing with this godforsaken identity thief." Coincidentally, the customer service representatives at Experian, TransUnion, and GFY Debt Collectors seemed to have developed a profound personal investment in how Mandy (who looked like a harlot in that see-through sundress) and her husband barely touched each other at the neighborhood barbeque on Sunday, and how Renee's twenty-year-old son was sporting a tattoo on his bicep that looked satanic, which isn't surprising because that whole family needs Jesus.

By the time her last dispute with a collections agency was filed, the rest of the office was utterly fed up with her complaining and her dereliction of work responsibilities, including the attorneys who had been her staunchest allies up until then. Truly, this gave me almost as much joy as the money itself.

Because the firm was so stingy with my salary, I had started supplementing my income by transferring small sums from their cash-on-hand into my dummy bank accounts. I also used the firm's credit card for minor charges and created phony expense reports on behalf of different attorneys to cover it up. At a mid-sized firm like this one, a lot of client money flows in and out every day (for retainers, legal fees, sums being held in escrow, money laundering, and so on), and a lot of random attorney expenses are incurred and reimbursed (client meals and drinks, governmental filings, firm-sponsored events, continuing education classes and materials, more money laundering), but we had only one dedicated payroll person, who also managed all the firm's compensation and benefits issues on top of that. By necessity, some of the mundane payroll-related work got pushed down to the secretaries, and they often pushed it off to me. Few of us had any emotional stake in the firm's long-term viability or financial welfare beyond receiving our next paycheck. It was an environment conducive to opportunity, if you were clever enough to figure it out.

I may make it sound easy, but after a while my efforts to evade detection made it start to feel less like a fun and lucrative way to stick it to my bosses and more like a second full-time job. First of all, I felt like I could never take a spontaneous vacation or a sick day. My one notable trip during my tenure there—a week in Miami—was meticulously timed to take place after a six-week lull in any corporate malfeasance. Suffice to say, my little multi-state adventure with Alex never would have been feasible if I had been working at the firm rather than at The Roosevelt at the time. God forbid some try-hard busybody took over one of my responsibilities while I was gone and noticed the discrepancies in my work. Certain inconsistencies I could have justified by pleading incompetence or admitting to making a sloppy mistake in my haste to meet an impossible deadline, but most of the charges I had falsified wouldn't stand up to scrutiny and couldn't be explained away by confusion or human error. And so, I needed to be physically present at all times to guard my work from nosy, "helpful" eyes.

I had no idea how our payroll girl decided which expenses to audit or which debits to review, so I erred on the side of purloining smaller sums. I avoided round numbers. Think about it: a series of deductions of, let's say, $103.83, $97.54, $62.03, and $133.26, is less likely to draw attention than a whole bunch of $100 transactions, regardless of how they're spread out over time. And none of those transactions will draw the attention that a single $500 debit would incur.

My prudence helped me remain undetected, but taking these little amounts over the long term in lieu of planning and executing one big score was exasperatingly time-consuming, and it was time spent around people I found repugnant. In retrospect, I can fairly say that my actions were motivated more out of spite for them than by the relatively paltry sums of money I procured. At its core, the firm's business model was premised on finding ways for rich white-collar criminals to evade their taxes, defraud regulatory agencies, and rip off their business associates and employees, so regardless of whether the money was coming out of the clients' or the partners' pockets, I knew I wasn't harming anyone who didn't have it coming.

I'm humble and I know my limits. I'm not a hacker so I didn't try to commit any kind of convoluted computer fraud. At worst, I lifted a few passwords from the truly moronic colleagues who left their login credentials on sticky notes next to their desktops, and when I accessed their accounts, I only did so on the firm's intranet (and never on the computer at the receptionist desk, duh!). The firm contracted out its IT work to some third-party vendor, and the nerd who was assigned to assist us seemed to be googling and guessing whenever he came into the office to troubleshoot computer issues, but I didn't want to risk the possibility that he was smarter than he let on (since playing the fool can be a great strategy to avoid incurring extra pointless responsibilities). For all I knew, he'd realize immediately if I were logging onto a coworker's account through my personal computer at home, and he'd probably use it as leverage over me, as a way to blackmail me into accepting a date with him. I learned as much as I could from perusing internet chat forums about how IT geeks operate and the diligence they conduct with respect to network access, but I still felt precariously under-informed. As such, I limited the use of my coworkers' credentials to those circumstances in which it was strictly necessary to create an electronic paper trail to align with the story behind an otherwise indefensible account deduction.

I never told anyone inside or outside of the firm what I was doing until now. It's amazing that I need to point this out at all, but you'd be shocked by how stupid people are, how inclined they are to spill all sorts of incriminating information to anyone who is willing to listen to them with a neutral, encouraging smile as they disclose all sorts of sordid details. And by the way, if you think that's what is happening right now, I'd caution you against feeling too smug. I already told you: I have my reasons for being totally transparent, which I'll get to soon enough.

Anyway, aside from my generally superior strategic thinking, my discretion is probably the biggest reason I was able to get away with fleecing the firm for so long. I was impeccably dressed and I showed off my expensive bags and jewelry at work, for sure, but I always had a story to tell about some rich guy I was dating who showered me with gifts. Accommodating the latest Don Juan's schedule was a great excuse to avoid after-work drinks with people I held in contempt, and it justified how I could afford such nice things on a salary that everyone knew was unworthy of my talents. Besides, I was surrounded by people who were old, washed-up, overweight, bitter, and miserable, whereas I am young and gorgeous, so it was easy for them to believe that I'd have some rich prince at my beck and call. Frankly, all the secretaries and paralegals (aside from Arlene, of course) got off on living vicariously through my epic stories. Supplementing my income with the firm's ill-gained excess, and then using the fruits of my labor to create a fantasy that provided hours of entertainment for the rest of the staff, was a boon for firm morale. I was practically performing a public service.

My aspirations grew commensurately with the tales I told, and I began to dream about haughtily buying a forty-thousand-dollar oil acrylic and ink painting off the walls of one of Miami's trendy art galleries, or paying the six-figure lump-sum initiation fee for membership at one of Atlanta's finest country clubs. Having already amassed almost thirty grand of credit card debt in Arlene's name and growing frustrated with the limited amounts I was able to extract through payroll and expense reimbursement trickery, I then turned directly to the firm's clientele as an entirely separate treasure trove of opportunity. None of the attorneys at my firm practiced criminal defense law, but as I've said, ninety percent of our clients were up to something nefarious, be it screwing over their business partners, screwing over the federal government, screwing over their employees, or screwing over their spouse. Watching how these shitbags operated, and seeing how my firm facilitated their deviance and duplicity, removed any compunction I otherwise might have felt about taking as much as I could from both. It underscored a lesson that I had learned during my retail days, or rather, a truth that I had known since birth but which would be reinforced again and again throughout my life: all rich people are crooks. They have no morals. It's a zero-sum game, and their wealth is someone else's poverty. They had already stolen from me, directly and indirectly, and so all I was doing was taking back what was rightfully mine.

The law firm had its policies and procedures intended to protect client data, of course, but haste and distraction and incompetence and indifference meant that attorneys and staff alike constantly diverged from what the hyena-faced office manager referred to as "best practices." A social security number that was supposed to be contained in an encrypted attachment might accidentally end up in the body of an email instead; a dozen different replies and forwards later, the entire exchange winds up in my inbox as part of a to-do item because the billing partner can't be bothered with figuring out for himself how to digitally store the message under the client's file. Or an Excel spreadsheet containing all clients with delinquent account balances, using their SSNs as their unique identifiers, accidentally gets saved down to the general corporate drive instead of the password-protected file space where it was supposed to be. By clicking the "preview" view of the file in the system, I didn't even have to open the document. All the information I needed showed up on the right side of the screen, without leaving any digital record that I ever had access.

Ninety percent of my work was done for me at that point. Do you know how easy it is to fill in the gaps of someone's residential and employment history through public records? To figure out their birthday based on their public Facebook wall, where all their friends and family send them the obligatory "happy birthday" post? Plus, our firm tried to maintain reasonably complete records of every client's personal and business addresses, telephone numbers, the names and contact information of any spouse or kids, and sometimes even the details for their personal assistant, accountant, secretary, and financial advisor. They kept all this data in the HR drive, which was accessible to me on the assumption, I suppose, that I ought to be able to expeditiously reach all the people connected to high-value clientele.

But even when I wasn't blessed with all these details, even when I was dealing with a particularly shady individual who didn't seem to want to give even his attorneys too much information about how he could be found, you'd be shocked how much you can get a person to tell you just by posing as a utility company or a financial institution and calling them from a burner phone. Have enough information about them to prove that you already know what you're talking about, and speak with a mix of confidence and indifference (much like the way a legitimate customer service rep speaks to you), and tell the person on the other end that you're calling to "verify" or "update" their records. If they don't disconnect within the first twenty seconds, you're golden.

But I digress. Ultimately, identity theft was more of a hassle and high-risk proposition than it was worth. As much as I enjoyed punishing assholes and expanding the scope of activities with which I could support myself, the small-sum ventures were taking up far too much of my time. And the bolder I became supplementing my income directly from the firm's coffers, the more reserved I was forced to be in other ways. I didn't suddenly convert into a goody two-shoes, but I cut back on griping about all the shit beyond the scope of my job description that the attorneys made me do anyway, I reined in what Raymond refers to as my "sass mouth" even when a lowly secretary was trying to give me orders, and I followed the basic rules around stuff like dress codes, no matter how absurd or demeaning or inconsistently enforced.

It was destroying my spirit.

So I quit. It was time anyway. As a receptionist, my access to the firm's real money, primarily held in client escrow accounts, would remain strictly limited; and given the number of clients I had swindled over the course of the preceding nine months, to say nothing of how I had manipulated our internal expense reimbursement process and abused the corporate credit card, I decided it would be prudent for me to disappear immediately and completely while I was still ahead. I think I told them that I was resigning in order to pursue my dream of owning my own food truck, but first I'd be going to culinary school in Tennessee. It was something outlandish like that, and their enthusiastic response to my "bravery" was hilarious.

One of the junior paralegals brought in a cake on my last day to congratulate me on my "big move." I had to spend twenty minutes in the conference room making small talk while it was served, but it was a thoughtful sentiment, I suppose. Arlene took all of the leftover dessert back to her desk without asking anyone for permission or forgiveness. Thirty minutes later, as her final parting gift to me, I overheard her, between heaping mouthfuls of chocolate-frosted butter cake, bitching to one of her church cronies about her ongoing battle against unauthorized charges. I was ready to applaud myself on causing her continued aggravation, but then she went on to describe a bunch of random medical and prescription drug expenses incurred under her name and social security number that were categorically not my doing. So, as I watched her plod around the office for the rest of the day, always with a fresh plateful of cake and a plastic fork in hand, I merely scoffed and let it go, content with the knowledge that someone else was continuing to do the Lord's work against her even after I had moved on.

It was time to return to my old standby: ripping off douchebag men.

Chapter Twelve

While I was still working various desk job gigs, I ran my honeypot schemes almost exclusively online. My primary function, at both at the apartment complex and at the law firm, was to greet clients and to answer phones, but my supervisors had no clue how long any of my secondary tasks should have taken me to complete. All my predecessors must have idled away their days too, because I was never reprimanded for spending six hours on an assignment that could have been handled in forty-five minutes.

This, in turn, meant that I could use all of that superfluous time during which I was expected to be physically present but not otherwise required to do anything of value, to try to hook fools and dorks through Tinder, OkCupid, Instagram DMs, Facespace private messages (especially for cheating forty- and fifty-year-old men whose profiles were littered with family photos), Match, eMelody (these guys were all so desperately lonely, it was hilarious), Plenty of Guppies (although I'm pretty sure two-thirds of my intended targets were also catfish who lived outside the U.S. and were trying to scam me back), Christian Mingle... hell, I had fake profiles on everything, which I constantly had to tear down and rebuild using new names and locations depending on which personas got burned, which panned out so lucratively that they needed to be retired completely, what accounts were pulling alternate profiles with different info when I ran my reverse-image searches, and so on.

It was a well-organized numbers game, complete with hand-written notes and charts kept in an attractive teal-colored Shinola journal (which, if necessary, I could tear out, tear up, and set on fire in a trashcan at home, leaving behind no evidence of the extent of my electronic machinations), and sitting behind those desks all day gave me the time I needed to pursue multiple options at once. My identity-theft ventures hinged on the necessary information becoming available to me at an opportune time, and since this occurred only intermittently, and since both Bradford and my supervisors at the law firm scolded me whenever they caught me reading a hardcopy book during work hours, the only alternative to my dating app schemes was to spend eight hours a day staring into space or scrolling through Instagram.

For the most part, I used my own pictures on my dating profiles, but everything else was a fabrication. I quickly learned to choose jobs that made me seem professional and competent but not so smart or fancy that I'd be emasculating, and which also provided me with a good excuse to be away from home (whatever city I had decided that "home" would be) most of the time. Sometimes I was a traveling nurse or a marketing consultant who advised clients on-site, but pretending to be a flight attendant was my default approach. It gave me a reasonable pretext for being out of town whenever the guy proposed that we meet in person ("what a bummer!"), and naturally they all got off on the thought of me in a cute stewardess's uniform. It was such an effective character that I splurged on (or rather, one of the law firm's idiot clients with a penchant for bribery and misappropriating competitors' trade secrets unwittingly splurged on) two real flight attendant uniforms that I found on eBay. I took selfies in the parking lot and bathroom of the Indian Creek MARTA station and while riding on the blue line, and sent them to particularly promising prospects to let them know I was thinking of them from the staff bathroom at Hartsfield-Jackson or while riding the Plane Train.

Being a flight attendant also broadened my options for extracting money from an overeager mark. Maybe I could use my flight privileges to fly to meet him... but I still needed money to cover the fees and taxes associated with my ticket, plus all my other travel expenses. And I'd still have to fly standby, which I know from experience is always risky proposition to or from his home city, and sometimes it takes a whole day of sitting around to finally catch a seat, and we'll only have forty-eight hours together as it is, so maybe if you just wanted to pay for a real plane ticket (in first class, please) for me?

A lot of these guys had the sense to demand that we Face-Time before any money was exchanged, and although I couldn't do that on a burner phone (and certainly wasn't about to give out my real mobile number), I offered to Skype instead. Then I adjusted the info associated with my phony Skype account as needed, put on one of those absurd eBay uniforms if I had it with me that day, and flirted my way through a five-minute call before claiming I had to rush back to work. There were a handful of generic-looking spots around both The Roosevelt's and the law firm's lobby and exterior that provided suitable backdrops, able to pass as a random airport or out-of-state hotel as long as I was careful about my framing.

A single Skype session was, consistently, enough to assuage their concerns. My face and outfit matched my online pictures and profile, and since they wanted to believe it—since each one of them was convinced that he deserved a gorgeous, perky, obedient woman who was stoked to suck his dick, notwithstanding that he had nothing to offer in return—the video chat was all the confirmation they required. I'd get the money and then I (or rather, Nicolette or Natalia or Alessandra or Ghislaine) would vanish. No risk. My name, city, job, age, alma mater: all of it was a fiction, leaving him no way to find me. Besides, most rounds of this game netted me between fifty and five hundred bucks, which was a pleasant supplement to my income, but hardly enough to induce some guy to fly across the country from Bumfuck, Montana, or Shithole, Texas, or wherever he was stuck living, even if by some miracle he did figure out my real name and address. It never happened, and I'm sure I could've talked my way out of it if it had.

One of the uniforms I bought was from Lufthansa, which was a perfect way to convince these fools that I was actually Italian or French or Spanish and working internationally. I made myself a European citizen who went to a bilingual international preparatory school, thus my lack of a discernable accent and my expert command of the English language. Sometimes I got sloppy (I'm pretty sure there are not now, nor have there ever been, any direct flights from Paris to Kansas City), but my ability to think on my feet is unparalleled, and on the very rare occasions I was questioned about an ill-conceived assertion, I always eked out a convincing explanation or excuse with a poker face. Indeed, sometimes the tale was an opening to squeeze even more money out of them:

"Actually, I quoted the wrong price because I didn't want to admit that I needed to pay a rush fee to process my visa renewal, because it was my own stupidity that got me into this situation. I'm so embarrassed. I must have missed the notice when I was traveling for work, and then when I came home, I was preoccupied because my grandpa had died. I never got to say goodbye because I was in the air when it happened, and I don't think my mom will ever forgive me for it. I barely made it back for the funeral, and then I had to pick up an extra international shift when a senior flight attendant called out last-minute in order to get back in my boss's good graces. The first notice is probably still sitting in a pile of mail, but I only ever saw the final warning. I guess I didn't pay one of the initial fees, and now there are penalties for that, even on top of the rush fee. Oh, you must think I'm so silly and harebrained, listen to me carrying on. This is not your burden. I can't believe someone who has his life so together like you would be interested in a foolish woman like me."

They got such a boner from being the hero and feeling superior to me that I didn't need to ask them to help cover the costs of my fictitious crisis; they freely offered to wire me whatever amount I needed.

One guy, Chuck, had such an outstanding hero complex that he offered to contribute the full $4,500 I needed to finish paying off my uncle's gambling debts by Saturday, four days away. I was playing Emilia Giordano from Naples, Italy, at the time, and this dumb fucker must have rewatched *The Godfather* movies a few dozen too many times, because every outrageous thing I said, he ate it up. It got to the point where I was basically seeing what I could get away with. I told Chuck that after selling nearly all of our belongings, the family had managed to pull together $45,500 of the $50,000 we needed to repay Jimmy the Mower (the lawn maintenance guys were cutting the grass across the street at that particular moment) by the end of the week. But if we were even one cent short at the stroke of midnight, Uncle Tommy would be dead before sunrise, and then Jimmy the Mower's crew would start knocking off the Giordano clan one by one (possibly including me!) until Uncle Tommy's debts were satisfied.

Five thousand dollars was wired to me at 10:00 a.m. the next morning. I cut off contact with Chuck immediately, so I never found out for what purpose he intended I use the extra five hundred bucks. Thanks to Chuck's heroics, I enjoyed a week pretending to be a socialite in Miami. I guess Uncle Tommy is sleeping with the fishes.

That Miami trip was how I came to understand that sometimes you have to spend money to make money. I liked the Emilia Giordano identity so much that I decided to stick with her for the duration of my trip, with some slight modification from her online dating persona to make her more upscale. I was still Italian, but rather than being the victim of the mafia, I made vague allusions to having family connections to powerful men. I was still a flight attendant, technically speaking, but now I worked as an independent contractor servicing private jets and exclusive clientele (Arab sheiks, tech billionaires, famous movie stars), but of course, due to the strict nondisclosure agreements I was required to sign to protect their privacy, I couldn't name names or share photos or tell stories. It was a job I did because I loved to travel and I loved to meet interesting people, not because I needed the money. The "family" had me taken care of completely in that regard.

I continued to explain away my so-called Americanized accent and proficiency in English by claiming that I had attended The Anglo-Italian School and The American International School in Naples, and I added a bachelor's degree in Art History from Brown University to Emilia's résumé. In retrospect, given all the pompous wannabe art-douches that frequented the same set of Miami's swanky lounges and bars as I, the choice of major was reckless, but those supposed four years at an Ivy League college provided a basis for my familiarity with American culture and further helped to explain away my flawless English. And besides, I'm genuinely interested in art, and I'm a quick study. Whenever someone asked my opinion on anything relating to the art world—to challenge me or to try to humiliate me, not because they gave a shit about my thoughts—I replied using the all-too-familiar tone, imbued with unfounded confidence and tinted with disdain, so popular among men when they speak to women about... well, pretty much about anything.

And even those same men who, mere moments before, had spent several minutes condescendingly explaining to me what Bitcoin is or how exchange-traded funds work, generally refrained from further debating my always critical, always haughty remarks on matters of art, culture, and design. With my phony credentials and very real confidence, opining on the arts turned into a fun game of MadLibs, which I played with near-total impunity:

> *Yes, of course I'm familiar with that work. The suggestion of* [covert texture] [temporal discourse] [oscillating emotion] [transcendent dogshit] *evokes in the viewer* [instability] [manufactured rage] [cultural disorientation] [explosive diarrhea], *while* [challenging] [emphasizing] [bum-fucking] *the* [universality of being] [collective unconscious] [objecthood of man] [synthetic nature of reality] [limpness of your dick]; *it's a* [daring] [provocative] [sublime] [decadent] [fucking idiotic] *reflection of* [the zeitgeist] [man's eternal struggle against himself] [the humility inherent in personal evolution] [the fact that all of you have fully bought into your own bullshit]. *I'm baffled that anyone could misconstrue the artist's intent otherwise.*

On the rare occasion that someone managed to rebut any of the ostentatious nonsense spewing from my mouth with a modicum of intelligence, it was easy enough to deflect. I always had a "brilliant professor back at Brown" who shared his or her "esoteric interpretation," and you know, it's really impressive that someone who doesn't have an extensive formal background studying this material can make such insightful reflections into

such a complicated topic, and why don't you tell me more about...
or, what do you think about... and since these buffoons zealously
milked any and all opportunities to hear the sound of their own
voice, suddenly a situation that could have exposed me would
become completely neutralized.

It was enough to make me wish I had some semblance of
artistic talent. I'm thinking about moving on from the Atlanta
area anyway, after my current situation is resolved, and maybe
I'll return to Miami. I can claim my utter inability to paint is "an
avant-garde rejection of the norms and strictures of society and
of the very art world itself, and if you can't see that, it's probably
because you're unwilling to engage in the potentially devastating
discourse with the work, and indeed with yourself, that revelation demands." It took me two hours of thumbing through an
art criticism magazine in the airport lounge and another couple
of hours spent wandering around the Perez Museum of Art and
ICA Miami to master their language and mannerisms last time I
was there. Imagine what I could do if I were fully immersed in
the scene?

And lest you think that I'm uncultured swine or too stupid
to get it or something, let me be clear that I wasn't mocking the
artists or the artwork itself. I just told you, I personally have a
tremendous appreciation for the fine and contemporary arts.
Rather, my problem was exclusively with the pretentious twits
who pretended to reverently marvel at, or be moved to tears by,
these works, conspicuously gasping and swooning both inside the
museum and when they recollected the pieces after the fact. It
was the functional equivalent of Alex's claim that he and Shannon
felt their feelings more deeply than everyone else. These assholes
were equally convinced that they interpreted, understood, and
connected to art more profoundly than anyone around them
could—or at least they were dead-set on convincing the rest of us
this was true.

They were the ones I liked to jerk around while I was
otherwise trying to enjoy a cocktail in peace. Everything they said
and did was calculated to impress the same people who were
trying to impress them back. It was a corrupted, distracting, poorly

executed version of the way I sometimes fine-tune my own image in order to attract wealthy men, done with an unwarranted self-satisfaction that rendered them more repugnant than the fools who putz around Miami's museums and public displays taking inane selfies with each piece and moving on to the next without pausing for a single moment to glance at the artwork they'd be posting to their Instagram account later that day. At least those dunces shamelessly embrace their ignorance.

I typically prefer to keep my headphones off in public so I can overhear the conversations around me, but after twenty minutes at the Institute of Contemporary Art, I was so disgusted by the other museum patrons' chatter that I fetched my Bose earbuds from my purse and turned up Intervals—this badass instrumental metal band that I'd recently started listening to, because unlike Alex Montalvo-Moore, who will forever remain a mediocre guitar player performing mediocre country songs, I am willing to evolve in my musical tastes—in order to tune them out.

With their fatuous observations blocked, I was able to relax and focus, and I was surprised to feel spontaneous and unexpectedly deep connections with certain creators—genuinely, and without the need to boisterously announce it to everyone around me. Perhaps what I do and what they do are manifestations of the same underlying instinct. And the best of the best in the art world manage to monetize it, so why shouldn't I? My peers are told to define themselves, to focus on two key characteristics—always a banal, forgettable, and ultimately meaningless adjective/noun combination like "innovative authenticity" or "authentic innovation"—and are advised to make their online and real-life identities match up with this personal brand. They have no room to deviate or to explore. No room to try something different and fail. No room to contain multiplicities.

But this trip, inspired by a coffee-table book I had picked up in the PAMM gift shop on the performance artist ORLAN, I decided, "I am OLIVIA, among others." Maybe I initially pursued my vague interest in art because it seemed like a viable way to meet high-net-worth individuals and to keep the strivers in check, but by the second or third day of the trip, I was toying with the art-world identity because it was fun and fascinating and because I could. I've created that freedom for myself. I've taken what was meaningful to me, what spoke to me, what improved my chances of meeting my objectives or morphing into a new objective of its own, and I've left the rest behind.

For a moment, I thought about Alex, and how if he hadn't been crazy and if I had adopted the personal brand of "rockstar girlfriend," I would have missed out on the Miami trip and on so many other opportunities. And it would have been that much more stifling because it was an identity forged by and through my relationship to and status derived from someone else. Thank the Lord that version of me fell apart before it had the chance to take hold, and thank the Lord I had grown so much wiser in the interim.

On the flight back to Atlanta, as I was enjoying my third cocktail in my cushy first-class seat (sadly, seated next to a stern-looking woman wearing a bright red pantsuit and a gaudy gold wedding ring, who was unlikely to be amenable to my advances even if I were prepared to expand my options to the sapphic sphere), I reflected on the preceding week and had the self-awareness to realize that my approach to men in Atlanta was going to have to change. Superficially, the trip might have seemed like a failure. Of course, I never had to pay for a drink, but the most expensive gift I was given the entire time was a pair of $635 Chanel tortoise-shell sunglasses that some tanned retiree in a golf shirt randomly bought me after I smiled at him while browsing in Icons Miami Eyewear. According to him, I looked like a modern-day Jackie O, and South Beach needed more elegant young women who appreciated vintage style and understated glamour. Gramps didn't even use the gift as a pretext to ask me to dinner, although if he had, I probably would've accepted. They're a great pair of sunglasses.

But that was it! Those designer glasses were my most notable acquisition, and I earned them simply by pleasantly existing within some rich old dude's milieu. I didn't snatch cash out of anyone's wallet, I hadn't convinced anyone to transfer my hotel charges to his credit card, and I wasn't returning with some sucker's bank account information memorized off an open browser tab and jotted down in the Notes app on my phone. That hadn't been the point of this trip! I had paid for my first-class flight and my luxury hotel myself (I mean, technically it was Chuck's money, but you understand my point), which meant that I was indebted to no one. My time there was my own, and I used it to study how the men who resided three steps up in the social hierarchy thought and behaved. I returned to Atlanta with a renewed appreciation that I could pursue my ambitions in ways that didn't involve me hunched over a desk all day, making a pitiful salary and trying to scrounge up scraps from the electronic trail left by wealthy clients or shitty coworkers or entitled philanderers. Miami taught me that if I were willing to shift to the longer-term strategy that wealthier men required, ultimately I'd get more for less effort, leaving me more time to do as I pleased without any male interference or input at all.

Even before the trip to Miami, it was clear I had a knack for in-person seduction and what you would probably label "extortion" or "swindling" or "theft," and what I would rather describe as "inducements to give me what I'm due." But my prior endeavors into this sphere had been amateurish, with corresponding results. Miami was an unequivocal success because it proved to me that I belonged with the rich and cultured. Atlanta-rich and Miami-rich are two different breeds, of course, but I had newfound confidence that I could adapt and integrate among any brand of wealthy, and with that access I would be able to acquire what I deserved.

I immediately retired the use of my own pictures from the online dating game. Objectively, it was unlikely that any of the men I wanted to start pursuing in person in Atlanta would stumble across my image under a phony name on one of those disgraceful dating apps, especially if I restricted my profile location and preferences to cities outside of Georgia; but at the same time, the caliber of man I was after was likely to travel often and to have friends or colleagues across the country who could match with me, and I didn't want to risk it. I couldn't find many details about how the apps' algorithms generated potential matches, and I was getting bored with those schemes anyway. It was a lot of work for minimal rewards, and I mostly did it to pass the time at my real job.

Incidentally, after I had shut down all my phony accounts, I briefly used a few pictures of Raymond to create the dating app profile of a successful man seeking a bisexual or straight woman between the ages of twenty-two and forty-eight, with no restrictions on race, religion, height, or weight. It was more of a social experiment than anything else. I thought it'd be interesting to view the game from the perspective of a heterosexual man. Raymond is kind of old now but he's still a handsome enough guy, and in all the pictures I used he looked polished and well-dressed with a friendly smile, so I figured that with a simple bio suggesting that he was educated, stable, and reasonably well-off, I'd probably get a handful of decent matches.

What actually transpired, however, was horrifying. Most of the women who matched with him were even more desperate and trusting than the whackjob guys who matched with me. Several of the white women couldn't be bothered to disguise their creepy, fetishy obsession with Black men, in the full range of despicable manifestations this can take, which gave me particular glee when I was able to twist their psychological defects into money in my pockets. After extracting $489 (the cost of a plane ticket) from some herpes-ridden hag with over-processed hair from Oklahoma City who proposed a variety of appalling race-play scenarios for "our" first meeting, I bought Raymond an iPad for Christmas. It was by far the best gift anyone in the family gave or received that year. Like I've said, Raymond is one of the only halfway-decent men I've ever known, and I'm proud I was able to do something so generous for him.

My brief endeavor into catfishing as a man clarified why it had been so easy for me to hook guys using my fake female profiles; from shuffling through an endless array of ridiculously filtered photos and shameless "follow my Instagram!" plugs from unremarkable girls with delusional aspirations of becoming influencers, to reading the embittered sob-story profiles of nasty women who'd be better served abandoning their search for a husband

and resigning themselves to adopting their seventh cat, my quest for true love as Raymond proved that these apps were a cesspool of humanity for heterosexual men and women alike.

It was time to operate in the analog world. Immediately prior to my revelations in Miami, I had been spending a lot of my downtime at dive bars. To be fair, the music was better and the atmosphere was a needed change of pace from my stuffy day jobs. Plus, since I hadn't been interested in real dating since the Alex debacle, I mostly hung out with Milo and Jana on the weekends, and they refused to show up anywhere with a cover charge or a dress code unless it was a special occasion. Upon my return to Atlanta, however, I finally acknowledged that, notwithstanding my handful of minor victories with online cons and moderately clever wire transfer schemes, I had grown complacent. These tactics were adequate for generating short-term income, but unless I made a conscious effort to continuously surround myself with the people who already had the money and status that I ought to have too, I would stagnate.

I decided to focus my energies on Buckhead, with a job and a social calendar that would position me to be surrounded by wealthy men every single day. I considered abandoning my apartment in Sandy Springs for a luxury high-rise in Buckhead Centre but concluded that, at least for the time being, I could achieve what I wanted without incurring the additional expense of another move simply by relocating my professional and social life. I didn't resign from the law firm receptionist job immediately, but I used some of the time I formerly spent on online seduction and drip-bleeding the firm's vulnerable credit lines to search for new employment that would place me in locations that rich men frequent.

As I recentered my approach, there was one key question I needed to answer first: what could I give these men that no other woman could? As I rose up the rungs of the social ladder, simply being hot and amazing in bed would no longer suffice; there were too many other attractive women giving out enthusiastic blow jobs to their keepers for me to distinguish myself on those attributes alone. I tried out different identities at bars in Milton, Dunwoody, and Alpharetta, and gauged how men reacted to each. These self-proclaimed gentlemen weren't quite my target demographic, but I wasn't yet prepared to commit to a single character, and I couldn't risk any of the regular patrons at Buckhead establishments noticing that my career, style, interests, or even my first name, were changing between visits. These suburban men were convenient to my apartment and office at the time, and they were decent enough temporary surrogates for me to formulate my initial impressions about their initial impressions of me and thereby develop my basic game-time strategy.

At first, I was Amy, the worker's compensation attorney in private practice at a boutique law firm. My time at Ballsack, Jerkoff & Cockwhore LLP had taught me enough legalese to pass a cursory bullshit exam, and I figured that my purported practice area was sufficiently obscure as to avoid generating questions from some overeager asshole who happened to be having a crisis relating to the exact subject matter of my supposed expertise and who had no qualms about soliciting free legal advice. For a few days, I honestly thought that I could intrigue these men by presenting myself as their equal, as someone who could be a potential partner in achieving shared financial, career, and personal goals in a power-couple marriage.

What a joke. Without exception, as soon as I told the targeted man that I was a lawyer, I could see the interest visibly drain from his face. These guys clearly thought that my tight business skirts and suggestively unbuttoned blouses were sexy, but only if the body and brain underneath was that of a physical therapist or a dental hygienist or "a communications major starting my first-ever job at a PR firm." Someone who was sort of smart, but not intimidatingly so. Someone who worked diligently but without undue ambition to achieve modest success in a feminine career, but who, deep down, knew that she was naïve and helpless and a bit of a ditz, and who therefore remained properly insecure about her inferior intelligence when humbly presenting herself before a man. I could get away with being an entrepreneur, but only if my business was geared exclusively toward other women (selling a line of high-end athleisure or cellulite-melting Brazilian butt cream on the internet, running a one-woman interior design firm focused on children's bedrooms, baking gourmet cupcakes), and only if I was struggling (but not too desperately!) to stay afloat. Ultimately, this is what I had expected and had known all along. In a twisted way, given my relative lack of fancy schooling, I suppose it was for the best. In the long run, it's easier to feign being a nutritionist or a preschool teacher than an actuary or a neurosurgeon.

Since my character's intellect and ambitions needed to hover right around average to make it to the next step with these men, I needed to distinguish myself in other ways. Inspired by the deviously clever way that fat bitch Arlene found an "in" with the firm's attorneys by attending the same church as the beloved junior partner Jessica Fitzgerald, I too found God. A few times I was proudly Jewish, on a few other occasions devoutly Catholic or Christian, and one time, on a night when I was happy to abstain from alcohol anyway, I claimed that I had been called to the teachings of the Latter Day Saints and was actively considering conversion. These "discoveries" of shared religious faith did indeed lead to immediate common ground and implicit trust, but since ultimately it only mattered one way or the other to a relatively small segment of men, mostly I was areligious or blandly "raised Episcopalian" if necessary.

When the men commented on my toned physique, I used their unsolicited feedback as a way to generate interest by crediting my fitness to a noteworthy hobby. The aesthetic benefits were a bonus, I claimed, resulting from my love of yoga (a fan favorite), weight lifting (met with skepticism and condescending advice about not getting too big or not hurting myself), jogging, ballet or modern dance, "cardio classes three times a week at the gym with my girlfriends, and then we get pretty pink cocktails together after [giggles]," or golf (another fan favorite, and a fantastic segue for me to learn at which country clubs they and their golfing buddies were members).

As a result of those conversations, I applied for the open hostess, assistant pool manager, and banquet bartender positions at Capital City Club, Cherokee Town & Country Club, and Atlanta Athletic Club, respectively, but despite my experience with high-end clientele at The Roosevelt, none of the opportunities panned out. You'd think that my experience at a law firm would have been beneficial too, but in retrospect any hiring manager at a ritzy country club would know that the shithole office I worked at in Dunwoody was a far cry from the AmLaw 200 firms in Midtown. I'm certain that's why my applications were rejected. The country clubs' corrupt, miserable members may have comprised a portion of the law firm's clientele, but no one wants to acknowledge any affiliation with that sleaze, just the obscene wealth that results from it. That's what I get for trying to be honest on my résumé. Whatever. Now I know that as the hired help, I never would have been more than a quick fuck for those men anyway. Whatever additional financial access and opportunity to observe the elite's behavior in a posh leisure environment that those jobs would have provided, I could obtain elsewhere through less degrading means.

Testing out characters in suburban bars was an enlightening experience, and for a couple of weeks, it was almost fun. But "fun" doesn't pay the bills, and the truth is, I had grown attached to the Emilia Giordano persona. Even during the weeks of experimenting in the suburbs, she kept reemerging, evolving and deepening in ways that would be critical to a long-term con. But unless and until I moved out of metro Atlanta and far away from the overwhelming majority of my high school classmates who remained in the area, changing my first name to anything other than some derivation of Olivia was too risky. I knew I could quickly get rid of someone from my past if they approached me in public, but probably not quickly enough to prevent them from using my real first name.

So now, I would become Olivia Giordano. If I ever got confronted about the change, I could make up some story about a previous marriage. In order to explain away the Georgia driver's license and U.S. passport, I was now a dual citizen. A significant portion of the wealthy men I wanted to pursue were likely to have access to corporate aircraft or memberships with Jet Linx or Magellan Jets, so my "private airline stewardess" shtick was no longer viable. But I liked how well-traveled it made me seem (and so did most of the men), so I claimed that I had recently retired from that line of work for a job that would "let me put down roots for a while."

I continued to make occasional allusions to mob connections and family money, suggesting that the primary reason I worked was because I enjoyed talking with interesting people and because it added structure to my days, and certainly not because I was desperate for a paycheck myself. A well-timed tip with a crisp hundred dollar bill, retrieved from my sleek black-and-gold YSL wallet, cemented the illusion in the real world. How could they not be intrigued? Olivia Giordano: wholesome but with an edge of danger, an exotic Italian goddess who nevertheless spoke perfect English, a level-headed gal who chose to work despite her family's wealth, with a pedigreed education that was limited to the matters of fine arts and culture appropriate for a female mind.

I even took Italian language courses online in order to learn basic conversational phrases and a few racy remark. Eventually I became proficient enough to understand and respond competently to anyone who happened to truly be fluent and was excited to show off his skills with me. I figured that, if questioned, I could follow up whatever Italian blather I managed to recite with a self-deprecating joke about how disappointed my relatives back in Naples are about how Americanized I've become, even though my parents were the ones who elected to enroll me in English-speaking schools in Italy, who sent me to college in Rhode Island (have I mentioned that I attended Brown?), and who rarely spoke Italian around the house specifically so that I would grow up fluent and without an accent in the lingua franca of the globalized world. And then I'd shrug and make a flippant, flirty comment about how I still remember how to say the good stuff: a seductive whisper of "ho voglia di te" for the conservative old guys, and a bolder "voglio le tue mani su tutto il corpo" (or, as my language skills improved, something far more explicit) for the cocky younger ones.

My wardrobe was already at the forefront of fashion thanks to the contributions of Marissa, Arlene, and a half-dozen other idiots who unwittingly shared their good credit with me, and my Rent the Runway "unlimited swaps" membership provided the remainder of the clothes and accessories that an Atlanta socialite would require. I had swiped at least a dozen different pairs of designer shoes over the course of my retail days, all of which were still in great condition. A surprising number of (ostensibly straight) men in Buckhead possessed an uncanny ability to discern the true luxury-brand bags and shoes from the knock-offs, but I had stolen most of my accessories specifically because of their time-lessly elegant style and these same men proved to be less skilled at knowing which pieces were from a past season and ever-so-slightly off-trend. In most circumstances, a meticulously maintained pair of black Manolo Blahnik pumps and a sleek leather Balenciaga satchel could withstand the passing of a half-dozen years without betraying my act. Suffice to say, the most seamless aspect of my transition to the Buckhead project was looking the part.

As I said, men didn't want me to *be* too smart or ambitious, but they didn't seem to mind me looking like the television version of a female lawyer or advertising executive: sleek blouses (with one too many buttons undone), pinstripe skirts (cut two inches too high), and suit dresses that hugged my curves more tightly than any real professional woman would be comfortable flaunting in the courtroom or the boardroom. Despite their protestations to the contrary, none of these morons wanted "a laid-back girl who sips beer and watches football in jeans and a white t-shirt," nor were they interested in any of my edgy, female-friendly fashion ensembles. Even the aggressive displays of sexual availability that worked so well for me in Miami (thigh-high boots, skin-tight sleeveless club dresses) occasionally floundered here. Somehow, I was most approachable and desirable in the costume of a PornHub librarian. Fuck it. This was a numbers game, and if that's what Atlanta's high-end market demanded, I would abide.

I suppose you want to hear about the men themselves. I'm sure it all seems fascinating to an outsider. In truth, my stories about dating Buckhead men bore me. Notwithstanding their conviction that they have been specially chosen (whether by birthright or by the higher power they profess to believe in for appearance's sake) for greatness, ultimately these men are interchangeable. The most exciting thing about being in their presence was that it occurred in expensive restaurants or exclusive lounges or members-only clubs.

Imagine. Imagine being so unflinchingly, intractably convinced that the promise of the three-and-a-half-inch, perpetually flaccid appendage hanging between your legs could cure flu symptoms, depression, the common cold, migraines, hell, probably even cancer and atherosclerosis. That a few wheezing thrusts of His Majesty could resurrect a deceased grandparent or bring a beloved old dog back from the dead, or at least would leave any woman quivering in such ecstasy that she would forget she ever cared about anything other than that glorious dick anyway. That even a teeny, tiny lady-brain would understand how blessed she was to be chosen as his receptacle. That such honor would eclipse the pain of any type of personal or professional setback or suffering, be it a mass layoff, a foreclosure, a bankruptcy, an auto repair she couldn't afford, a falling out with a family member, any blight in her day or year, no matter how trivial or severe: all would be rectified by a good boning courtesy of His Most Holy Cock.

After all, that risible sack of skin and tissue had imbued him with a natural aptitude for math, science, spatial reasoning, and logic, so much so that, notwithstanding his struggles to maintain a B-average in high school algebra or chemistry, he was more qualified than a woman with a Ph.D. in Applied Mathematics or Theoretical Physics to opine on the very subject matter of her dissertation. That pathetic, clumsy, capricious protuberance was the reason and the justification for why he deserved not just the promotion and the raise and the nice house and the ability to walk the streets drunk and alone at night without fear or blame, but the love, respect, admiration, and obedience of any woman whom his dick decided was worthy of his attention, including and especially, the hot chick. And if that supreme, almighty, heavenly dick decided that one hot chick was not enough, then it could, should, and would acquire others, as many as necessary or useful to satisfy his ego and his whims.

I could have remained as pathetic and impotent as their stubby, sagging johnsons in my anger over the injustice of it all, but

I'm not the victim of society or of any specific individual therein. I observed and adapted. And as a result, men like this became a godsend for me. I had turned myself into the hot chick. Not the Snellville-hot that I used to be, but Buckhead-hot. Maybe-a-wife, maybe-a-whore, I'll-spend-whatever-it-takes-to-find-out hot. He wouldn't worry about me overhearing his conversations about a shady private placement deal of unregistered security-based credit swaps or an unlicensed import/export transaction he was orchestrating with a trading partner from an embargoed country, because I was too dumb to understand Big Boy concepts like that anyway. My nescience was a given and my fidelity could be bought with pretty, shiny trinkets. I would be another toy to show off to the people who were simultaneously striving to impress him back, and he would be so preoccupied with that dick-measuring contest that, as long as I shoved down my contempt with a vapid smile, giggled at his jokes, and kept myself slim and enviably dressed, I could rob him blind and he wouldn't suspect a thing.

In the eighteen months between when I resigned from the law firm and when I met Raj, I'd estimate that I got involved in a meaningful way—which is to say, I put in at least a couple weeks of effort—with about ten different Buckhead men. I cannot emphasize enough how unremarkable they all were. The only thing noteworthy about them is that they were all, to a person, conmen and criminals in their own right. But whereas my actions are condemned, theirs are praised as "bold," "aggressive," "ambitious," and "boundary-pushing." No matter. Thanks to them, I didn't have to pay for a single month's car payment or rent, for meals or gym membership dues, for vacations or clothes or trips to the salon, or for much of anything at all, during that entire stretch of time. And when those allowances and gifts were no longer sufficient for me to tolerate their gilded mediocrity, I took the knowledge I had gained from eavesdropping on their conversations with a blank stare and a confused smile, and used it to abscond with as much money as I thought I could get away with. Those who noticed were either too embarrassed or too concerned about the risk of what would be uncovered if law enforcement started poking around their finances, that I was never so much as questioned.

I exclusively pursued new-money men, primarily white guys who were generally between the ages of forty and fifty-five (although occasionally I ventured into younger or older territory), who were recently divorced or who were enduring irreparably broken marriages until their kids went to college or until more of their assets could be hidden from their spouse. The men in this demographic wanted to flaunt their wealth, and I quickly realized that I didn't want to conform to the stodgy, racist, incestuous world of southern old money anyway.

I considered playing the dutiful girlfriend role long-term so that I could score an expensive engagement ring (which I would promptly sell after breaking the engagement two months later), but who knows how long it might have taken for any one of these idiots to pop the question. The thought of a public proposal sickened me, but I'd have to feign that it was the happiest moment of my life. I didn't think that being a fiancée would give me much additional access to the average mark's funds or would induce him to spend materially more money on gifts for me compared to being his girlfriend or his favorite mistress. And given their access to fancy divorce lawyers and their inevitable insistence on a prenup, pursuing marriage as my endgame was a ridiculous proposition financially, even if I had been able to get past my countless personal and philosophical objections to the institution. The best part is, none of the other single women in this scene seemed to understand the fundamental underlying dynamics at play; they were all desperately trying to get married, either by inducing their target to abandoned bachelorhood or by convincing him to divorce his current wife. There was an ample, underserved market for exactly what I was willing to offer.

After that, it's simply a numbers game. It's a matter of learning where the key players prefer to go for their morning workouts, their business lunches, their after-work drinks, and their late-night extravagances, and then showing up at those places repeatedly. Men of their means have the money and power to hire an in-home personal trainer, to decline invitations to social events they don't feel like attending, and to opt for quiet nights at home with their ugly wife and disappointing children. If they are out in public, it's because they want to be, and women like me are the reason why. When you understand that, you understand that the whole "trick" to snagging a wealthy guy is nothing more than being in the right place at the right time, with an elegant appearance and approachable smile. If you can listen to him brag and complain without rolling your eyes or caring that he doesn't respect you or give a fuck about you in any real way, you'll be golden.

I don't mind sharing my secrets. The market is glutted with middling dick. If you beat me to one target, I'll move along to the next. Or I'll just wait until you're done! You'd think they'd learn their lesson, but most of them are either too oblivious to realize what's happened or, more likely, their ego cannot countenance the idea that a woman has outsmarted them and they'll create any justification or convoluted explanation necessary to avoid confronting that horrifying truth.

Besides, I have only another five or so years left of this particular hustle. It's never long after we women turn thirty that men start to think that they're doing us some sort of favor by dating us. The whole balance of power shifts, and although I'm certain that there is some sort of dynamic there that I'll be able to exploit when the time comes—men who date women over age thirty probably fancy themselves to be more mature or open-minded or generous for forgoing the plethora of more nubile options that they imagine remain a realistic possibility for them, and surely I can twist this self-deception to my advantage—hopefully by that point I will have accrued enough wealth of my own that I won't ever have to pander to these clowns again. They've unwittingly taught me about all the amoral business practices they utilize to expand their empires and screw over their competitors. At my current rate of growth, I'll have a million-dollar net worth by the time I hit "past her prime" territory, and I'll be able to employ the very tactics I've learned from them over the years to displace them in any industry in which I choose to focus my efforts.

For now, though, I am still squarely in my twenties, still gorgeous, and as long as the presents and cash keep coming, still able to repress my disgust for long enough to execute the con.

Chapter Thirteen

You've been giving me a perplexed look, as if you don't understand why I'd be so transparent about everything that has unfolded over the past ten years. I'm not stupid. I understand that, technically speaking, I've admitted to the commission of various crimes. Can't you see that was a strategic decision? Perhaps you're not used to the people sitting in this chair being quite so clever. You can't offer me immunity from prosecution and then arbitrarily retract it. I declined legal representation because I don't want you assigning me some moron public defender who is juggling thirty other cases, and if I had done anything that could get me in real trouble, I would take Raymond up on his offer to pay for a defense attorney for me. But you've been reiterating since I got here that you're more interested in understanding what happened with Raj than you are in pursuing charges against me. So I realized, if I tell you everything I've ever done now, you won't be allowed to come after me for it later. I guess you didn't think of that little loophole, did you?

But ultimately, we're on the same side here. You want to know about Raj, and I'm happy to tell you. I suppose you already know how it ended, so I'll start with how it began.

Raj approached me. Let's be clear about that. I've been more than forthcoming about how I targeted other men, so I have no reason to lie about this. I was at Porter Beer Bar in Little Five Points, of all places. I wasn't working an angle. Don't get me wrong: I am well aware that some of those dirty hipsters have far more family money than your average Buckhead douche, and they're riddled with their own set of insecurities that I could capitalize on and monetize, but what I do is part art, part science, and I have perfected my methodology for a certain type of man in a particular type of neighborhood. Maybe I'll go to Little Five or East Atlanta if I need a one-night, heavily tattooed palette cleanser in between three-month blocks dedicated exclusively to nasty semi-retired investment banker old-man balls. But the day I met Raj, I wasn't even doing that!

No, as I remember it, earlier that day I'd had an interview downtown for a secretary position at one of the city government offices. I was toying with the idea of focusing my energy on men with political power, rather than just money. After three hours of submissive glances and phony smiles at middle-aged men in ill-fitting suits—whose spheres of influence in the city of Atlanta, it rapidly became apparent to me, did not now and would not ever extend beyond the four walls of their tiny windowless offices lit with flickering florescent lights—I needed to pacify my anger with a drink or two before I spent another hour in my car trying to get home.

This was back in late February, maybe early March. I could give you the exact date, since I programmed the interview itinerary into my calendar app, but the big Asian dude with the moustache out front made me turn over my phone almost immediately after I got here. I remember it was a nice day. It was a little after 4:00 p.m. when I found a parking spot for my car maybe a half-mile down Euclid Avenue, and I didn't mind walking because the sun felt so good on my face and shoulders.

I had started leasing a dark red Mazda MX-5 Miata the prior November so that I'd have it for holiday parties. Its presence is conspicuous under any circumstances, but especially in that neighborhood; I know the houses there cost a fortune, but most of the cars using street parking are trash. My baby has tinted windows, but I was concerned about some random junkie or opportunist peering in anyway and smashing a window or cutting through the soft top to get to my suit jacket and my USB cord. At the same time, I didn't want to lug that crap around with me, and I certainly didn't want to look frumpy, even if my only plan was to sit and have a single beer by myself. So into the trunk they went, and I was free at last to stroll unhindered in a conservative grey sheath dress by Derek Lang (a temporary acquisition, courtesy of Rent the Runway) that hugged my curves without being too garish about it.

If you've been to the Porter before, then you're familiar with the layout. It's a nice place for a casual date, or to go sit in the back with a group of friends and share appetizers or whatever, but with the way the bar area is laid out, it's not particularly conducive to approaching or being approached by strangers. Again, for me, on this particular afternoon, that was part of the appeal. I wanted to sit in a stool staring straight ahead, sipping a ridiculously filling, obnoxiously high-gravity coffee stout, and strategize my next move, since my test run at Atlanta's political high-rollers had been a total bust. At most, I expected to flirt with some hot, bearded bartender with shitty forearm tattoos, who probably would invite me to his metal band's show at 529 that night. And, with the full understanding that had I remained on the path set out for me in Snellville, this would have been the pinnacle of the type of man I could have hoped to obtain, I might have been tempted to allow myself a single evening in which I scrapped my ambitions, changed into an outfit that was actually comfortable and cool, and spent a few hours having fun in East Atlanta.

But that's not what happened. Other than the staff, the bar was almost completely empty. A cute lesbian couple, on what I'd guess was their third or fourth official date, was sitting at one of the tables behind the bar and adjacent to the bathrooms, sharing goofy smiles and a bowl of salt & vinegar popcorn, and otherwise oblivious to their surroundings. A hot Korean guy with multiple facial piercings was editing photos on his laptop by the front window. A tall, gaunt, white man in a tattered brown coat, who could have been in his late thirties or his late fifties for all I knew, was hunched over at the far end of the bar, occasionally raising his head to take another sip of his drink before immediately returning to his resting position.

And then, Raj.

I noticed him in the same way I noticed the other patrons. They were present but immaterial. I was conscious of, but indifferent to, their existence. Raj was dressed in a stylish silvery-grey button-down shirt with the sleeves pushed up his forearms, untucked over a pair of darker grey jeans, no tie, no belt—it struck me as the attire of a man cognizant of the fact that he was approaching the final few years in which he could troll Moondogs and hit on newly minted twenty-one-year-olds before it became prohibitively creepy—although I didn't notice his very un-L5P outfit until after he approached.

"Did I hear you order the Peche Mortel Bourbon stout?" he asked from his seat, three stools over. "I'm impressed. We don't see too many girls like you drinking that kind of beer."

I raised an eyebrow. "I'm not sure what you mean by that."

He stood up with his drink and situated himself in the stool next to me. For however irritated I was that some random guy was invading my space and disturbing my peace, I can acknowledge that this was a ballsy move on his part. Still, I maintained my poker face.

"You're fit. Feminine. Well-dressed. And that's a heavy beer. I would've expected you to ask if they have any Whiteclaws in the back."

"I didn't realize that my appearance and drink choices would be subject to such strict scrutiny when I entered the premises," I replied flatly.

He paused, looking at me intently. Then he smirked.

"It's standard procedure, but it only applies to those of us who have fewer than three facial piercings or five visible tattoos. Believe me, wearing a shirt like this, I was subjected to it too."

Despite myself, I cracked a smile. From one pickup artist to another, I had to give him credit for his ability to realize that his initial strategy was failing badly and for his willingness to change his technique on the fly. I wasn't interested in pursuing any further conversation, but he seemed to be encouraged by my slightly softened expression.

"My name's Raj," he said. He pushed back his sleeves, partly out of habit and partly to make sure that I noticed his rose gold and alligator skin Jaeger-LeCoultre watch. If it had been a Rolex, I probably would have questioned whether it were a knock-off, but JLC timepieces have always struck me as a more refined display of wealth and status, and therefore generally outside the scope of the average poser's awareness. Raj's good taste rendered him marginally more interesting. "Raj is fine, but a lot of my friends know me as Rich, or R-Money. My family owns the Mirage chain of BMW dealerships all throughout Atlanta and North Georgia. Plus we have locations in South Carolina, Florida, and Texas. We had the grand opening of our eighth location today, in Alpharetta. We also own a bunch of pickup truck dealerships. We tend to make more money off those, if you can believe it. It's all in the financing."

Maybe not so refined. I might as well have been talking to a freshman from Westminster High School who was looking to pick a fight about whose dad was richer. Or caught in a tacky auto dealership ad produced for public access TV on a six-thousand-dollar budget. I half-expected '80s-style computer graphics promising "out-of-this-world discounts" to zigzag in and pinwheel next to his head.

"I'm Olivia," was all I said in reply.

"Olivia, it's a pleasure to meet you," he continued. "No one else from my company was interested in having a drink to celebrate this early in the day, so I came here alone. Are you meeting anyone here? A pretty girl like you must be meeting someone. Either way, please let me buy you your beer, at least. I don't expect anything in return for it."

"Okay, sure," I said, exhaling. If nothing else, it would be a fun little game to try to figure out whether he was so jumpy and overeager because I made him nervous, or because he had done a bump of cocaine in the bathroom five minutes before my arrival. "Thanks."

"So, you're not meeting anyone here?" he asked again. He stood up from his stool and looked me over from head to toe—it seemed guileless, I might add, done with an almost fawning admiration, possibly outside his conscious awareness that he was doing it at all—and then sat back down. I remember very clearly thinking to myself, what an odd man he is. He was a few inches taller than me, but slightly less than six feet, and I suspected that he might have lifts hidden in his classic Oxford shoes. He wasn't exactly hot, but he wasn't unattractive either. He had a full head of hair with no evidence of plugs, and although it was gelled, it didn't look too slick or sticky; his eyebrows appeared professionally groomed; his skin had that nice glow that's only possible with the aid of a professional aesthetician; when he lifted his glass, his hands looked smooth and soft, and his nails were trimmed uniformly, without a speck of dirt or a jagged edge; and when he flashed a smile, his teeth, indubitably porcelain veneers, overpowered his face, but in a way that wasn't entirely lacking in charm. His dimples were objectively cute. His physique seemed the type earned by doing six shirtless rounds of biceps curls on the balcony of his Midtown penthouse, blasting the same three Linkin' Park songs on repeat while sipping a Sam Adams between sets, before heading to the clubs. He smelled like birch and black currant. He smelled like money. And that was probably why, notwithstanding his quirks, I didn't leave my beer half-unfinished on the counter and walk out right then.

"No, I came here by myself," I replied. "This was a spontaneous decision. I had a job interview downtown and I needed a drink before the drive back home."

"That bad, huh? What do you do?"

"I didn't bomb the interview, if that's what you're implying. They weren't what I expected, and I'll turn them down even if I get an offer, but I'm not, like, trying to drink away a humiliating experience or anything pathetic like that."

He had momentarily stopped fidgeting and was looking at me expectantly, so I continued.

"I worked as a flight attendant for private aircraft for a few years. I was an independent contractor, so I did corporate gigs and worked for all sorts of VIPs, mostly in the music business. It paid well, but I didn't do it for the money. I just liked the experience of traveling and meeting successful, charismatic people. I don't need to work, but I like the structure it provides, as long as the job is fulfilling and my coworkers and clients are interesting. So I can afford to be as picky as I want with my future employer. Today I was being considered for the position of a personal assistant and confidant to a powerful Atlanta political figure, but neither the offices nor the role itself was up to my standards." Up until that point, I wasn't sure if I was going to be Olivia Fletcher Ray or Olivia Giordano with him. Olivia Giordano it was.

And Olivia Giordano knows how to elicit the information she needs. Within thirty minutes, I had learned that Raj was thirty-two (he enjoyed the conceit that he could pass for a decade younger) and an Emory MBA grad, with an independent net worth that was probably less than seven figures but which could prove to be substantially higher if his family's assets, as well as the many allowances that his parents continued to give him, were incorporated into the analysis. He mentioned multiple times (unprompted by anything I had said) that his heritage was one-half Indian, on his mother's side. *Only* one-half. His father was white, and more specifically, German and British. Again unprompted, he underscored that the latter was how he self-identified culturally and ethnically.

He had one sibling, Dinesh (also known as Danny), who was captain of the men's rugby team as an undergrad at Georgetown, which was where he also went on to earn his Master of Science degree in finance. Dinesh was married to a "short but surprisingly hot" systems engineer who had "given him" three sons, and he recently had been promoted from controller to CFO of the family's BMW businesses. (Raj artfully dodged the question twice when I inquired into his own job title.) Dinesh sounded like their parents' golden child, but Raj didn't express much envy over his older brother's accomplishments. Indeed, despite the fact that they worked together on a daily basis, after Raj had covered the impressive basics of Dinesh's life story, he grew disinclined to talk about his brother any further. He said that their parents were conventional and conservative but also loving and supportive, and the four of them owned and operated the family's business empire together relatively harmoniously. Raj wasn't wearing a wedding ring, and he expressly stated that he didn't have kids.

"I don't even have a dog," he had said. "I'm too busy with the dealerships and with my club promotion business to give a pet the attention it deserves."

I'm sure I couldn't fully repress the flash of disdain on my face. Yet another party promoter/social media guru in Atlanta? As if the city wasn't already crawling with those cockroaches?

But it turned out that Raj's business, Alpha Buzz Co., was at least semi-legit. He acknowledged that he wasn't making a ton of money off it yet, but he was well-connected and, despite his father's misgivings, he was convinced that it was a worthy investment of his time and funds. I assumed this was all bluster until he offered to put me on the guest list for the private party at Ogesana Lounge that night. The event was invitation-only and was bound to be attended by wealthy men looking for their next mistress or side piece. Alpha Buzz Co. was co-sponsoring the evening and providing the models staffing the event: a dozen girls in their early twenties with implants and extensions, who would make forty bucks each to flirt with strangers all night, but who would be firmly instructed not to hook up with anyone on the premises. It should go without saying, that kind of work is entirely beneath me, even if it would have gotten me in the door. Raj's company also was handling all the event's marketing, promotion, and press.

Typically, I have trepidations about attending nightclub parties. From a professional perspective, obviously. Atlanta's club scene is filled with men who lord it over their VIP tables, toss around their cash, invite women to sit on their laps and enjoy their bottle service, and generally give the appearance of vulgar wealth... until you look a bit more closely and realize that they're watering down drinks to make the bottles last longer, tossing and tipping singles (not tens or twenties or hundreds), and scooping the money off the floor or the bar top and back into their pockets when the dancer or bartender doesn't notice their "generosity." These fools will catch you if you charge your drink to their card, because they're going over every line item on their receipt and arguing with their server if the bill is fifty cents over what they anticipated. You can't take cash from their wallets, because all of their disposable income has already been dedicated to financing the illusions they're perpetuating that night. And when it's all over, they climb back into the clunker of a car that they left on a side street because they couldn't afford valet, and drive back to Forest Park or Norcross or, hell, to Snellville, to tell their three roommates about how wild the night was, how hot the girls were, and how that's going to be their life every night someday.

But Raj's party at Ogesana Lounge altered the calculus. Statistically, I was less likely to waste my time on a broke poser because most broker posers can't weasel their way into these kinds of events. Raj seemed harmless, and I assumed that he wouldn't have any shady expectations of how I ought to "thank" him for putting me on the list. The reciprocity was in my presence. That's not arrogance, that's how it works. Technically, Alpha Buzz Co. was being paid to promote the event and to staff it with generically hot bimbos, but there was an implicit expectation that his company would ensure that the party was attended by a higher caliber of women—women like me—as well. Any schmuck with a few thousand Instagram followers and a couple hundred bucks in cash can pull off the former; in the long term, having a reputation for the latter would allow Raj to command high fees for his services and let him mingle with the elite. This could be a mutually beneficial relationship, even though no sex or money would ever be exchanged between us.

Or, at least, this was how I thought through the decision to attend as I drove back to my apartment an hour later.

When I got home, I drank a bottle of charcoal lemonade to detox. I scrolled through the day's headlines in the *Atlanta-Journal Constitution* and the *Wall Street Journal* online. I did a twenty-minute language lesson in Italian. I flipped through the latest issue of *Jezebel* magazine, which I had picked up when I got my brows threaded earlier in the week.

The society pages clinched my decision to attend. The standard Buckhead-housewife cocktail of Sculptra, Botox, and lorazepam suppressed all semblance of human emotion except for the smug sense of superiority that pervaded every face in every picture. How dare they? Dressed in all-black to hide the lumps and sagging that no amount of lipo and CoolSculpting can fix; their crinkling necks and speckled hands betraying their losing battle against senescence; adorned in guilt-gift jewels, the shameless manifestation of an endless cycle wherein an entitled man cheats on a repulsive vagina and offers a shiny, perfunctory apology when caught; and yet, these women somehow think they're better than me because they managed to nab and "keep" a wealthy husband (a man who, in fact, has simply performed a rational cost/benefit analysis and determined that staying married, even to a wretched old hag, will cause him far less damage than what a divorce settlement, and all the dirt that would be revealed in the attendant court proceedings, would cost him)? Don't they understand that it would take me no effort—none!—to steal their husbands away from them for good, and that they should count their blessings that I'm not interested in raggedy old-man dick for any longer than it takes me to extract as much money as possible from the useless appendage's owner in the shortest amount of time? And yet, there they were, plastered on the pages of *Jezebel* as if they were icons. All I needed to do was show up, and they'd be forced to realize how misguided, how delusional, their self-important conceit was. Irrespective of whether I found a new mark, the satisfaction of putting those women in their place would be enough to justify my attendance.

In anticipation of weekend scouting, I had ordered cherry red sleeveless jumpsuit from Rent the Runway, but I decided to debut it a few days early with some delicate gold jewelry, three-inch nude pumps (notwithstanding Raj's directive, indeed the last thing he said to me before I left the Porter, to "wear your sexiest heels tonight"), and a sleek beige and gold clutch from DeMellier (also rented). I did my eyes in a neutral palette, left my skin free from powders and foundations to let my youthful glow shine through, and dotted my lips with a bit of colored gloss from Bobbi Brown, which was the only cosmetic I tossed into my bag for the night. Perhaps you don't appreciate the brilliant strategy behind all this, how perfectly I calibrated my image that evening not merely to stand out amongst a crowd of Buckhead Betties who were past their prime, but to emphasize the specific, myriad ways in which they fell short of what I offer. I was youth and elegance personified. I was the embodiment of wife-material, with all the benefits that such status confers, but with the luxury of never having to bear the burdens attendant to that role. My only concern when I left my apartment was that an inferior man would attach himself to me too early in the evening and scare the better prospects away.

I showed up forty-five minutes after the event started. Perhaps this seems like a foolishly premature appearance, like something an amateur would do, given that a majority of the major players wouldn't grace an event like this until it was several hours under-way. And if your entire approach to snaring men is based off of articles you've skimmed in *Cosmo* magazine while perusing the airport newsstands, and you're content with being the booty call of some flashy clown whose only interest is one-upping other men, then you're right to show up at the point in the night where blood alcohol levels are at their highest and standards are bottoming out. I hope you're satisfied with enjoying a façade of status for the three hours that you're some guy's arm-piece accessory, without ever realizing a cent of his money. I don't care. Ultimately, it's less competition for me, not that someone with such a short-sighted, impulsive perspective would be much competition for me under any circumstances.

Of course, the usual try-hards were at Ogesana Lounge when I arrived: the awkward third-year associates from Atlanta's B-list law firms who think their $160K salaries (after bonus) make them ballers; the ditzes in their late twenties and early thirties who briefly banged an NBA benchwarmer or a random NFL defensive end when they were ten years younger and who are desperately trying to resurrect the memory of being something WAG-adjacent; and that one sad divorced guy who's at least forty-five years old but still gets zigzags shaved into his beard and rocks the same rhinestone-studded jeans he's owned since the early '90s, who greets both the venue staff and the models-for-hire as if they're all old friends. Fortunately, these losers are always easy to spot and discard.

Two of Alpha Buzz Co.'s fourteen promo girls were already visibly hammered, and three of the others were huddled together in a booth, sneaking shots of tequila and ignoring the guests. Raj was talking to a lanky white guy, probably in his early twenties, who was wearing an otherwise-decent houndstooth suit that unfortunately had not been tailored to his narrow shoulders and girlish waist. Two of the (relatively) more attractive promo girls were standing behind Raj, one on each side, where I'm certain they had been directed to remain for the duration of the night. The redheaded white girl looked bored senseless, stealing furtive glances around the room and staring longingly at her martini glass, as if she could will it to refill itself with straight vodka through the strength of her contempt alone. The shorter blonde, in contrast, smiled stupidly at no one in particular and bobbled her head up and down eagerly as Raj spoke, her ample cleavage jiggling along with her thick skull whenever Raj made what she appeared to think was an especially salient remark. At least the dumb bitch was doing her job, I suppose.

Based on his gesticulations and body language, Raj seemed to be pitching something to the goofy kid dressed up in his obese father's suit—possibly the merits of buying a new BMW from one of Raj's parents' dealerships, or maybe the opportunity to invest in Raj's new record label or to hire Alpha Buzz Co. to plan the next Kappa Zeta Douchebag frat mixer. Regardless, Raj was sufficiently preoccupied that I was able to slip past him and make my way to the bar unnoticed.

The bartender hadn't had the chance to hand me my cocktail before I sensed a masculine presence looming behind me.

"Put her drink on my tab, Dave," the man said with a slight southern drawl.

The bartender caught my eye for confirmation that this was acceptable. I rolled my eyes (out of the man's line of sight, of course), smirked, and nodded my head. Then I turned to face Prince Charming.

I was pleasantly surprised. Despite his grey hair, the man's tanned skin and blue eyes gave him a relatively youthful appearance. He was probably in his early fifties (I never forget that these chumps are the same age as Raymond), and if I could tolerate his presence for more than five minutes, at some point in our conversation he would probably boast about how many miles of cycling on his custom Trek Madone road bike he accrued per week. He might even lift up the pant leg of his suit to show off his calf muscles: "You might not know this, but some men pay ten thousand dollars for calf implants to get their legs to look like this." He was a mélange of bravado and insecurity in a bespoke suit, and exactly the reason I show up early to these things.

"Thank you," I said, as additional details came into focus. Hand stitching on his notched jacket lapels, which lay smoothly against his chest; a crisply folded pocket square that was color-coordinated with his tie; dress shoes polished with military precision; the faintest scent of hibiscus palm and vanilla, as if he'd teleported directly to Ogesana Lounge from his beachfront estate in Charleston, South Carolina. This was a man who fancied himself a modern-day southern gentleman, while simultaneously holding an unshakeable belief that "bitches only want men who treat them like shit," and who therefore, as one of the rare remaining Nice Guys™ of his age, status, and stature, was doomed to an endless series of failed romances through no fault whatsoever of his own. Ensnaring him would be easy enough. "Chivalry is a lost art these days," I continued. "I appreciate the drink."

"Men these days don't know how to behave around real women like you anymore," he started in enthusiastically. Nailed it. "You deserve to be treated like a lady. Someone like you should never have to open your own door or pick up a check or pump your own gas."

"Well, it makes the men who were raised right all the more appealing when I find them," I cooed.

"Most girls your age don't know what's good for them," he continued. "I think you're just as pretty as any of the event models here tonight, but you have more class."

He was absolutely correct about that, of course, and it was insulting to imply that anyone might think otherwise, but it still made me vaguely uncomfortable that his preferred method of seduction was ripping on the other women present, as if he were comparison-shopping and I was the least-flawed option. Still, I smiled and murmured, "How sweet."

His name was Rhett and he was charmed to meet me. Not so charmed, however, that he could fully suppress his impotent rage for longer than a few minutes at a time.

"I can only imagine the bozos that those girls are dating." He kept turning his head toward a group of three of the promo girls and scowling with disdain. "It makes me feel sorry for women like you. Women who know what it means to be feminine and ladylike and sweet. The good guys still want someone delicate and gentle, someone we can protect and take care of. But you probably have to fend off hundreds of assholes to find one classic gentleman like me. You shouldn't feel sad that you're not married yet. If you focus your energy on more sophisticated men with traditional values, you'll find a husband in no time."

Listen, I don't mind humoring these idiots' conceit. It's part of the job. But I have never been anyone's victim. The thought that I could be the subject of someone's misplaced pity makes me want to vomit. The thought that I could be in a position where legally binding myself to one of these imbeciles is my best option, with or without a sound exit strategy, is my nightmare scenario. Normally, a guy like Rhett would have been easy to hook and even easier to rip off. Two weeks of vacant smiles and unprompted giggles, a few conversations in which he prattles on about finance or politics or science and I feign that he is *so* smart and doing *such* a good job explaining such a challenging topic that my silly little lady-brain can almost understand, and I'll be twenty thousand dollars richer without so much as having to see or touch his withered peapod, which is the only thing in this situation meriting pity. Because, remember, I'm a "good girl" befitting such a "nice guy," and I don't jump into bed right away.

It is incomprehensible to men like this that I—or any woman, for that matter—could outwit them, and so I am able to oper- ate with impunity. Rhett could have been a goldmine. But his self-righteous condescension grated at me. I was not in the mood to pander to a man twice my age who fancied himself a martyr, having convinced himself that he was the last paladin of tradi- tional Southern manners, and that this was the only reason why he couldn't get his dick sucked. His meandering little speech was so stupid that I found myself taking the side of the floozy promo girls, most of whom probably *were* indiscriminately dating losers and fuckboys, which was perhaps the most infuriating part of it all. Pass.

Unfortunately, it's only practical for me to laugh in a man's faces or to walk away from him mid-conversation when I'm at a location and surrounded by people that I have no interest in seeing again. A scorned man is a spiteful one, and a veneer of chivalry doesn't change that fact. I would have to indulge Rhett's vanity for a bit longer, pandering to his ego in order to protect myself and my reputation, until I could gracefully exit the conversation in a way that left him convinced that both my departure and his decision not to further pursue me accorded with his own volition.

But I'm not whining. These events aren't meant to cater to me. They're designed for the men who attend them, and I know that going in. I make the best of the situation with the resources and options at my disposal.

With Rhett, I got lucky. I allowed him to bloviate for another four minutes uninterrupted, first as he continued his tirade about how women don't understand the type of man to whom they ought to be sexually attracted, and then as he transitioned to a diatribe over a perceived slight by one of the caddies at his country club, until some colleague of his mercifully approached us. They started talking about the stock redemption provisions in a shareholders' agreement for a REIT corporation in which they were both minority owners, which obviously was far too sophisticated a topic for my lady-brain to comprehend, and thus I was able to excuse myself and escape without incurring his ire.

This cycle repeated itself twice more before I had the chance to say hello to Raj. We only exchanged a few words at first. By then, the party had picked up significantly, and we quickly separated to find other conversations. But somehow, we kept finding each other at the ideal moment. Raj was as anxious to mingle with the right people as I was, and we instinctively fell into a natural rhythm throughout the night. More than once, he rescued me from a piddling douchebag. In turn, I introduced him to random men whose greed and liquid assets far outweighed their business acumen, which is to say, exactly the type of individuals who would invest their money in one of Raj's schemes. I still wasn't attracted to Raj in any meaningful way, but it was impressive to see him in his element, and our unspoken collaboration helped me elevate my own game.

The event formally ended at 1:00 a.m., but I stuck around for another hour while Raj wrapped things up on behalf of Alpha Buzz Co. I spotted one of his business associates gesturing in my direction and nudging Raj with approval and envy, and Raj was more than happy to propagate the illusion that we were somehow together. I was tipsy and in good spirits thanks to the new contacts I had generated that night, so I played along and reciprocated his harmless displays of affection. We did seem to make a good team.

Raj called me the next day while he was taking a lunch break (a three-hour lunch break) from one of his sporadic in-person visits to his family's Smyrna BMW dealership location. The oldest of the geezers I meet are reluctant to make dinner plans via text, so I've made my peace with voice calls, but I was surprised to hear from Raj again so soon, especially via telephone. Nonetheless, after three rings, I decided to pick up.

"Liv!" he started. "What a party last night, right?"

"Hey, Raj. Yeah, it was pretty fun, I suppose. Good crowd."

"It was epic! Amazing crowd. So many beautiful people." Was he trying to convince me or himself? "Atlanta's elite showed up for Alpha Buzz Co. You can't put a price tag on that. After an event like that, Ogesana Lounge is going to make all the Hot Lists next month."

"Yeah, it was cool. Thanks for the invitation. I'm glad I went."

"I'm glad you did too. I was going to see if you were interested in doing paid promotions for me, but I think it's better to have you as an attendee."

"Do you really think that I'd prance around in a tube top and neon booty shorts offering tequila to randos for forty bucks a night?"

"I'm not a hundred percent sure I could convince you to do that for any amount of money," Raj chuckled. "But for the record, my girls always look classy, and I pay them a minimum of fifty dollars for four hours of work. Most of the girls last night made eighty in cash."

"Okay, okay. I'm not hating." I smiled despite myself. Raj had instinctively mastered the optimal combination of deference and confrontation needed to maintain my interest. "I'll admit that the outfits you had them in last night were pretty cute. The skinny redhead with the shoulder tattoo and the Black girl with the pixie cut were killing the game. Men were actively seeking the two of them out, not just tolerating their interruptions because they're hot."

"That's Brianna and Noelle! Wow, you have a great eye." Raj seemed genuinely excited. "They're two of my best girls. They get first dibs on all our events, and I pay them a small premium to show up. They're the kind of girls I need to stay loyal exclusively to me. What did you think of Mirabel? She was the only other redhead there. She was with me for most of the night."

"She was probably the most conventionally pretty of all of them, but she has a bitchy face. If she were a little taller and lost five pounds, she could have been a model. But, you know, she's not. So she could stand to check the attitude."

"You are too much," Raj replied between laughs. "I should pay you for your consulting services. Mirabel is signed with one of the agencies in town, but she only does commercial modeling. Not editorial. I told her to wear higher heels. It was her first event with me. I think I'll give her one more try."

"You'd be better off putting her on the guest list and having her sit by the bar. If she knows how to dress, she'll elevate the scene, and she can be as snotty as she wants."

"I agree in theory, but I don't think she'll show up if she doesn't get paid."

"Then she's being short-sighted. How many opportunities would someone like her get to plug into Atlanta's social scene otherwise? If she or her parents had any money or status, she wouldn't need to supplement her catalog modeling gigs working as an after-hours booth bunny."

"Fuck, that's harsh. But you're probably right. I want her affiliated with Alpha Buzz Co., but getting to attend our events in her own clothes and getting free drinks all night should be enough incentive."

I was getting bored, so I didn't say anything in response.

"Right, so speaking of inviting gorgeous women to attend the elite events that my company puts on, what are you doing next weekend? Not this upcoming one, but the weekend after, starting next Thursday?"

"Well, I suppose that depends. I have soft plans with a few people, but I haven't finalized anything. What are you proposing?"

"That you come to Miami with me. We leave Thursday around noon and get back probably late Sunday. Unless the Sunday parties are going to be hot too, in which case we'll stay until Monday. We need you to be flexible, or else you'll have to pay your own way back."

"I might be able to make that work. Who is 'we'?"

"It's the whole crew! My boy, Iron Troy—he sold off his nutrition supplement company a year ago, and one of the first things he did with all that cash was buy a twenty percent stake in Alpha Buzz Co., he knows we're going places—he's chartering a private jet, and we're taking our four best girls from Atlanta there with us. The other ones we'll fly down on a commercial airliner. Iron Troy is the real deal. He's hooked up with all the hottest chicks on the east coast."

"I hope you don't expect me to fly commercial," I scoffed. "That'll be a hard pass."

"No, of course not! You'll be one of our top four on the private plane with me. I guess the mystique will be gone for you, but flying private is exciting for the other girls on their first trip."

It took me a moment to remember that I had told him I was formerly a private-jet stewardess to the stars. "That's cute," I said with studied nonchalance. "I'll try not to judge them too harshly. The flight attendants or the girls who think private airliners are some kind of a big deal. What are the accommodations in Miami?"

"We're renting a mansion on South Beach. It'll be me, Iron Troy, and about twenty other girls in addition to you. You'll need to share a room, but you won't be sleeping much anyway. We'll have dinner at Miami's best restaurants and the clubs are going to be out of control."

"Right. What's the catch?"

"Nothing sleazy! If anything, it's the opposite. I don't want you hooking up with anyone publicly. If you're interested in someone, or if someone important is interested in you, you should check with me first and I'll arrange it. And you're forbidden from going near any of the other promoters. Most of them are shady, so it's really for your own good."

"Sure," I snorted. "Anything else?"

"You'll be expected to drink and party and look like you're having a good time, but do it without getting sloppy. You won't have to pay for anything. These rules apply to everyone. None of my girls are allowed to be trashy. Iron Troy and I are creating a vibe. On this trip, we're only inviting models and a few regular girls like you who are especially beautiful and fit. But you need to pack your stilettos. Four inches minimum. I let it slide at Ogesana Lounge last night, but anything less than four inches will be unacceptable in Miami."

"You let it slide? Are you for real right now?" I was willing to ignore most of the bullshit he was spewing in exchange for the free trip to Miami, but this was getting ridiculous.

"You know what I mean! I didn't say anything because you were mostly just my guest last night and it was a weekday party. But there's a different set of expectations in Miami. We're curating a certain look. One that would translate to New York or St. Tropez. High-end clientele expect tall and thin and flawless."

I didn't say anything.

"You're almost there as-is. I'm not asking you to lose weight or get plastic surgery! And I really want you to come. It's a nice touch when a few of my girls can form coherent sentences at dinner. And then at the club, you can just smile and dance in our section and you won't have to speak at all."

I understand how absurd this arrangement must sound to an outsider. Like, you're probably thinking that it must be a front for a prostitution ring, or that R-Money and Iron Troy were going to make me smuggle a couple ounces of crank in my cooch before I could get on the plane back to Georgia or something. You simply haven't been initiated into the ways of the rich and beautiful. I'm as skeptical as they come about other people's intentions, but nothing about Raj's proposal caused me concern. I love Miami. Olivia Giordano is a star in Miami. And the weather in Atlanta that day happened to be gloomy, damp, and unseasonably cold.

"Okay," I said after another long pause. "As long as we understand each other. I'll make you look good and I'll charm the shit out of whoever you need me to impress, but I want it to be perfectly clear that I am not sleeping with you or this Troy guy or any of your other buddies. And I'm fine with your little dress code. Sexy but not slutty, and I'll only wear my Louboutins and Jimmy Choos."

"Four-inch minimum."

"Yes! For fuck's sake. Do those designers even make two-inch heels?"

"Okay! Sick! So you're in?"

"Yes. Miami is one of my favorite cities in the States. I'll come."

"I'm so happy, babe! I'm so pumped." There was a huge crash in the background and more of the muffled voices that had been distracting me throughout the call. (He told me later that he had left the BMW dealership to drive one of his models to her cosmetic dentistry appointment and was trying to work in the waiting room, despite the presence of two random unsupervised toddlers crawling around his feet and causing general havoc in the absence of any adult supervision.) "I'm going to have a special gift for you on the plane," Raj continued. "I'll text you all the details. We'll be VIP in all the hottest clubs and we'll make appearances at all the best after-parties, and everything is going to be super-exclusive and high-end. You'll fit in perfectly."

It took him another two hours to get around to texting me the details as promised after we hung up, but overall I was pretty impressed with the itinerary he had planned, assuming we really would be VIP and comped for everything like he claimed. I had wanted someone to take me to the trendy steakhouse Grassfed on my last visit and I was bummed when I ran out of time before finding a proper date. Cerrado, which had opened at a prime location on South Beach six months earlier, would probably be packed with celebrities on Friday night. Plus, I was able to track down the Instagram accounts of two of the after-party hosts, both of whom had tens of thousands of followers and were living ridiculously lavish lifestyles in gorgeous mansions, so I'd get good exposure at those events as well. I hadn't heard any hype about Stopwatch, the club at which we were scheduled to appear on Saturday night, but I wasn't too concerned. If anything, it'd be easier to network at the dinners and after-parties than at the clubs themselves, so even if Stopwatch turned out to be lame, it wouldn't interfere with my overall mission.

Raj followed up with a second text informing me that I was required to attend everything on the schedule, "NO WHINING NO EXCEPTIONS HANGOVERS OR BEING ON THE RAG ARE NO EXCUSE TO BAIL ON YOUR OBLIGA-TIONS." I replied with the eye-roll emoji and he texted again: "Sry, i have 2 send that to every1. u wouldnt believe some of the shit my girls say." I replied with a simple "Bet" and went about my business. I still hadn't made up my mind about Raj, and I was hoping the Miami trip would clarify whether he was someone with whom I should align myself on an ongoing basis. The way he was barking orders at me was annoying, but counterintuitively it was also appealing insofar as it suggested that he was running Alpha Buzz Co. as a viable business rather than his own personal escort service. And if the rest of the women (excuse me, "girls") surrounding him were weak and malleable enough to tolerate it, it'd be that much easier to distinguish myself from them. I started picking out my outfits that night.

Chapter Fourteen

A week later, having told the temp agency I was then work-ing for that I'd be unavailable for assignments due to "personal issues" (and not giving a single shit if they dropped me as a result), I was boarding a private jet at DeKalb-Peachtree Airport with Raj, Iron Troy, and three other females wearing fake eyelashes and overpriced athleisure. Two of the girls were Brazilian and spoke only to each other, and only in Portuguese, for the entire flight. I'm going to assume that the third girl was eighteen, but I didn't ask her age because I didn't want to know the answer. It wouldn't have surprised me to learn that she was a high school sophomore who had snuck out of her bedroom window to make the flight. All three of them were five foot ten and rail thin. Other women might have been intimidated, but I had the prettiest face out of everyone and I know for a fact that most guys will choose nice breasts over bony hips any day, so I didn't care. Mostly, I spent the flight wishing that the jailbait would chill with the selfies and the squealing.

The mansion was more of the same. From the outside, it was gorgeous: a three-story, six-bedroom modern villa with a pool, hot tub, and incredible views of the downtown Miami skyline and Biscayne Bay. Alas, it was already chaos when we arrived, and within twenty-four hours the place was completely trashed with spoilt beer and discarded tampons and rotting food and broken glass. When we showed up, there were at least eight girls doing impromptu photo shoots around the grounds, and part of me wishes that I had joined them, because after that first day I might as well have been squatting in a shanty town. Everyone was white, except for one Asian-American girl who was about my height and two more fair-skinned Brazilians, who promptly secluded themselves with the Brazilian girls who had flown in with us from Atlanta. As much as I'd like to attribute the whitewashing to the fact that Black girls have too much sense to get embroiled in this type of trainwreck, the truth is that basically everyone with any power in this scene, including Raj and Troy, is racist, although almost all of them would vociferously deny it, citing their friendship with some random Nigerian or Jamaican promoter as conclusive evidence to the contrary.

I ended up sharing a room with three willowy platinum-blond Polish girls, two of whom barely spoke a word of English. If anything, the language barrier was a perk. I wasn't in the mood to engage in idle chatter or make new friends. The three of them squeezed into the queen-sized bed together, and I was assigned a blow-up mattress on the floor. I held my tongue and later slept in whatever bed was open for a few quick daytime naps throughout the weekend. It was fine. I hadn't gone there to rest.

I think Iron Troy was a white guy, but his hair had been dyed jet black and his skin was so tan that it rendered his appearance ethnically ambiguous. The only time he would respond to "Troy" (and not "Iron Troy") was when a particularly big spender beckoned him. I didn't ask for the origin story behind the "Iron" moniker. He looked 'roided out (or at least, the upper half of his body did), so maybe it derived from "pumping iron"; or maybe it was because he ruled the girls with an iron fist when it came to their interactions with other promoters. Zofia, the Polish girl who spoke the best English, told me that Iron Troy considered responding to texts from other promoters, as well as waving hello to them at the clubs, to be treasonous enough to merit the silent treatment for a week. Actually accepting anyone else's invitation to go out was a betrayal that would lead to an epic meltdown of rage-filled tears on Troy's part, and a permanent exclusion from all of his future events. Zofia had seen it happen, and she claimed it was terrifying.

"Is he beating his girls? Like, smacking them around when he feels like they've been disloyal?" I asked.

Zofia looked appalled and vigorously shook her head no.

"So then what is the big deal? It's emotionally manipulative, I guess, but there's no actual viable threat. It's not like he can blacklist you from the entire Miami club scene. Right?"

Zofia shrugged. "I guess not."

"Right. So it's bad business on his part. If he banishes someone like you from his table, you'll immediately have ten other promoters pestering you to go to their clubs or sit with them instead. And then they'll be the ones making money off your presence. And you're not even from here. Most of you aren't! You and Hanna and Milena can go back to Manhattan or Warsaw or whatever and never deal with him again, and it's completely his loss. Don't you get it?"

Zofia squirmed. "You make it sound so easy."

What could I do? I liked Zofia better than most of the girls in the house, but if she wanted to be helpless, I wasn't going to waste my time. I already knew that each of the clubs and the hosts of the after-parties in Miami would be paying Raj and Troy several thousand dollars to show up with us in tow, and we weren't making a dime. They crammed as many of us as possible into the mansion, and Iron Troy's sketchy friends came and went from the property as they pleased, so I barely count our lodgings as legitimate compensation. Our food and drinks were comped by the venues in exchange for our social media posts and the cachet our presence brought, so it's not like Raj and Troy were paying for that either. Raj would go back to Atlanta at the end of the trip with an additional six thousand dollars in his pocket, easily, even after expenses and Iron Troy's cut. When I really thought about it, though, I was more irritated with Zofia and the other regulars than I was with Raj or Iron Troy. It took me less than a day to understand the game and the players and to start figuring out how I could wield it all to my advantage. The willful ignorance of Zofia and the others kept them subjugated to the promoters' whims.

Raj had made it clear that none of the girls were obligated to sleep with him or Iron Troy, but half of the females in the house (and plenty of the bottle girls and hostesses at the clubs too) were fighting for the chance to bed them anyway. I was fine to remove myself from the competition, and Raj seemed to prefer that we devote our attention to wealthy patrons and other VIPs rather than to him whenever we were out in public, since their satisfaction ultimately translated into more money in his pockets. As an added benefit, when the girls in the house saw that I clearly wasn't trying to steal Raj's or Iron Troy's attention away from them, I escaped the petty sabotage (stained clothes, stolen makeup, rampant gossip) that plagued the mansion, and a few of the regulars even opened up to me about who in Miami was a major player in the international party circuit or otherwise good to know.

I don't think any of the girls in the house were so delusional as to expect that Raj or Iron Troy would be exclusive with them, but another one of the New York City models, a nineteen-year-old with waist-length honey-colored hair named Hadley, told me that she had "dated" Iron Troy for a while two years before (you do the math on that), and one of her best friends, who had declined to come on this trip, had been involved with Raj up until he ended things about three months prior. Hadley insisted both men were very generous with their recurring bedmates, which stood in stark contrast to the way they treated their one-off hookups and the girls who didn't sleep with them, who at most could hope for occasional small favors and erratic flirtatious attention.

Hadley wanted to brag about what Iron Troy had done for her while they were together (multiple CoolTone treatments for her concave ass, a sapphire ring which she had since pawned to make rent, an admittedly gorgeous hunter green Bulgari clutch that she brought with her everywhere we went, and unlimited access to his Uber account to spare her the indignity of public transportation, among other things), but I was far more interested in the perks that Raj might offer. According to Hadley, he was even more munificent than Iron Troy, covering her friend's share of rent in a Tribeca apartment and allowing her unrestricted use of his black card to buy clothes and home décor (provided that Raj found her selections aesthetically pleasing), until their undefined relationship came to an end. I pushed her for the cause of the breakup.

"I dunno," Hadley mumbled. "They weren't really a couple to begin with, so how could they break up?"

"You know what I mean," I said, trying to hold my temper. "Why did they stop sleeping together? Why did he cut her off? It sounds like it was a good deal for your friend. Why did Raj end it?"

"I dunno," Hadley repeated. "She caught feelings, I guess? She knew Raj was fucking other people. He basically did it right in front of her face sometimes. Not in a mean way, it just happened."

"So she scared him away?"

"Yeah, I guess so. She wants a real boyfriend. She says she's done with promoters and she's focusing her attention on investment bankers now. Why do you care?"

"I don't," I snapped. "I'm just making conversation with you."

Dinner wasn't for another three hours at that point, so I wandered off to see if anyone had some weed to share. All of the girls in that house were working my last nerve and I was in dire need of something to take the edge off.

The thing about being part of Miami's VIP scene—or being one of the elite in any city, for that matter—is that if you're in, you understand. If you're not, you don't. There's no point in trying to explain it to the masses. I'm sure you can imagine the basics: no fatties, no uggos, no poors, blinding lights, thumping bass, sweat and lust in clothes that are worth more than the blue book value of your crappy car. But when you're VIP at the best spots, at a certain point in the night, the atmosphere shifts into something sublime. We're having too much fun to dissect it in the moment, but on some subconscious level we recognize that we're modern royalty. We're the most beautiful women in the world, and exceptional men with exceptional wealth are vying for our attention. It's transcendent.

Or, hell, maybe it's just all the good drugs.

I decided that Raj was someone worth pursuing on the private jet back to Atlanta, and I want you to understand the frame of mind I was in when I arrived at that decision, but I'm not sure there's much use in rehashing the details of the whole weekend there. If you win the lottery or something, maybe someday you can afford to experience it for yourself.

Suffice it to say that I ate at better restaurants and drank for free in even better clubs than when I had gone to Miami alone almost two years before. Keeping things platonic with Raj and enjoying the perks of his access while searching for superior men to pursue was a viable option. Although Raj and Iron Troy had no trouble getting laid, a significant portion of the girls in the Miami mansion—including several of their respective recurring fuck buddies—also clearly thought that both of them were a joke, and on some level everyone was using them for free travel and adventures that would otherwise be out of reach. It wasn't uncommon for these girls to fly somewhere cool on Alpha Buzz Co.'s dime while their real boyfriends were busy (probably cheating on them, to be fair) back in New York or Rio de Janeiro or wherever. Somehow, everyone involved in this arrangement seemed convinced that they were benefiting from it.

But Atlanta's scene is structured differently than Miami's, and Raj would be far less useful to me as far as making a name for myself in the former. The handful of Atlanta events for which he could get me an invitation that I wouldn't necessarily be able to get myself weren't worth the indignity of him barking orders at me about what to wear or where to stand or who I was allowed to talk to, if I retained my status as merely another one of his "girls."

But if I could enjoy the benefits of Raj's connections and put myself in a position to get access to the one thing I cared about—his and his parents' money—the calculation would shift. And based on my conversation with Hadley, for that to happen, I would need to start sleeping with him. It could have been worse. It *has* been worse. Over the years I've slept with plenty of idiots to whom I felt no attraction. Some of them were downright repulsive. At least Raj was kind of cute and kind of cool. That was dangerous for some of his other girls, who wound up falling for him and trying to force him to be exclusive, but there was absolutely no risk of that scenario materializing for me. Being with him was more fun than investing time with most of the men I had "dated" before, but otherwise he was no different than any other mark. I needed to take what I could get and then get out.

Chapter Fifteen

The transition to something relationship-adjacent with Raj was as smooth as I could have hoped. The fact that he met me at a bar in Little Five Points while I was wearing a suit dress, the fact that I wasn't actively pursuing a career as a D-list catalog model or an Instagram prostitute, the fact that I wasn't throwing myself at him at the end of the night, and the fact that I wasn't broke or addicted to drugs or pills, all served to distinguish me from almost every other female in his social circle. Quickly, even his words intimated the distinction he had drawn in his mind: they were his girls, but I was his woman.

Within three weeks of our return from Miami, I had become Raj's primary girlfriend and was reaping all the benefits that Hadley had described. Raj regularly handed me his credit card and told me to buy whatever dresses, bags, and shoes I wanted for the events he had planned the next week. If he noticed that I was adding a few thousand dollars worth of electronics, jewelry, and home goods to the tab, he never complained. He was obsessed with Agent Provocateur and Coco de Mer lingerie, and he spent easily three thousand dollars on bras, thongs, and bodysuits for me just to see me model them for him. One afternoon I made an offhand comment about needing to schedule my next Brazilian waxing appointment, and he immediately offered to pay for as many rounds of electrolysis as I needed to get my entire body completely hairless.

I never pestered Raj about who he was with or what he was doing when we weren't together. This wasn't some grand exercise in self-restraint; we used protection and he got tested for STIs every month or two, so as long as the other women didn't cause him to be stingy with me, I genuinely didn't care what he and his dick got into in my absence. I knew how to bolster his ego and make him look good in front of his clients and business associates, but when we were in private, I pushed him and kept him on his toes. He needed it to keep his interest, and he certainly made it easy. Beneath the cocaine-fueled exuberance, Raj was a deeply flawed and insecure man.

Rarely did a South Asian guy—or any male with brown skin, for that matter, other than perhaps a spray-tanned white guy—walk past us without Raj muttering some sort of jab about his appearance or cologne, or his reputation or pedigree. He seemed to think that this was a way to distinguish himself from them, but much like his constant references to the fact that he was "half-white," it only served to underscore his Indian heritage and the fragility of his social stature. I didn't give a shit about his ethnic background either way—say what you want about me, but I'm not a bigot—but his anxiety over it was pitiable and discomfiting. It was, sadly, also understandable. The simple fact was, the owners of most of these bars and clubs assumed that if they attracted too many non-white people, their business would be deemed "ghetto" or "sketchy." It doesn't matter whether this was fair or paranoid racist bullshit. From their perspective—the perspective to which Raj needed to pander—having a few of the "right kind" of minorities would make the scene "cool," but "too many" was undesirable. And desirability was Raj's life blood.

I'm not here to be anybody's savior, and I'm not about to let some twisted white guilt get in the way of me living my best life. But every once in a while, I did think about Finn and Matilda. Even a little shit like Finn doesn't deserve what will be coming to him in a few years when he tries to visit these places with a group of his friends and they get turned away on a pretense, probably for some purported violation of the dress code. Or Matilda, who won't have half the opportunities that I've had to run these kinds of scams, because the Black girls are mostly relegated to shilling shots of flavored whiskey at the same venues where I am welcomed as a queen. I've told you from the beginning, I've never conned or stolen from anyone who didn't deserve it. The men in these venues, almost by definition, deserved it. Raj was a victim of it, but he perpetuated it too, and I have no remorse about manipulating that duality to my advantage.

I didn't know about Anika until two weeks ago. I don't think I have any way to prove this, but I've been honest with you about everything else—honest to a fault, honest even when it makes me look bad—so I'm assuming you'll give me the benefit of the doubt. I'm obviously a perceptive person and I've made my living off of my ability to read people. But this, I missed. Built into Raj's personal narrative was the foundation for living two separate lives: one life as the dutiful son, working diligently for the family business with the promise of someday inheriting it with his older brother; and a whole other life as an aspiring club promoter and record label owner and entrepreneur, a life in which he fancied himself a self-made man, even though his parents generously funded his stupidity notwithstanding the fact that he vehemently repudiated their traditional values and his Indian heritage at every turn. From this, I assumed that he strategically placated his parents and extended family whenever necessary to maintain a steady flow of project financing and spontaneous gifts, but nevertheless kept them at an arm's length in order to conform to the image he thought he needed to have in order to ingratiate himself into the social scene in which he aspired to gain acceptance.

Actually, convoluted though it may be, I still think all of that is accurate. But I didn't realize there was more to his story.

I'd seen him with a wedding ring on a few times. I asked him about it once, and he explained that sometimes he wore a phony wedding ring if a potential male client was a family man, or if he needed to make a female client or vendor or whatever think that he was spoken for. He said that he and his brother and cousins had been doing it for years. This probably sounds like a blatant fabrication to you, but I do the exact same thing. Years ago, I invested in a cubic zirconia solitaire, set on a platinum-plated sterling silver wedding band, and it can fool anyone other than a true expert inspecting it with a handheld loupe. It functions perfectly whenever I need to pretend that I'm engaged, married, or recently divorced. I originally got it when I was working retail, to try to fend off the creeps who hit on me while I was trapped at the job and was supposed to be polite no matter how sleazy they were to me. So, I didn't think twice about Raj's explanation. I knew from experience how pretending to be married can be useful at customer-facing jobs. He wasn't defensive or nervous when I asked him, and it never came up again. Most of the time we were together, he had it off.

I never met Anika in person. We spoke on the phone once. Like I said, that was two weeks ago. I had combed through Raj's bank accounts online a dozen times, and all of them were titled in his name only. The way he circulated his cash and credit through multiple accounts at multiple banks every month was dizzying and almost impossible to follow, even for me. The only thing that was clear was that he was up to something. I assumed that he was either embezzling from the family business or trying to hide his liquid assets from creditors, and most likely both. I knew that Raj spent an insane amount of money on cocaine every week, and that a lot of the deals he did outside of his parents' automobile empire were cash-only, so at first I wasn't too concerned, strictly speaking, that his account balances were rapidly dwindling. It simply meant that I needed to shift my strategy and lift a couple hundred in bills from his wallet more often, while making fewer direct transfers from his banks to my dummy PayPal, Venmo, and off-shore accounts. This wasn't a sustainable approach, but Raj still had regular access to lots of wealthy men, so it was in my best interest to hang onto him until I found someone new.

Whenever I wired money out of his accounts, I followed the same logic that I explained to you from back when I was transferring money to myself from the law firm, only now the inconspicuous numbers I chose were an order or two of magnitude higher: I avoided withdrawals of round sums like $5,000.00 because they tend to catch the eye, but a withdrawal of $4,805.07 looks like a monthly mortgage payment and is easily glossed over. Given the way Raj ricocheted money between his banks and frenetically opened new credit lines to pay his debts on older ones, he would have had to do a thorough self-audit to catch on.

But then, a few days before Anika and I spoke, I was using Raj's laptop, ostensibly to check my work emails while he got ready for the night, when I realized that he hadn't actually made a mortgage payment in months. I checked every account of his that I knew of—and I'm pretty sure I knew them all, since he never erased his browser history and he kept all his passwords stored and auto-filled on each website—and despite the fact that all his account balances had been shrinking and shriveling, not a single payment had been made to a mortgage lender, or to cover any of his utility or credit card bills, for that matter.

Then it finally dawned on me. He was, almost certainly, renting the apartment in which he was currently primping and peacocking in the bathroom and in which I was sitting on an eight-thousand-dollar loveseat in the living room, staring at his laptop aghast as I realized how blind I'd been. How could I have missed it? Plenty of Atlanta men have their family house in the suburbs and a bachelor pad in Buckhead or Midtown for hosting their side pieces. But they tend to be upfront about it, at least with the mistresses. After all, most of their wives are banging their tennis instructors or exploring their long-repressed lesbian inclinations with their equally restless, unsatisfied female neighbors, and there's an unspoken etiquette that everyone will keep themselves in a state of blissfully medicated willful ignorance.

This revelation meant two things. First, Raj was probably married. To be honest, I didn't really give a shit one way or the other, except to the extent that it impacted my calculus of how much of his cash I could take and at what intervals. A heretofore unknown wife meant that there could be an extra set of eyes on all of Raj's accounts, but it also meant that Raj would be a lot less likely to pursue legal or extra-legal means of justice and vengeance if he ever caught on to how much money I had taken from him. Doing so would mean near-certain disclosure of the entire affair to his spouse, as well as an admission of how reckless with the family's savings he had been, all of which would likely end up costing him much, much more than the few tens of thousands of dollars I had appropriated. To say nothing of the scandal! Raj's marital status would require further investigation and possible strategic adjustments, but it didn't affect my non-feelings toward him beyond that.

The second and more important realization I had was that Raj either had another bank account that I had yet to discover, or his financial situation was far more precarious than I had thought. This issue required immediate resolution. If Raj was hiding his vanishing assets (under his wife's name? in an offshore account? in cash somewhere in the apartment?), I needed to know and to determine whether, when, and how that money would be accessible to me again.

And if not? If there was no secret cash stockpile or shell limited liability company shielding all his holdings in the Cayman Islands? If what I was seeing as I clicked through the twelve open tabs in Firefox was a fair and accurate reflection of Raj's current financial condition? Then Raj was fucked. He was fucked in a way that there's no coming back from. Frankly, for as much as he boasted about his daddy's wealth, I was unconvinced that his parents would bail him out of this disaster, particularly if they realized that a significant portion of his debts could be attributed to his cocaine habit and his compulsive need to share his drugs with strangers who scoffed at him as soon as his back was turned; to his idiotic desire to participate in underground poker games with five-figure buy-ins, even though I told him bluntly and repeatedly that he can't gamble for shit; to his even more idiotic business ventures, which were always all hype and which always failed or puttered out despite regular injections of his and his parents' money into the enterprise; and of course, to all the money he had dedicated to constructing the life in which I knew him, a life totally separate from and secondary to his parent-approved life with a spouse who, for all I knew, his traditional South Asian maternal grandparents could have arranged for him to marry, and the betrayal of whom would only further provoke his entire family's shock, disappointment, and ire. Any part of this mess might be enough for them to decide that he had gone too far, he had abused their trust and generosity and he had made too many terrible decisions along the way, and so he would be on his own to fix it.

For a fleeting moment, I sincerely felt bad for him. He had brought all of this on himself, of course, so my compassion was misplaced. And I quickly snapped out of it. But if both of my suspicions were true—if he was indeed married, and if his finances were as disastrous as they looked—then I needed to take whatever I could and disappear. Why shouldn't I? His wife (probably soon to be ex) and the credit card companies and the mortgage lenders and the federal government and all the utilities companies and, hell, probably his dealer and the landlord of this absurd bachelor pad apartment, would all be coming after him for whatever scraps remained. He owed almost two hundred thousand dollars total across nine different credit cards. He had personally guaranteed two small business loans. His house would go into foreclosure and his meager remaining assets would be divided in bankruptcy court. Why shouldn't I get my share too?

I was spiraling. I could hear him moving from the bathroom to his walk-in closet. It would take him another twenty minutes to finish getting dressed, but I needed to wrap this up. I needed to be typing out a staged reply to a nonexistent business contact while elegantly sipping a vodka martini, garnished with two Roquefort-stuffed olives, when he exited the bedroom. And I needed to maintain my cool. I needed to monitor his behavior throughout the night and hold off on taking any decisive action until I had more information.

I don't know what signals I thought he'd unconsciously give off. I knew he wouldn't be so dumb as to, like, try to make me pay for my own drinks that night, much less ask me for a loan or confess that he was screwed and solicit my advice. If anything, he was even more profligate in his spending and more wanton in his cocaine use than usual. We went to Affinity, where he bought three bottles for the table. He shared his blow with anyone who asked and tipped the waitress enough in cash that she pretended not to notice when he did lines at his seat. The two of us left for Ruby Lane before the third bottle had been opened. But Ruby Lane didn't have space for us in VIP that night, and Raj was livid.

He threw a few hundred dollars in twenties at the doorman's face and called him a "broke-ass little bitch boy" before grabbing my hand and storming back to the valet. His ridiculous outburst didn't tell me much in itself; I'd seen him react similarly when his pride had been wounded before. Mostly, I was counting my blessings that Raj hadn't tried to throw a punch at the bouncer, who was easily a half-foot taller and seventy pounds of muscle heavier.

"Ruby Lane is played out anyway, baby," I told him. "I'd rather go to Pearl 49. We won't even have to drive."

"Of course we have to drive. I don't make my bitches walk. Not even one block."

This was the first time he had referred to me as one of his "bitches." Yes, it's disrespectful. And coming from a guy like Raj, it sounded downright absurd. I don't have a good explanation for why it didn't affect me more in the moment. He was so agitated, pacing around in front of the valet stand while some kid in a red jacket silently observed us with glazed-over eyes, waiting for instructions, that I guess I barely processed his words. I did consider asking the valet if we could bogart a few puffs of the weed he must have had stashed somewhere nearby to help Raj balance out.

Before I could say anything, however, Raj was cramming his valet slip and a twenty into the attendant's hand, still angrily mumbling nonsense to himself. I waited without speaking. I remained silent in the car, not that Raj could have heard anything over the pulsating bass of the 21 Savage album that he immediately turned to full blast as soon as he started the engine.

We pulled up to Pearl 49, a full six hundred feet down the road. By the grace of whatever higher power you believe in, the doorman working that night was one of Raj's good buddies. They had some sort of mutually beneficial arrangement between them—something involving the circulation of cash, ecstasy, beautiful women, and prime locations in the club—which Raj tried to explain to me as we skipped the line and walked toward a table near the DJ booth at the back of the venue. The music was too loud and his thoughts still too disjointed for me to fully understand the connection. I do remember that whatever he said was enough to make me think that I should be careful about how I ended things with him, and careful about covering my tracks. If he were truly ruined, it wouldn't matter much, of course. But in that moment, Raj seemed to me to be a cockroach. He might be able to survive whatever storm was approaching.

Pearl 49 was fine. It was fun. It was the same unremarkable shit that goes down there every Thursday night, even though we all gush about how "epic" it was the next day. Whatever. Raj and I left a little after 2:30 a.m. He had calmed down and was in marginally better spirits than he'd been in after the slight at Ruby Lane. His cocaine baggies had been depleted in their entirety, but he didn't mention any after-parties where he could score more. I certainly wasn't going to bring it up. Notwithstanding the half-bottle of vodka he had consumed essentially on his own over the last ninety minutes at Pearl 49, he insisted on driving us back to his apartment.

I figured that he was still amped up enough that he'd spend the next several hours pacing around his living room, but to my surprise he joined me in his bedroom. I took off my dress and climbed into bed in my thong. He made a perfunctory attempt to remove it. I brushed him of by telling him that I was still sore from the pounding he had given me on Tuesday morning. This was a risible assertion, of course, but it pacified his ego enough for him to take several swigs out of the bottle of whiskey he had set on his nightstand and turn off the light. I would be spared the hassle of his coke-dick and would get to sleep before 3:30 a.m. Everything else could wait.

I left Raj's apartment at 8:00 the next morning without waking him, and we didn't speak again for the next two days. This was completely normal. I knew he was rotating through three or four other women whenever he wasn't with me. We didn't talk about it much, but it wasn't a secret either. He assumed that I was loyal exclusively to him, mostly because that's what he wanted to believe. I did nothing to disabuse him of that notion, and in fact, for most of the time we were involved, I wasn't actively pursuing other men anyway. There were a few wealthier older guys that I kept on simmer with sexy texts and the occasional flirtatious happy hour drink, but since I had met all of them while attending events that Raj's company had sponsored or promoted, it seemed too risky to pursue anything more aggressively. Besides, the optimal approach for those geezers was to play the long game. Assuming they didn't croak before I was ready for them, my mysteriousness and unavailability would make me all the more desirable in their eyes.

But now I had reason to believe that, in addition to the random promo girls—who, with their caked-on foundation, discount lip filler, and calcified boob jobs, were no threat whatsoever—Raj was dividing his time with a wife as well. I looked for her on social media and Google Images, obviously, but without a first name, she could have been any one of the hundred different women with whom Raj had posed for pictures over the years. There were a handful of repeats, but I also was a repeat, and I sure as shit didn't qualify as even a serious girlfriend, so there wasn't much to read into there. For all I knew, his wife could have been deeply religious, or perhaps she had a social anxiety disorder, or maybe she was South Asian too and continued to strictly abide traditional cultural norms. Whether at Raj's behest or because of her own distaste for the scene, this woman might have separated herself from the Buckhead/Midtown nightlife crowd entirely, which would render it nearly impossible for me to connect her to Raj through online research alone, unless and until I obtained more concrete information about her elsewhere.

I also needed to reexamine Raj's finances but, in contrast to some of the men I had been with who left all their usernames and passwords on a Post-it Note, allowing me to stealthily snap a photo and sign into their accounts from any location after the fact, Raj kept his passwords saved and auto-filled on his browser. I needed direct access to his laptop to continue my research. He was usually so drunk, coked out, or otherwise distracted that it had never been a problem before, but now I was stuck. The more I thought about it, the more I realized that I was probably going to have to cut my losses and move on. Maybe one more fund transfer.

Maybe one more online splurge using one of the two credit cards that I had memorized, although even that was a dicey proposition given how close he was to maxing out all his accounts. Maybe I'd be lucky to snag five hundred dollars in cash from Raj's wallet one last time, on the assumption that he wouldn't remember whether or not he'd already spent that money on drugs.

I used those two days away from him to plan dates with three different older guys—all in their late forties or early fifties, all white, all nominally Christian, two in finance and one in real estate development—for the following week. I reviewed my own assets and recurring expenditures over the prior twelve-month period. It's been a good year for me. I haven't brought in as much as I deserve, mind you, or taken nearly as much as any of those clowns could have afforded to spare, but I'm already well above six figures. That's without counting the value of any of the gifts I've been given, most of which I'll eventually resell, or the rent or car payments that were covered on my behalf, or any of the other perks that men offer up willingly in exchange for my complicity in the delusion they're still virile and important.

So I wasn't too worried about Raj. He'd been a waste of my time, but ultimately they're all wastes of time. I take what I can for as long as I can, and then I move on. I went to Raj's apartment on Sunday, assuming that I'd party with him one last time that night and then cut my losses and break up with him the next morning. The rest was his wife's problem now. Cheers to me for not being one of those stupid bitches who think that marrying up is going to solve all their problems, you know? Imagine: Raj's façade of a business empire is disintegrating; he can't ask his parents for the family money he needs to extricate himself from the debts he's incurred for frivolities and in pursuit of his self-indulgent ambitions without conceding to them that he's an abject failure; his reputation in Atlanta and Miami will be ruined and all the vultures he's deluded himself into calling his friends are going to delight in his downfall; and if I were his wife, I'd be expected to diminish myself "for the good of the marriage," so as to not further emasculate this shell of a man and add another burden to a disaster entirely of his own making. Fuck that! The cowering, meek, obedient women who marry these chumps and stick around even after the charade is exposed are too foolish or stubborn to acknowledge that they had it exactly wrong.

Anyway, Raj and I went out in Buckhead that Sunday. Most of it is a blur. I'm not big on cocaine, but I took a few bumps that night. Raj's mood hadn't changed much since Thursday. He was still throwing money around, still picking fights over imaginary or inconsequential slights, still manic. I was happy to see it, as it would give me reasonable grounds for ending things with him the next morning over brunch. Depending on how much he remembered, I could claim he got aggressive with me at one of the clubs. Or I could say that he had made it clear that he was never going to move on from his polyamorous party-boy phase, and I realized I was looking for something more serious. Or whatever. I wasn't sure exactly what I was going to say—there's an art to these things, to making these guys feel like the decision to end the "relationship" is at least as much their choice as it is yours, lest they turn vengeful or start ruminating on what went wrong and wind up uncovering whatever you might have done to or taken from them over the preceding few months—but Raj's antics would make my job that much easier.

Somehow, he busted his lip. Like I said, I was pretty drunk and coked out myself, and he was stirring up shit wherever he could with men who outweighed him by fifty pounds, so I honestly have no idea what happened. He didn't know either. He kept claiming that he got punched by this tall Black guy in a classic pinstripe suit, who got into Raj's face after Raj grabbed his girlfriend's butt. Unfortunately for Raj's narrative, however, that was the one incident that I did remember perfectly from start to finish. Raj had never met either of them, and the girl had done absolutely nothing to indicate that she would appreciate having her buttocks spontaneously fondled by a stranger. The guy would have been fully justified in knocking Raj onto his ass, but he held his temper with a nobility that Raj did not deserve. So when Raj was still accusing the guy of being a "thug" the next morning, I told him that he was being a fucking racist and a liar.

"You've pulled shit like this with Black people before," I told him. "They're either your 'homies' or they're 'low-life gangstas.' It's obnoxious and I'm sick of it. I have no interest in being with someone who is a bigot."

"I am not a fucking bigot, bitch," Raj said. "I'm Indian. How are you going to call me a racist when I'm brown-skinned myself?"

"Oh, so you *are* Indian now?" It was too early in the morning for Raj's brand of bullshit. "All you ever do is talk about how white you are. How your dad is white. How fair-skinned you are, and how your perfect older brother is even lighter. How you only identify with your British and German heritage. Every other day you bring this shit up. It is your prerogative how you choose to self-identify, and I usually wouldn't give a fuck either way. But now suddenly you're a proud brown-skinned man, when it's convenient for you, when I'm calling you out for being prejudiced against Black people? Give me a fucking break, Raj."

"Listen!" He grabbed my wrist and yanked me toward him. It's faded away now, but for a few days I had a bruise. He had never been so forceful with me before. To be honest, it startled me. I know how to handle myself, so I wasn't scared. But it was unsettling. "Listen, Olivia," he said again. "Where the fuck do you get off judging me? What, just because your step-dad is Black and you have a couple biracial siblings, you think that you have the slightest clue about my lived experience?" I couldn't recall when or why I would have *ever* told him anything about Raymond or Finn or Matilda, but he was too worked up for me to interject. "You think you realize one-tenth of the horseshit I have to put up with trying to pursue my dreams, when the entire industry can't seem to make up its mind about whether I'm white enough to belong?"

Then his phone rang. He has a Pavlovian response to that thing. I could be topless and on my knees, blowing him to completion, but if his cell so much as buzzes, his attention is immediately diverted. He'd shove my head away to lunge for it. So whatever fight we were about to have was no match for the allure of his mobile phone.

But when he picked it up and looked at the caller ID, he hesitated. He held his breath. Then he swiped it on to answer.

"What do you want?" he barked. "Now is not a good time."

Immediately a female voice started laying into him in a mix of English and what I'm assuming was a Hindi dialect. She sounded far too young to be his mother, so it had to be his wife. From the fragments I was able to overhear and understand, it was unclear whether she was angry about money or about me. I guess both. He put her on mute while she was carrying on.

"You need to tell her that you're an investor and a co-owner of Inception Wealth Company," Raj demanded. "Tell her that a majority of members in our LLC voted to approve a capital call, and tell her that you had to liquidate your assets in order to meet it. Make sure you emphasize that part: you had no choice either, you had to liquidate your assets too. Explain to her that we'd both be in default under the operating agreement if we didn't, and that we got together this morning to meet with a corporate attorney to talk about our options to invoke dissenter's rights."

"Raj! What the fuck are you even talking about?" Look, like I told you, I am very well-versed in legal terms and concepts because of my time as a receptionist at that godawful law firm, and although what he was describing wasn't precisely the kind of legal predicament that they usually handled, I'm intelligent enough and I had learned enough from listening to other businessmen that I understood the gist of it. But he was springing this on me out of nowhere and I can't be expected to recount the nuances of a complicated fact pattern like that without warning! "Who is on the phone right now? Is she mad about me or is she mad about money?"

"She is fucking furious about fucking both!" Raj was panicking. "It's my wife, bitch. Give me a fucking break, Olivia. I know you're a smart girl. At some point you must have realized that I'm married. You need to help me."

"If you call me 'bitch' one more time, the only thing I'll tell her is that I'm just one of the eight different women you're currently banging, and you can deal with the consequences of that. Quit being a prick and just be honest with me for once."

"I am being honest with you, bi—... Liv. She's my wife. I have a cash flow situation right now. It's resolvable. I'm not broke. I can fix all of this. But somehow she knows we're together—you specifically—and I need to fix both of these problems before she ruins everything. If she leaves me now, I'm fucked. I won't be able to recover from it. I need another six months. That's it. After that, I'll initiate the divorce myself. You and I can be together. But we have a prenup with an infidelity clause, and I need to transfer funds that I don't even have yet, and..."

He paused. He looked desperate, and he didn't seem to notice that his wife had stopped yelling a few seconds before and was now silently awaiting his response.

"Raj?" she snapped. "Raj, are you still there?" She said something else in the foreign language I didn't understand.

"Please," he whispered as he took us off mute and began speaking into his phone. "Babe, of course I'm still here. But I'm with one of my business partners right now. The majority interest-holders are trying to push us out. I'm the one who started this company, and you can't imagine the stress I'm under trying to hold them off from stealing what I've built."

"Your business partner? Do you think I'm stupid? If you're really with him, then prove it. Let me talk to him."

"I told you," Raj mouthed at me.

"Fine, just give me the fucking phone," I whispered back.

And that was how I wound up talking with Anika. I spent a full ten minutes with her on speakerphone, with Raj listening in. The situation was so absurd that I can barely recall the details of the conversation now. I explained that the reason Raj and I had been spending time together lately was because of this venture—even though I had no clue what type of business Inception Wealth Company was engaged in or where it was headquartered or how long it had been in operation, or frankly whether it existed in reality outside of Raj's warped brain at all—and I repeated Raj's speech about the operating agreement and capital call and all that crap as best as I could remember. It was brutally obvious to me that she didn't believe a word of it. She feigned that she did, but I saw through her act.

Raj, however, did not. When I handed the phone back to him, they spoke for another three minutes, during which he vowed that he'd be back to their place as soon as we finished up with the lawyer, probably around 2:00 p.m. that afternoon.

"That was a close one," he said after he put the phone back down. "Do you think she suspected anything?"

"No," I replied. "I think we played that really well. I think you're in the clear."

I'll never forget the cocky smile that dumb fuck had on his face in that moment. I stuffed the most expensive of the random shit I had left at his apartment over the past few weeks into my handbag. There wasn't a doubt in my mind that Anika would be cleaning out whatever was left in any and every bank account to which she had access while Raj and I were at brunch. I figured that I could end thing between me and him by text some other time. This was my gift to Anika. While I was distracting Raj over a hair-of-the-dog bloody mary, I was allowing her to take what I could've had myself.

CHAPTER SIXTEEN

I don't really know what happened after that. Everything up until the last time I saw Raj is hearsay. And not even hearsay coming from Raj's mouth. Hearsay from the people who have pieced together what transpired. When Raj pulled up to Lillian and Raymond's house in Snellville, he didn't explain much of anything.

The doorman at my apartment in Sandy Springs has since said that some guy who roughly fits Raj's description was looking for me that same afternoon, but I haven't asked to see security footage or anything, so I can't know for sure it was him. I'm guessing he went there first, but I have no idea how it occurred to him to look for me in Snellville next.

The temp agency didn't have a work assignment for me that day, so I had driven over to my parents' house to hang with Milo and eat their food. Finn was in his room playing videogames. Milo and I had been together in the TV room for most of the morning, but by sheer luck, he had gone to Finn's room to play Horizon Zero ten minutes before Raj showed up. Matilda was at her friend's house, or maybe she had gotten called in to her part-time job at the Chick-fil-A. I'm not sure. Raymond and Lillian were out. While we were eating lunch, Raymond offered to set me up with an interview for a secretary job in Snellville's city hall, which is so far beneath me that I was almost offended, but I knew he meant well. My mother got jealous of the attention he was giving me, so she interrupted us and started whining about how they needed a new couch for the TV room, even though all the stains on the old one were the result of her and her friends' drunken bullshit. But Raymond was, as he usually is, willing to oblige her whims, so they had left together to go shopping at one of the outlet malls.

When Raj pulled into the driveway, it didn't occur to me that it could be him. He knew nothing of my real family. None of the men I was with ever did. Not ever. I was always Olivia Giordano in that world, so Raj couldn't have known my real last name. At least, I hadn't thought so. Maybe while I was fishing through his computer files, he was rummaging through my wallet and found my real driver's license. I have a fake that says "Olivia Giordano," and it's good enough to fool any guy that hasn't worked twenty-plus years as a bartender or a bouncer, but maybe I got sloppy and left my official Georgia ID somewhere in my purse and he stumbled upon it. Maybe someone from my high school saw me at a club and used my real name or said we knew each other from Snellville, and Raj overheard. Maybe I said something suspicious in my sleep; if it happened during one of Raj's paranoid 4:00 a.m. cocaine-frenzies, he would have started investigating right then. I don't know. He never brought it up.

I remember thinking to myself, "that's the same model BMW that Raj has," and also, "who else in the Fletcher-Ray family knows literally anyone who can afford a car that costs a hundred thousand dollars?" But I could see from the TV room window that the front bumper was smashed in and the left side of the car was severely scraped up, whereas Raj's car was always spotless inside and flawless outside. He gets the damn thing detailed at least once every six weeks. So in the moment, my guess was that some nineteen-year-old asshole with a thing for underage girls was looking for Matilda. For a second, I almost felt protective of her.

I had sent Raj a text the week before to officially end things. He didn't reply, and he hadn't contacted me otherwise since, so I figured that he was swallowing his pride and moving on. All the better for me. He had gone totally silent on social media, which was a huge aberration for someone who normally posted at least four times a day on every platform. I assumed that I had broken his heart and maybe he was trying to work shit out with his wife.

Or whatever. My focus had shifted to the three new guys I'd gone out with over the preceding few days, particularly the real estate developer, who seemed especially willing to compensate me fairly for making him feel like a big-dicked stud.

Like I said, what I know about what happened before Raj arrived at my parents' house comes entirely from what I've overheard, or what I've been told here. I saw the photos after the fact. When his car pulled up, I knew nothing.

He stumbled a little as he got out of the vehicle and slammed the driver's side door shut. I was still half-absorbed in my phone until that point, but when I realized it was Raj? Frankly, I was irritated. That's it. I guess on some level I was concerned that he might file a police report if he had realized how much money had been transferred out of his bank accounts, but I also knew it would be pretty damn difficult for him to prove it was me and not his wife or one of his other side pieces. Besides, his ego would not allow him to suffer the humiliation of admitting to a police detective, much less to his own father, that he had been grossly irresponsible and he had been duped. Mostly, I figured he was there to try to win me back, and I didn't want him to make a scene in front of the entire neighborhood or to say anything that would give Finn reason to snitch to Raymond about how I've been supplementing my income.

I tossed my phone onto the table and went to meet him outside before he could start banging on the door. Milo and Finn had turned up the volume on the PlayStation, but I know how loud Raj can get when he's worked up, and if my brothers heard his asinine declarations of love for me, I'd never hear the end of it.

Notwithstanding his initial stumble out of the vehicle and the fact that he seemed to have smashed his precious BMW into something during the drive over, Raj didn't look drunk or strung out, per se, when I first got to the patio and shut the front door behind me. This was something different. He was pacing in front of his car, but he wasn't staggering. He was drenched in sweat. He was muttering something to himself, but I couldn't make it out. He must have heard me come outside, but he hadn't made eye contact with me yet, so after twenty seconds or so of observing his bizarre deportment, I finally hollered at him, "Raj, what the fuck are you doing here?"

Now I know. I know that before he found me in Snellville, he had been at his home in Alpharetta. His real home. I know that Anika had intercepted a notice that their house had gone into foreclosure. I know that earlier that morning, she had packed up her car with clothes, jewelry, toys, and diapers. Now I know that she and Raj had two kids together. Someone told me that she confronted him while the two-year-old was already strapped into his car seat. The five-year-old, I guess, was puttering around the driveway, even though he was supposed to be getting himself buckled up in the car too.

Am I really supposed to continue here? Raj didn't tell me about any of this while he was traipsing around Lillian's driveway, mumbling and gesticulating like a madman.

So be it.

What I've been told is that Raj stabbed Anika eight times in their kitchen, and then he shot her in the chest. I was shown the photos. She had her car keys in her hand. She had almost gotten out. She looked nothing like what I had imagined. She was much younger and slimmer and more attractive. Her outfit, before it was destroyed, had been fashionably preppy. I had correctly assumed she was Indian after hearing her berate Raj in what had sounded to me like a Hindi dialect on the phone, but after listening to that interaction, I started envisioning her as matronly and frumpy and bitter. As someone who, through appearance and demeanor, had driven Raj away. Instead, Anika looked like one of the pretty, carefree, slightly-snobby Emory undergrads that I see wandering around VaHi sometimes. She probably sat at the popular kids' table in high school and rode horses at a private equestrian center on the weekends before she became a mom. She probably baked blueberry muffins with her kids, and then chased them around the backyard in an impromptu game of tag so they'd burn off their sugar high before their father returned home. She probably daydreamed about writing and illustrating her own children's book once her sons got a little older and more self-sufficient. She was a catch. Except now, she was dead.

I've been told that Raj shot his two-year-old in the head while the kid was sitting in his car seat. Your detective spared me the photo of that, but he did show me a picture of the boy in the morgue. What fucking purpose did that serve, by the way? Raj never said a word to me about his toddler or his other son. Not once while we were involved, and not once while he was in my driveway either.

Your detectives told me that his neighbors called the police, and witnesses report that the five-year-old realized something bad was happening and tried to hide behind a bush, but Raj found him and shot him too: once in the stomach, once in the head. They showed me a picture of his body in the driveway, and a close-up of his face in the morgue. And then, apparently, Raj got into his BMW and sped off down the road at eighty miles an hour before the cops showed up. Presumably to come find me. What the fuck do you want me to say about this? I didn't see any blood on him when he was in my parents' driveway. Maybe he changed his shirt, I don't know. All I saw was the sweat.

You think I'm callous. I'm not callous. I'm trying to be factual here. Accurate and honest, like I have been since we started talking. Understand: I never met Anika, except for that one phone call when Raj forced me to pretend like I was an investor in his business. I tried to help her by distracting Raj over brunch, so she'd have enough time to take the rest of his money for herself and get away. I could have taken it myself, easily, but I was compassionate enough to let her have whatever was left instead. And I really, truly did not know for sure that he was married until that day. I never, ever knew he had children. He never mentioned them. Never even hinted at it. One time I overheard him bragging at a nightclub about how he had "no baby mamas," and he constantly acted like men who had to dump half their earnings into paying child support were chumps.

Even if I had known, what could I have done differently? Would you rather that I feign grief over the death of total strangers, however gruesome it might have been? Would you rather I blame myself for the murder of two children that I didn't know existed until some dickhead detective started shoving photos of their dead bodies in front of my face? Raymond told me that he could dip into his savings and work overtime if he had to in order to pay for a lawyer for me. I thought we had an understanding that I'd tell you everything in exchange for total immunity, but now part of me is wondering if maybe I shouldn't take Raymond up on that offer after all.

But I need you to realize that I didn't do anything wrong here. I've been completely honest with you about everything. So I'll finish my account, and then I'll talk to Raymond about whether I need a lawyer going forward. I have nothing to hide.

So: Raj was in Lillian and Raymond's driveway, sweating and sputtering and acting like a lunatic, but not like a lunatic who had just killed his entire family. I'm not being flippant. If there had been the slightest indication that he was so deranged that he'd do such a thing, do you really think I would have gone outside? Do you think I would have started yelling and cussing at him about what the fuck was he doing there and how the fuck did he find this place? But I did. And he finally looked up at me. His eyes bore into me with full intensity, and yet they were totally vacant. He didn't say a word.

Then, he burst into tears.

I don't think I've ever seen a man cry like that, ever. The closest I can think of is the crazy temper tantrums that Finn used to have until he was about eight years old, when he would become so unhinged that nothing could get him under control—bribes, spankings, threats, ignoring him, consoling him, nothing—until he eventually wore himself out. Raymond could hold him tightly and carry him out of the store or church or wherever, if he was around when it happened in public, but if it was just Lillian, all we could do was wait it out. She didn't have the upper body strength to restrain him, or the pain tolerance to withstand his frenzied blows.

That's the only comparison I can make. And if you have kids of your own, then that's what I need you to imagine. Think back to the worst tantrum your kid has ever thrown. Was he expressing his thoughts in a rational, coherent way? Could you understand half of what he was screaming? Would it have mattered if you did? Think about that, and maybe then you'll understand why it's so absurd that I keep getting grilled about what Raj said to me in that driveway, and why it's so unfair that you all are acting like I'm hiding something from you. I'm sure the neighbors did hear him screaming his head off. But were they able to make out a word of it? Have any of them been able to report to you a single sentence that came out of his mouth? It's not because they were too far away, or at least not solely because of that. Raj's thoughts weren't logical, and his words were choked out between sobs. None of it made sense.

He said his life was destroyed. I remember that. In the moment, I thought it was because I had dumped him, and also because he had squandered all his money on drugs and vanity projects and other bullshit, including maybe a few gifts and treats for me. And for his other club girls too. They were probably stealing from him as well. I thought that this whole spectacle was a desperate ploy from a desperate man to get me back. He wailed Anika's name several times, but he kept covering his face with his hands so if he was confessing his crime to me then, it was too muffled for me to discern it. I still don't know his kids' names. No one has told me. So if he cried them aloud, I wouldn't have known it then and I still don't know it now.

Try to have some sympathy for me here. I have a thirty-something-year-old man who has tracked me down at my step-dad's house on the other side of town, and I don't know how. He is having the type of conniption that is otherwise only seen in movies. His car is smashed up, he's not making any sense, and I have every reason to believe that this is his pathetic, possibly drug-addled attempt to try to convince me to get back together with him. And all I wanted was for him to get lost before Lillian and Raymond came back with their new couch, or before there was a lull in Finn and Milo's videogame and they heard the commotion, or before one of the nosy neighbors called the police. Which, I guess it turns out, one of them did anyway.

So without leaving the front patio, I screamed at him, "Get it through your head, Raj! It's over! Go back to your wife or one of your club sluts, I don't care anymore. Just get out of here!"

It seemed to take a couple seconds longer than it should have for him to process that I had spoken and for him to react. But then, abruptly, his tears stopped. The howling and the lamentations stopped. He looked at me again. And then he pulled out the gun that had been tucked into the back of his jeans.

I hadn't noticed it. He was wearing a baggy t-shirt, which wasn't at all his normal style, but everything else about the situation was so strange and unexpected that I hadn't had much opportunity to reflect on the potential significance of a sartorial deviation. It was a pistol. That's all I can tell you. Raymond has taken me to a shooting range in Norcross a few times over the years, with the objective of making sure that I know how to operate a firearm safely and effectively if it's ever necessary. But neither of us are gun nuts. I can't confirm for you the make or series of Raj's weapon, if that's what you're hoping. He started waving it around so frantically that it was impossible for me to get much of a look at it anyway.

I don't know why I wasn't more afraid. I'm tough, obviously, but at this point it was clear that either Raj was on something significantly more potent than his standard morning eightball, or he had gone mental. I don't know why I didn't run back inside and lock the door. I bet that subconsciously, I wanted to protect Milo and even Finn from him. And I knew that I could talk him down. I'd always been able to handle things whenever Raj got out of control before, and even though this situation was an entirely new level of insanity, I could manage it.

He wasn't pointing the gun at me or at anything in particular until we heard the police sirens, so I guess in that sense, it's really the cops who are to blame for what happened next. It was obvious that they were coming toward us. All of the normal noises of our neighborhood—cars with the bass cranked up, dogs barking, shirtless pot-bellied retirees mowing their lawns for the third time in a week, folks hollering hello to each other from across the street—had vanished all at once. It was as if everyone within a three-block radius had stopped what they were doing to listen in on Raj's breakdown and my attempts to pacify him. But then I faintly heard Milo and Finn inside the house, each yelling and groaning about how much the other sucked at Horizon Zero, both without a clue as to what was transpiring in the front yard. If they were oblivious, then maybe the sirens were a coincidence. Maybe there was a domestic dispute or a drug deal gone wrong down the road. Maybe it had nothing to do with me and Raj, and maybe I'd be able to get him off the property without it turning into an official incident.

But Raj panicked. Or maybe this was his plan all along, I don't know. As soon as the sirens registered into his conscious awareness, he stopped waving the gun at the sky and started pointing it in my direction. He wasn't aiming directly at me, mind you, but he'd brought the weapon down to shoulder level. He was shaking and screaming things about me that were objectively false, so why bother repeating them here? The worst thing I did to him was exaggerate the truth. Fine, maybe a couple of times I outright lied, but he was lying to me too, and about things far worse than me, like, telling him that I used to work with celebrities and billionaire sheiks as a private flight attendant. Our relationship wasn't one where he cared to hear about my past—or where he showed much of an interest in my present or future, for that matter. The only thing true about our connection involved him giving me gifts or offering me drugs to induce me to be another one of the accessories he'd carry around with him to impress other men on any given night. We both entered into the exchange voluntarily, and if you're going to moralize the transactional nature of our relationship, then he's at least as culpable as I.

Most of what I have from him, he gave me willingly, or with willful ignorance. He made so many promises about what he could do for me, so many boasts about what he could afford, and I simply ensured that those claims were fulfilled. I took less from him than I've taken from others. And I certainly wasn't the only woman he was sleeping with. Are his other promo girls and club bunnies being grilled like this? He was bawling that I took everything from him, but he did this to himself.

It sounded like the cops were less than a minute away at that point, so I told him, "Raj, you better run, you idiot. Those cops are coming here for you."

The gun fired. I swear I saw a flash of surprise on his face. I don't think he realized that the safety was off. If he actually was aiming for me, then he's a terrible shot. The bullet hit the side of the house, a few inches above the dining room window.

"You asshole!" I snapped. "You're going to have to pay to patch that up."

"With what?" he cried. It was the most intelligible thing he'd sputtered out since he arrived. "With what money, Olivia? It's gone. Everything is gone."

Four cop cars were pulling onto the street. He was whimpering. And then he turned the gun on himself. Right there in the driveway, Raj shot himself in the head.

He immediately crumpled onto the ground. I didn't rush to him. The bullet definitely had punched a hole through his front windshield, and I couldn't tell from where I was standing whether there was shattered glass everywhere. I mean, technically I didn't even know for sure if he had actually shot himself. It looked like blood was pooling onto the pavement, but all of this could've been a ploy to get me to come down to him, and even before I knew about Anika and his kids, I had a sudden premonition that he could try to abduct me or kill me too.

Besides, the police had pulled up and now Raj's screaming was replaced by theirs. They had the nerve to tell *me* to get down on the ground, as if I were the criminal. Once those morons realized that it was my parents' house and I was the one under attack, they helped me up and started being a lot nicer.

One of the first things the cops asked me was if anyone else was on the property. I told them "my brothers," and had the foresight to mention that if Milo and Finn were playing videogames with their headsets on, they still might not realize what was going on. God forbid the police snuck upstairs to Finn's room while he and Milo were screaming about guns and kill-counts. But the two of them answered immediately when the cop—the heavier one with the beard and the nice smile, I don't remember his name— knocked on the front door. Officer Nice Teeth didn't even have to twist the handle; both boys were standing right there in the front hallway.

I guess Milo and Finn had heard the first gunshot go off, and they'd been trying to break into Raymond's gun safe so they could come outside and help me. Finn has always been kind of a coward, but Milo insists that he was right there with him as they were trying to crack Raymond's locks, so I guess I believe that my half-brother finally stepped up for me. Hearing that makes me happy I've resisted the temptation over the years to open credit cards under Finn's name and SSN. I'm not mad that they didn't come out earlier to protect me. Like they said in their statements to the officers on-site, they were in Finn's room, upstairs and toward the back of the house, with the door shut and the videogame's sound on full blast. It took actual gunfire hitting the wooden siding just below the second floor for them to realize that there was a crazed man out front threatening my life.

Meanwhile, Raj was bleeding out all over Lillian and Raymond's driveway. My step-dad is going to have to spend his next day off from work repaving the whole damn thing, and from what I understand, he'll be paying for that out of his own pocket. If Raj survives this, I'm thinking about suing him for that, and for the costs of patching up the house's siding, and above all for the emotional distress he's inflicted on me with all of this. He might not have any money left, but his parents still do.

Or maybe they don't, or won't. I can't imagine what his medical bills are going to be. The idiot had gotten himself so worked up, that he managed to partially miss his own brain and failed in his suicide attempt. Like, he shot himself in the head, but not straight through. He hit it on a tangent. I know this because when the ambulances got there a few minutes later, they were shocked that he was still alive and were hollering out to each other and also giving the cops updates on Raj's status via their radios. The whole situation was chaos, but I'm brilliant at being able to keep my cool and focus my attention on extracting key information in exactly these kinds of environments.

So I knew that Raj was alive but critical. They were taking him to Grady even though Northside Hospital in Gwinnett is closer, because Grady happened to have a neurosurgeon with expertise in treating gunshot wounds on premises at the time. Last

I overheard, he's currently in a medically induced coma with a fair prognosis of survival over two months. They expect that if he makes it, he'll be permanently blind, but with proper rehabilitation he won't be paralyzed. No one has said anything about how much plastic surgery he'll need to fix his face.

The police officer who was next to me at the time, the ginger guy with the Irish last name, told me I was lucky to be alive. After Raj was on the stretcher, a different cop handcuffed him to the metal bar on the side and got into the ambulance with him. It seemed a little ridiculous since Raj was unconscious at the time, but given the damage to his car, I assumed he must have pulled a hit-and-run on the way to my parents' house and was being arrested for that. Officer McIrishface asked me what my relationship to Raj was, but neither he nor anyone else had said a thing to me about Anika or her kids yet. I explained that I had dumped Raj by text the week before, because we weren't that serious to begin with, and that I supposed that this was his sick way of proving that he couldn't live without me.

Raymond and Lillian got back about two hours later. Most of the scene had been cleared at that point. Milo had called Raymond and told them to come home, but they'd gone all the way to the outlets in North Georgia, out past Cumming, so it took them a while to drive back. And Lillian had wanted to finish her purchase before they left. The new couch was delivered yesterday. It's not as nice as the chaise sectional I got from West Elm courtesy of some retired law firm partner that I "dated" for about two weeks, but it isn't bad.

The two police officers who had stuck around explained to Raymond what happened. They told him about Anika and the children, and then Raymond told me later that night. I don't know why they didn't tell me directly.

And that more or less brings us to today.

I don't understand why you felt the need to do this in an interrogation room, as if I'm somehow culpable for Raj's sins. I think I've made it pretty clear that, if anything, I am the true victim in all this, and I don't adopt the "victim" moniker lightly. I told you from the beginning, I've never taken anything from anyone who didn't deserve it. Give me one single example of anything I've said that suggests otherwise.

Are we done here? If we could wrap this up now, that'd be great. I've told you everything I know, and I have a date tonight. Another real estate developer, Kenneth something, who I met last week at Bones, and without any introduction from Raj, if you're wondering. Kenneth is a different class of man. A step up. Maybe I'll never find a man truly worthy of me, but I'm getting closer. Besides, if I were to jump back into the trendy half of Buckhead's social scene right away, I'd have to deal with all sorts of gossip and speculation. But Kenneth is so far removed from this bullshit that I'm not worried about him bringing it up at all. On to the next.

www.ingramcontent.com/pod-product-compliance
Lightning Source LLC
Chambersburg PA
CBHW051921110726
47902CB00002B/368